Jesus ††† Judas

ALSO BY RALPH E. JARRELLS

ILL GOTTEN GAIN

FIERY RED HAIR, EMERALD GREEN EYES, AND A VICIOUS IRISH TEMPER

JESUS
JUDAS

Best Friends Forever
A NOVEL

RALPH E. JARRELLS

WordCrafts

*Jesus * Judas: Best Friends Forever*
Copyright © 2020
Ralph E. Jarrells

ISBN: 978-1-952474-12-5

Cover concept and design by David Warren.

Published by WordCrafts Press
Cody, Wyoming 82414
www.wordcrafts.net

Dedication

This book is dedicated to all of the teachers, preachers and lay people who have affected my life. Those who taught me. Those who challenged me. Even those whose stories I found to be incorrect. They all contributed to this book in some way. To all of them I say, Thank You. Most of them are no longer with us on this plain. Rev. Bill Faircloth, Rev. William Conner, Rev. Ryan Eklund, Rev. Phillip Ellen, Rev. Dr. David Dalton, Rev. Dr. Kaye Dalton, Rev. Dr. Lanny Lanford, and many more.

My writing is always dedicated to my loving wife, Sybil E. Jarrells and to two public school teachers, Elsie Lamar and Frances LaBorde.

No writer can be successful without great readers and editors, so, here's to Harriette Edmonds, Pat Mullins, and Judy Powell.

A special note of thanks to the Biblical History Center in LaGrange, Georgia. Thanks, Carlos and Christy.

Last, but in no way least, Jesus Christ, without whom there would be no story and no heaven.

STATEMENT OF BELIEF AND INTENT

This story is a work of religious and historical fiction. As such, I use the facts, as we believe them, as a skeleton. The King James Version of the Bible is the primary source for the material in this story. But, as with any fictional story, other sources are utilized as well as my imagination. It is not my intent to challenge the scripture. Nor is it my intention to start a divisive discussion. This is a story. You know the outcome. What we don't know are the events leading up to and surrounding the crucifixion. This book presents some possible scenarios.

My intent is to make the reader think. If it does, good. My intent is to present possibilities. If it does, good. If you, esteemed reader, enjoy the conjecture and the possibility, good. And, if you consider the work as "bunk," that is your right, and that is good, too.

Regardless, the story presented here is possible, but it is still a story. By the way, Jesus used parables or allegory (stories) to make His points. Maybe He will use this story to His benefit as well.

So, with that, I present the story of two Best Friends Forever: Jesus & Judas.

NOTES

1. Passages that are in italics are from the KJV Bible.
2. Usually, when someone is mentioned, a short biography follows.
3. The appendices are information to help understand the events in the story.

Introduction

THE STAR

I t was a magical night.
Clear. So clear that you could see forever.
A million, million stars filled the blackness, the moonless sky, from border to border, from north to south, from east to west.

The stars seemed so close, as if you could reach out and touch them. Like you could reach up, swirl your hand around and capture a handful of them. So many stars they must have multiplied just for that special night.

Then... a sudden flash... in the East. A blinding flash as bright as the sun. It brightened the eastern sky. As the light faded, there was in the same place a star, ten times brighter than any other. Was it a sign? What could it mean?

This celestial manifestation was an announcement of the birth of a man who would change the world.

Judah bar Simon was born in Alexandria, Egypt, to an elite Jewish family. He was the son of Simon bar Simon, legendary woodworker and furniture maker. Simon's furniture was highly sought after by the elite of that Egyptian city and most of the known world for that matter. Simon was happy to add a son to his family. Judah would soon follow in his father's footsteps, just as he had followed in his father's. The addition of a son would expand Simon's business.

Judah bar Simon, later called Judas Iscariot, was destined

to make an indelible mark on history and change the world.

††††

At the same time... *There were in the country, shepherds abiding in the field, keeping watch over their flock by night.* The chill in the Judean air was unseasonable for September, but not sufficient to require a woolen cloak. The sheep were quiet. The shepherds were sleeping, save for a single young boy keeping watch. A sudden flash of light in the eastern sky. The flash caused the sheep to be uneasy. Their bleating awakened all of the shepherds. There, replacing the bright light was a star, ten times brighter than any other. A fast-moving streak of light emanating from the star was heading directly toward the field where the sheep and shepherds were standing. It looked like a comet hurtling to earth. Fear was in the eyes of the sheep as they looked toward the light; the same fear shown in the eyes of the shepherds. What was happening? As the light reached the ground, the shepherds could see a winged being, unrecognizable, in the center of the light. He glowed brighter than the light that carried him. There was no movement of the being's mouth, but all present heard his soft commanding voice. The shepherds started to run, but with a simple gesture, the being stopped all of the shepherds... frozen in their steps. His words calmed them.

"Peace be with you. I am Gabriel, Archangel of the Lord God, most high. *Fear not: for, behold, I bring you good tidings of great joy, which shall be to all people. For unto you is born this day in the city of David, a Savior which is Jesus Christ the Lord. And this shall be a sign unto you; Ye shall find the babe wrapped in swaddling clothes, lying in a manger.*

"And suddenly there was with the angel a multitude of the

heavenly host praising God, and saying, "Glory to God in the highest, and on earth peace, good will toward men."

As quickly as the light appeared, the Archangel, the singing angels and the light were gone, leaving only the bleating sheep and the mystified shepherds standing in the field. Silently dumb-struck, the shepherds stood staring at the star that had replaced the celestial phenomenon. The silence that followed was quickly shattered by a cacophony. The shepherds all talking at the same time. The incessant bleating of the sheep added to the confusion They all finally quieted. A vote was taken and the decision was made that they should herd their sheep to Bethlehem and find this Christ Child Jesus which the Lord had made known unto them. They came with haste, and found Maryamor, and Joseph, and the babe wrapped in swaddling clothes, lying in a manger just as the angel had said.

Two births on that special night that would change the world for all time.

Author's Comments

I believe that as we read and study the Bible, we have a tendency to take the events, the stories, even the words out of the context in which they were written and put them in our modern time. We fail to remember that what we are reading happened over 2000 years ago. It was at a time and in a place that we have no personal experience with. Also, what we are reading was written in different languages and translated two, three or more times before the King James Version and hand copied by dozens of scribes since.

Understanding the Bible, especially the New Testament, is complicated by the fact that one person can be referred to by three, even four names. We have to understand that people living in Galilee and Judea in Biblical time would have their name translated into Aramaic, Greek and Latin because of the changes in government in the area.

Think about it this way. Everything in life was different. Nazareth (where Mary and Joseph lived) was 120 miles from Bethlehem (where Jesus was born). That's a reasonable trip today. But for Mary and Joseph it was four and a half days. In Biblical time there were no trips just to drop in for coffee with friends.

The roads were all dirt and rocks. So the act of foot washing was much more important than just a symbol of respect.

Think about that in today's terms. So you are the lady of the house and you have just finished vacuuming the living room rug. Guests arrive complete with dirty, or worse, muddy shoes and feet. What would you do? After you screamed, you might suggest removing the shoes and leaving them outside. You might also, bring a basin of water and offer to wash their feet. So, that puts foot washing in a different perspective.

Putting the Bible into perspective in other ways provides a greater understanding. Geographic perspective, for instance. Bethlehem is seven miles from Jerusalem. It may be helpful to know that Capernaum is on the northwestern shore of the Sea of Galilee and it is 118 miles from Jerusalem. The easiest route to travel, following the Jordan River, avoids the mountainous region and Samaria. It is my belief that we hear the names but have no idea where they are.

What about the weather and climate? Israel had two seasons. The hot dry season, generally *Adar* to *Cheshvan* (March through October) and the mild wet season *Cheshvan* to *Adar* (November through mid-March). But, you must remember that the Jewish calendar is a lunar calendar. See appendix.

Many modern day readers have a tendency to forget that Jesus was a practicing Jew. First of all, he was circumcised. Maryamor (Mary's Aramaic name) and Joseph would follow *Halakhah* Jewish Law—the *Torah* (the first five books of the Bible also called the *Pentateuch*), the Prophets (the 49 books in the Old Testament and the *Talmud* (the 613 laws that make up the Oral Law, best described as the way Jewish people are to deal with each other). Maryamor, Joseph, and Jesus would follow these laws, they would pray, they would follow celebration days, they would participate in sacrifices as dictated by the law, and attend synagogue regularly.

To compare the Jewish calendar (the lunar calendar) to our calendar, please see the graphic in the appendix.

So, with that background, let's get right to the story.

THE BIRTHS—CONTRASTED

Leah bas Ezekiel

The woman who would be Judah's mother, Leah bas Ezekiel, was the daughter of Ezekiel bar Jacob and was of the Jewish elite. She was from a rich and powerful Pharisee family. Her uncle was a member of the Sanhedrin, the Jewish Supreme Court. She was married to Simon bar Simon (son of Simon from Kerioth, a small village in southwestern Judea). Judah's father, Simon, was the premiere furniture maker in Egypt. Simon's family lived in a grand palace in Jerusalem, one of three he owned. Leah was at their Alexandria Palace awaiting the birth of her child so that she could have the assistance of Shifra and Puah, the finest midwives of the time. Her husband was at their palace in Cairo. He had been checking on the work at his Cairo workshop.

Preparations had been made for the impending birth. Simon had constructed a custom birthing chair for his wife. The padded chair, with the center of the seat cut out, had padded leg rests and an adjustable backrest. It was tall enough for the midwife to slip her chair under the seat so that she could catch the baby in her lap.

An extra bedroom had been set aside for the birthing process and *tumat yoledet*, the time of separation following a birth required by Jewish law, seven days for a son, fourteen for a daughter, as part of the forty days of being considered unclean. In addition to the birthing chair, there was a bed where Leah would sleep with the baby for the forty days of impurity. A horn of pure olive oil (for lubrication and to soothe the baby's skin), folded pieces of cloth for *fomentations* (compresses to alleviate pain), sea sponges, pieces of woolen cloth for modesty to cover her during the birthing process, bandages to swaddle the baby, a small clay pot of sea salt (an antiseptic to wash Leah and the baby), a fresh skin of wine (for its antiseptic qualities) and containers of penny royal (when crushed the leaves smell like spearmint to freshen the birthing room) and barley *groats* (to make a tea to relieve heartburn and stomach cramps) and platters of apples and quince (also to freshen the air in the room)... all of these items, necessary for the midwife and the impending birth, were already stocked on a table in the room.

Leah's friends were standing by to assist the midwives. The friends would work in shifts day and night to provide support and comfort, massage her during the labor and wipe her face and body with damp cloths. They had displayed the *Shir HaMa'alot* prayer over Leah's bed, as was the custom. *"I will lift up mine eyes unto the hills, from whence cometh my help. My help cometh from the* LORD, *which made heaven and earth. He will not suffer thy foot to be moved: he that keepeth thee will not slumber. Behold, he that keepeth Israel shall neither slumber nor sleep. The* LORD *is thy keeper: the* LORD *is thy shade upon thy right hand. The sun shall not smite thee by day, nor the moon by night. The* LORD *shall preserve thee from all evil: he shall preserve thy soul. The* LORD *shall preserve thy going out and thy coming in from this time forth, and even for evermore."*

This was to be the first thing that the baby should see. Everyone was experienced in her assigned job. Judah's birth was without complications. He entered this world crying loudly. It was almost like he wanted everybody to know he was here. He was washed with a combination of sea salt water and wine and wrapped in soft woolen strips. Leah was also cared for, washed, cleaned, rubbed with purifying oil, and covered in accordance with Jewish law. As was the custom, purifying oil was made of the finest olive oil containing tincture of myrrh, sandalwood, cinnamon and frankincense. It had a gentle aroma of sweet lemons. The purifying oil was massaged into Leah's skin, cleansing, purifying and hydrating her and emitting a pleasant aroma for her and her visitors. Leah was resting, Judah was sleeping quietly, and the attendants carefully cleaned the room, removing all of the remains of the birthing process save the birthing chair which they carefully cleaned. Only then were the men invited into the room where Leah would remain for the 40 days of *niddah*, the customary time of impurity.

Simon bar Simon was the first of the group of men, his friends and customers, that had assembled there to support him. Simon embraced Leah and was handed his son. He was proud of his two daughters but this was a son, his legacy. Judah began his loud crying one again. Simon looked at his friends and said, "He wants you to know he is here." Judah soon quieted and returned to sleep.

When all of the men were in the birthing room, Leah proudly announced the *Birket HaGoMel* prayer "*Baruch ata Adonai, Eloheinu melech ha-olam, ha-gomel l'chayavim tovot she-g'malani kol tov*" (Blessed are You, Lord our God, ruler of the world, who rewards the undeserving with goodness, and who has rewarded me with goodness.) Her loud voice awoke the sleeping Judah and he loudly pronounced his version of the prayer. Leah concluded by thanking God for protecting her in pregnancy. It was the custom to pronounce the prayer in the presence of 10 men. The assembled men replied, "*Mi she-g'malcha kol tov, hu yi-g'malcha kol tov selah*" (May He who rewarded you with all goodness reward you with all goodness forever).

Miriam bas Jochan

The two births couldn't have been more different. Nazarene born Maryamor, Miriam bas Jochan, was the virgin who had been chosen by God to be the mother of the Christ child. She had been espoused to her soon-to-be husband, Joseph bar Heli. The Roman Emperor Caesar Augustus had called for a national census as a way to prepare for a new round of taxes, so Joseph had to make the trip to Bethlehem for the census. It was close to the time that Maryamor was to birth the baby who was to be named Joshua bar Joseph and called Jesus. Joseph felt he had to bring Maryamor with him. They went from Nazareth to Bethlehem because Joseph was a direct descendant of King David and must be registered in the city of David, Bethlehem.

Joseph knew, that because of Jewish law, it would be most convenient for them to stay with family. So he went first to his close kin to inquire about a place for him and Mary-amor to stay. Many people had journeyed to Bethlehem for the census, and the town was overflowing with travelers, all seeking accommodations. By the time Joseph and Maryamor

arrived in Bethlehem, Joseph's relatives had already committed all of their available space to other relatives. Finding a
warm place for them was essential because Maryamor was
already in pre-labor.

His cousin offered Joseph an area in their stable. Since it
was the lower level of the inn and was warm and out of the
weather. They spread some new hay in a protected area and
provided extra cloth for Maryamor and small containers of
olive oil, sea salt, a skin of new wine and some fresh water. The
cousin's wife and some other cousins were the only women
available to help Maryamor deliver Joshua bar Joseph. The
women attendants expected the delivery to be fraught with
problems since Maryamor was a virgin. However, The Lord
God sent angles and put Maryamor in a deep sleep while
the unseen angels carried out the birth. The baby was born
with little ceremony and no problems. The attendant had
washed the baby Jesus with salt water and wrapped him in
strips of woolen cloth and placed him in a nearby manger
that was filled with clean, sweet-smelling hay. She cleaned
the sleeping Maryamor and massaged her with a spikenard
oil so that she would awake to a smell of frankincense. The
anti-inflammatory and antibacterial properties of the oil
mixture would be beneficial in Maryamor's healing process. It was then that the angels awakened Maryamor. Her
first words were the response to the *Barchu*, "*Baruch Adonai
hamevorach le'olam va'ed*" which is "Blessed be the Lord God
forever and ever."

With the baby cleaned and comfortable, the attendants
provided Maryamor with proper clothing to receive Joseph
and his cousin. There was great rejoicing at the birth of this
male child. Many prayers of thanksgiving were offered.

Within the same hour, there was a clamoring outside the stable. Joseph met a small group of men and young boys. They relayed the happenings of earlier in the evening and how they were told of the birth of a savior. They had come to pay homage and worship this divine baby. Many prayers were offered as well as blessings on the baby.

During this entire process, the baby Jesus lay quietly. It was like he was listening. There was what seemed a smile on his face and a sparkle in his eye. His countenance gave one the impression that he knew what was happening around him and why, and that he approved.

A young shepherd boy presented Joseph a newborn lamb for him to present at the temple for sacrifice. "This is for you, as an offering to God from all of us for this special child." The boy added, "We are honored to have been a part of his birth and pray God's blessings on you, the baby, and his mother"

The shepherds soon left, taking their sheep back to the fields where they had been told of the birth. The cousin and his wife returned upstairs to their other guests, leaving Joseph and Maryamor to bask in the glow of the infant Jesus and their shared happiness. The animals that had shared in the birth settled back into their stalls and joined the baby in blissful sleep. Maryamor looked at the baby and prayed a prayer of thanks to God for the honor of being selected to be this precious one's mother. Her gaze shifted to Joseph. She prayed thanks to God for providing this man who had willingly accepted her, even after he found that she was pregnant. Joseph was certainly God's gift to her. With those happy thoughts, Maryamor slipped into a restorative sleep.

Joseph gave thanks to God for the baby, the sheep for offering, and the goodness of his family for their place to stay. And, for being selected to be the baby's father on earth. He took a deep breath. The aroma of the fresh, sweet hay made him smile. It was a happy smell and closely matched his feelings. He smiled again and drifted off to sleep alongside his wife.

For that moment, all was right with the world.

Author's Comments

Maryamor

Maryamor was born in c.18 BCE in Nazareth to Joachim and Anne. Her original Aramaic name is translated Maryamor or Mariam. In the Greek translation it is Mapia which translates to Maryamor in English. When she was 3-years-old, Joachim and Anne took her to the Temple and presented her for service. She served as a member of the Virgin Group, sewing for the priests and cleaning the Temple. She would have been about 13 when she was visited by the Archangel Gabriel and about 14 when Jesus was born. Maryamor's pregnancy was announced to her by the Archangel Gabriel as she was drawing water at the central well in Nazareth. The idea was distressful for Maryamor since, although she was betrothed to Joseph, she was still a virgin. According to Jewish law, being pregnant before marriage was grounds for her to be stoned to death. The angel told her not to despair. Joseph's vision assured him that the baby she would carry was the Son of God. It was a miracle. Maryamor's cousin, Elizabeth, barren for many years, became pregnant. The angel told her she would have a son to be called John, and he would be the forerunner of Jesus.

Although some sources differ, Maryamor had at least four

sons and two daughters following Jesus' birth: James, Joseph, Simon, Judas, Salome and Miriam. Since Joseph had been married before, she had at least one-step son, James. Jesus' presentation as the "Son of God" was occasionally questioned because of his half brothers and sisters.

Maryamor was a direct descendant of King David through David's third son, Nathan, whose mother was Bathsheba. Jesus' official linage to David is as follows: Jesus was the son of Maryamor the daughter of Joachim, the son of Heli, the son of Matthat, the son of Levi, the son of Melchi, the son of Janna, the son of Joseph, the son of Mattathias, the son of Amos, the son of Naum, the son of Esli, the son of Nagge, the son of Maath, the son of Mattathias, the son of Semei, the son of Joseph, the son of Juda, the son of Joanna, the son of Rhesa, the son of Zorobabel, the son of Salathiel, the son of Neri, the son of Melchi, the son of Addi, the son of Cosam, the son of Elmodam, the son of Er, the son of Jose, the son of Eliezer, the son of Jorim, the son of Matthat, the son of Levi, the son of Simeon, the son of Juda, the son of Joseph, the son of Jonan, the son of Eliakim, the son of Melea, the son of Menan, the son of Mattatha, the son of Nathan, who was the son of David. David's lineage goes directly to Abraham.

THE CIRCUMCISIONS

In Alexandria: Judah's Circumcision

Eight days had passed since the birth of Judah bar Simon. It was time for the baby to be taken to the Synagogue for his circumcision. This was a job for Simon since Leah's time of *niddah* was still 32 days away. Simon had been working on a special order at his workshop in Cairo, the second of his three palaces. He had been alerted of the impending birth when Leah's pains indicated to Puah that the birth was expected within days. A servant was dispatched on a fast camel to tell Simon. Simon and the servant returned to Alexandria only hours before Judah's birth.

There were religious requirements for Leah, but Simon happily handled the arrangements for the *Brit Milah,* commonly referred as *Bris.* Since the birth coincided with the customary timing of the ceremony, most of the arrangements were a simple process. The *Bris* would be at the Alexandria Basilica Synagogue.

The Alexandria Basilica Synagogue was the largest, most beautiful and most expensive synagogue in the entire Jewish world. An inscription there gave high praise to Ptolemy II for the right to build it and for granting sanctuary to Jews. It was Ptolemy II's formal proclamation that synagogues were considered sanctuaries and were *out of bounds* for non-Jews. Ptolemy III and IV and Julian Caesar reconfirmed the proclamation.

Simon had approved the arrangements with the synagogue's kitchen staff and the menu for the celebration feast *Shalom Zakhar*, which was to be held *erev Shabbat*, the grand feast that would take place the evening before the Sabbath and the *Bris* ceremony. This was a special evening. Dozens of Simon's friends and leaders of the synagogue assembled at the synagogue. Wine was flowing freely, and the assembled were in high spirits.

All of the arrangements had been made for the *Bris* at the Alexandria Basilica Synagogue. It was Simon's opportunity to show off his new son and the success of his business. Hillel the Elder had been paid to officiate at the *Brit Milah*. Hillel had brought his grandson, Gamaliel, to assist. It would be an opportunity for Gamaliel to meet Simon and his son, Judah. The most trusted *mohel* in Alexandria had been retained to conduct the ceremony. Simon had asked 12 of his special friends to make up the *Minyan*. This group acted as official observers as required by Jewish practice.

The ceremony began with Simon and Judah, along with the *Minyan*, Leah's father Ezekiel, Simon's father Simon the Elder, the *mohel*, Hillel the Elder, Gamaliel and the priest of the synagogue gathering at the ceremonial place. Elijah's chair, the chair that would be used by Ezekiel, Leah's father, was near the table. He would act as *sandek* and hold the baby during the circumcision. As a part of the ceremony, he would be designated as the baby's godfather. Simon's father, with the baby, sat in Elijah's chair, signaling the beginning of the ceremony. With Ezekiel now seated holding baby Judah, the *Bris* ceremony began. Ezekiel carefully lifted the baby. Everyone, save Ezekiel, was standing. Simon was standing next to the *Mohel.*

"Happy is the man You choose and bring near to dwell in Your courtyard." As the *Mohel* continued his blessing, he signaled Simon to move in closer. "This is the Seat of Elijah the Prophet. For your deliverance I hope, O Lord. I have hoped for Your deliverance, Lord, and I have performed Your commandments. Elijah, angel of the covenant, here is Yours before You; stand at my right and support me. I rejoice in Your word, like one who finds great spoils. Those who love Your Torah have abounding peace, and there is no stumbling for them. Happy is the man You choose and bring near to dwell in Your courtyards. We will be satiated with the goodness of Your House, Your Holy Temple."

And, with that blessing, Simon performed his function, handing the ceremonial knife, the *Izmal,* to the *Mohel who* would use it to remove the foreskin. And, that quickly, it was done. Wine was dabbed on the cut both to numb and disinfect it. And with the closing prayer, all assembled, along with all who were watching, adjourned to enjoy the feast to celebrate the joining of the baby to the congregation. Leah and her attending women joined the men and the baby, now officially named Judah bar Simon. Tables lined the walls of the large celebration room. Wine was flowing freely. Many toasts were made. It was the social event in the Jewish community in Alexandria that Simon had wanted.

In Bethlehem: Joshua's Circumcision

It was the eighth day following the birth of Joshua bar

Joseph. It was the day that Jewish Law required circumcision of the newborn. Joseph and his cousin had already discussed the need for the *Bris*. Joseph had wanted it to be done in Jerusalem. After all, the baby was to take over the throne of David. They couldn't help that he was born in a stable in Bethlehem. Surely his circumcision should be kingly.

Joseph knew what the Archangel Gabriel had said to Maryamor, *"Hail Maryamor, thou are highly favored by the Lord God, most high; blessed are you among women. Behold, you shall conceive and bring forth a son, and you shall call his name* JESUS. *He shall be great, and shall be called the Son of the Highest and the Lord God shall give unto him the throne of his father David. He shall reign over the house of Jacob for ever and of his kingdom there shall be no end."* And he remembered what the angel had said to him, *"Joseph, thou son of David, fear not to take Maryamor as your wife: for the child she is carrying was conceived in her by the Holy Ghost. And she shall bring forth a son, and you shall call his name* JESUS: *for he shall save his people from their sins."*

Joseph and Maryamor had discussed the location for the *Bris* at length. Yes, Jesus was to lead the people of Israel. Yes, he was the son of the Lord God most high. Yes, it made sense for priests, Sadducees and the Pharisees to take notice. But Jerusalem was at least a 2-and-a-half-day trip. The baby was still suckling. Maryamor had just begun to heal from the birthing process, and she would not be allowed in the synagogue since she was still unclean. Joseph argued with Maryamor and with his cousin at length, but on the sixth day, he agreed with his cousin. The *Bris* would be held in Bethlehem.

Rebeka, an old Jewish woman who had lived in Bethlehem all of her life, was contacted. She often officiated at *Brit Milah* since there was no rabbi near by. She was readily available. Joseph's cousin had told him that she had performed most of the circumcisions done in Bethlehem. They agreed on a time. The *Bris* would be held in the stable so Maryamor could attend, for she was still *niddah*. Since Joseph was not the baby's biological father he would serve as the *sandak*. The ceremony was a simple one. Had the *Bris* been held in Jerusalem, two ceremonial doves would have had to be sacrificed. At the temple in Jerusalem, merchants had cages of doves available to be bought. In Bethlehem there were no doves to be found. Joseph was worried that not having the sacrifice would negate the ceremony.

Maryamor comforted Joseph. "Joseph, this baby is God's own child. The ceremony will be blessed, doves or no doves."

In addition to Rebeka, Maryamor and Joseph, Joseph's cousin and his wife attended, along with a variety of animals normally in the stable. They were uncharacteristically quiet during the entire ceremony. There was very little formality.

Joseph held the baby. Rebeka fixed the clamp.

"Happy is the man You choose and bring near to dwell in Your courtyard."

As Rebeka finished the ceremonial prayer, two doves flew into the stable and lighted on Maryamor's shoulders and watched quietly. Rebeka's Hebrew wasn't exactly correct nor proper but everyone there knew the prayer and, with one quick action of her well worn *Izmal*, the *Bris* was finished. A few drops of wine were dabbed on the cut as a disinfectant.

"What do you want to call this baby." Rebeka had directed the question to Joseph, but it was Maryamor who answered. *"His name shall be* JESUS: *for he shall save his people from their sins."* And with that, the doves flew out the stable door.

Rebeka had done many ceremonial *Bris* and heard many names in her time doing circumcisions, but Maryamor's pronouncement caused the old woman to stop and stare at Maryamor for a few seconds. With a shrug of her shoulders, she completed the ceremony.

"So, he shall be called Jesus." With that, Rebeka wiped the knife with a wine-soaked cloth, removed the clamp, checked the cut for any residual blood, wrapped the baby's penis with a strip of woolen cloth, and handed Jesus to Joseph. With no ceremony, she asked for the young goat that she had been promised for her services. Joseph quickly handed Jesus to Maryamor.

His cousin brought the young goat and gave it to Rebekah. Quietly, she ambled out of the stable, leading the young goat, and mumbling to herself something like, "Well, now I've seen everything."

But no one heard because the animals had started celebrating.

Joseph took the new skin of wine from his cousin and took a long swallow as if to say, thank God. He then passed it back to his cousin who took a long swallow. It had been a successful ceremonial ritual, even with little planning.

There was no Elijah chair, no *Minyan*, no celebration, no visiting celebrities, no Pharisees, no *Mohel*. The differences between the circumcisions of Judah and Jesus were as different as their births.

However, call it God's plan, fate, or just plain circumstance, these two births and the lives of these two men would be inextricably connected.

Author's Comments

Joseph

There is no documentation when Joseph was born, but for the benefit of this story we are estimating the year of his birth to be c.41 BCE in Nazareth. He was the son of a carpenter and followed in the steps of his father. He was called a *Tekton,* a Greek word indicating he was more than a simple woodworker. By definition, he would have been a craftsman with some education, and he was often called a *naggar* (a very learned man, highly literate in the *Torah*). He had married Salome when he was 19 and had one child James c.20 BCE. Salome died c.18 BCE, Joseph and his mother raised James. He was placed in synagogue school when he was five years old. Joseph perfected his furniture building skills during the day and taught his son at night. James joined his father when he was 11 years old. He showed a natural aptitude for building furniture, and with no help from his father, was building quality furniture before he was 14. Joseph enjoyed a full life even though he was not married. He was well respected in Nazareth and he was successful.

Nazareth was a small village of no more than 400 people. It was a warm autumn day in the month of *Tishri,* just before *Yom Kippur,* that the rabbi asked Joseph to meet with Joachim.

Joseph knew Maryamor. After all, Nazareth was a small town. The rabbi mentioned that it had been almost 15 years since Salome had died and wasn't it time for Joseph to consider taking a bride. Joseph said he had not considered it and was happy with just himself and James. The rabbi talked to Joseph about Maryamor's family, her beauty, how healthy she was and how she could take care of his house and have many babies. Joseph respectfully agreed but, since he had not considered marriage, he would pray about it and they would speak again on the next Shabbat. For the next week, Joseph thought about the offer and he prayed. He and James were happy and they had a routine. His house was comfortable just as it was. On the eve of the next Shabbat, Joseph had a dream, a happy dream of a loving family, a wife, five children, a very happy dream. God's answer to what Joseph should do? That is what Joseph believed. Joseph met Joachim and the rabbi, and the agreement was made. Joseph would take Maryamor as his wife after all. Joseph was of the line of King David, and he carried the responsibility to continue his heritage that had it started with Abraham.

When Joseph agreed to marry Maryamor, that began their formal engagement, generally at least a year before the official marriage. It was during that period that Gabriel appeared to Maryamor telling her that she was pregnant and that she would carry the son of the Lord. Joseph had some choices when he discovered the pregnancy. He could have quietly denounced the marriage and simply returned Maryamor to her parents. He could have publicly exposed the pregnancy, denouncing that he had any involvement. According to Deuteronomy 22:21, she could be stoned, *"Then they shall bring out the damsel to the door of her father's house, and the men of her city shall stone her with stones that she die.*" Thanks to Joseph's dream, Gabriel had prepared him for the news about Maryamor. So, he accepted her as his wife and his role as Jesus' father on earth.

Joseph's royal linage: David the king begat Solomon of his wife Bathsheba; Solomon begat Roboam; Roboam begat Abia; Abia begat Asa; Asa begat Josaphat; Josaphat begat Joram; Joram begat Ozias; Ozias begat Joatham; Joatham begat Achaz; Achaz begat Ezekias; Ezekias begat Manasses; Manasses begat Amon; Amon begat Josias; Josias begat Jechonias; Jechonias begat Salathiel; Salathiel begat Zorobabel; Zorobabel begat Abiud; Abiud begat Eliakim; Eliakim begat Azor; Azor begat Sadoc; Sadoc begat Achim; Achim begat Eliud; Eliud begat Eleazar; Eleazar begat Matthan; Matthan begat Jacob; Jacob begat Joseph, the husband of Maryamor.

Was Jesus related to King David and to Abraham? If you look at the lineage charts for Maryamor and for Joseph, you see that they were both on a direct family line to both King David and Abraham. Jesus was of the house of David from a physical line from his mother and from a legal line from his father.

Bethlehem

The town of Bethlehem had a population of 300 at the time of the census that was required by Emperor Augustus. The town was called the City of David since King David was born there.

Bethlehem was located 6.2 miles (10 km) south of Jerusalem. It was probably named for the Canaanite fertility god,

LeHem. At the time of the census, its economy was almost totally agriculture.

Bethlehem was an old city, even in Biblical terms. The earliest written reference to the town of Bethlehem was in 1350 BC (BCE). The Amarna letters mentioned Bethlehem as a town inhabited by the Canaanites.

The Hebrew Bible called Bethlehem "a fortified city built by Rehoboam" and identifies the city as where David was born and where he was crowned King of Israel.

"But you, Bethlehem, though you be small among the clans of Judah, out of you will come for me one who will be a ruler over Israel, whose origins are from old, from ancient time. He will stand and shepherd his flock in the strength of the Lord, in the majesty of the name of the Lord his God. And they will live securely, for then his greatness will reach to the ends of the Earth." Micah 5: 2-4 NIV

The Amarna letters are clay tablets dating from 1330 BCE. They were written by Abdi-Heba, Egyptian appointed governor of Jerusalem. They are mostly written in a script known as Akkadian Cuneiform, the writing system of ancient Mesopotamia rather than that of ancient Egypt, and the language used has sometimes been characterized as a mixed language, Canaanite-Akkadian.

MARYAMOR—SEPARATION & PURIFICATION

The stable where Jesus was born would be the family's residence for the next 40 days. But that was perfectly all right with Maryamor. She loved the sweet smell of fresh hay. She loved being near the animals. At night, she would nestle in the sweet-smelling hay next to her husband. The manger would be the bed for Jesus except when he was restless. Then Maryamor would nestle him next to her, and that is where he would sleep. He was almost always hungry and would nurse anytime Maryamor would accommodate.

It was a wonderful time for Maryamor. She was able to hold this little baby. It was something she had dreamed about. She had cuddled the baby dolls made of strips of cloth. She would whisper to them. She would hold them close to her breast like they were suckling just as the Nazarene mothers she had watched. Now, it was the same but better. It was real. A real baby. Her baby.

The marvelous feeling of providing milk to the little one. A real baby to talk to, who would make noises in response. And, this real baby was to be a future king, King of the Jews. It was almost too much for Maryamor's teenage sensibilities to handle. But she need only look at the babe she was holding. And she knew, it was real.

The baby's cry would silence the animals. The lambs were

especially watchful. She could walk in the area where the lambs were kept. She could sit with them. Their bleating would change. It was more a soft welcome than a demand for food. They would nuzzle her. They would gently lick the hands and feet of the baby.

"What are you doing, Maryamor?" It was Joseph's question.

"Watching the baby and the sheep. This is all so amazing. I never knew how wonderful it was to be a mother."

"Enjoy this time while you can, Maryamor. Very soon we will be going to Jerusalem and then back home to Nazareth."

That time came too soon for Maryamor.

The Trip to Jerusalem

Joseph and his cousin loaded a donkey with the supplies needed for the two-and-a-half-day trip to Jerusalem and the return. Joseph had planned to return to Bethlehem before heading home to Nazareth. Maryamor would ride the same donkey she had ridden on their trip to Bethlehem. Joseph would walk and lead the second donkey.

The easiest route would be the western road, the Via Maris. Even though the eastern road was shorter, it was also more mountainous. With advice from his cousin, Joseph had planned to make his way to Via Maris and stay the first night at the inn owned by a friend of his cousin near Caesarea. The second night they would stay at the home of Joseph's good friend at Emmaus. In Jerusalem they would stay at the home of an uncle.

With the plans made, Maryamor fluffed up the hay that was their bed and she and Joseph slept early. The baby was restless, so he soon joined his mother next to Joseph. The animals, too, were restless. It was as if everyone sensed the impending trip.

The sun made hits appearance early, providing a wakeup call for the family. Maryamor and Joseph said their farewells and began their trip with excitement and a bit of trepidation.

Via Maris was the country's main north/south route. It

connected the Persian Royal Road to Egypt. The Persian Royal Road was the main route for goods from the East to the ports in Lydia, and from there to the Roman Empire. Since the road was well- traveled, it was less likely for thieves to challenge a lone couple traveling. They took Via Maris to Caesarea. The plan was to overnight at the inn recommended by his cousin. It was a full day's travel. Maryamor had insisted that the young lamb given to her by the shepherd boy be her sacrifice, so the lamb rode on the donkey or around Joseph's neck. It was near the end of the day when Joseph, Maryamor and the baby reached the inn's location.

Maryamor was surprised that the inn was a two-story complex protected by a metal gate. The gatekeeper met them and, when Joseph mentioned his cousin's name, they were welcomed. The innkeeper graciously invited them into the front room of the inn. A young woman, the daughter of the innkeeper, washed their feet, and the wife of the innkeeper came to greet Maryamor and the baby.

There was much to do over the baby. The innkeeper's wife wanted to hold the baby and so did her daughter. While the women held the baby and talked with Maryamor, the innkeeper took Joseph to a room on the lower level of the quadrangle building. It was close to the well and it was very clean. He asked about the health of Joseph's cousin and his family and told Joseph of their close friendship and how happy he was that Joseph would choose his inn. The gate-keeper had already unloaded the donkey and taken the pair of donkeys and the young lamb to the stable where they were fed and watered.

By the time Joseph and the innkeeper returned to the front room, Maryamor had agreed, with Joseph's approval, to join the innkeeper's family for the evening meal. It was a pleasant meal. The daughter entertained the baby, giving Maryamor time to enjoy the meal. After the meal, the men talked while Maryamor helped clear the table. Everyone had eaten except Jesus and He made it clear that he was hungry. It didn't take long for the baby to be sound asleep. Seeing that, Joseph suggested that their conversation should end and they should retire to their room. Sleep came quickly and so did the morning.

The gatekeeper helped Joseph load the donkey. Maryamor completed the baby's morning routine and filled the water containers at the well. The innkeeper's wife had packed some bread and honey for their trip. Maryamor climbed on her donkey and took the baby from the innkeeper's daughter. Joseph picked up the lamb and draped it around his neck. They bid farewell and started on their way to Emmaus.

It was another long day on the road. Via Maris was busy with merchants and a few travelers. They arrived at Joseph's friend's house, and the entire entourage was made comfortable. Maryamor and the baby retired early. Joseph visited with his friend but very soon excused himself and joined Maryamor and the baby.

Day three on the road was more difficult. The baby had become accustomed to a schedule when they were in Bethlehem and the trip was changing his schedule. He was restless. He had slept most of the trip comfortably nestled in his mother's arms. But the final day of the trip, he was fussy, not comfortable even when suckling.

Maryamor was uncomfortable riding the donkey. She tried walking but couldn't walk as fast as Joseph. That was stressful for Joseph. The lamb wasn't happy, and his bleating started to be annoying. So, the day was stressful for all concerned. Everyone was happy when they neared Jerusalem and reached Joseph's uncle's house.

The donkeys were happy to be settled in their stalls with clean hay and fresh water. The lamb was happy to be in a small stall where he could rest from the road and nestle in clean hay. The baby was washed and happily settled in a cradle provided by Joseph's aunt. Maryamor had time to wash herself and change clothes. She was even able to wash her hair, so she was happy, refreshed, and comfortable. Joseph washed, changed clothes, and joined his uncle on the roof for some wine and cheese. The soft breeze and the setting sun were cooling, so Joseph was happy visiting with his uncle and enjoying the wine and cheese. And Joseph's uncle was happy to have family with him, especially with the new baby. Joseph took time to discuss the amazing happenings.

The women joined them, bringing fresh bread, more cheese, olives, figs and some dried meats. Joseph picked up his story with the visitations of the angels and the news of the baby. He told of the miracle of the birth. And how happy he was to have been chosen by God for these blessings. It was really the first opportunity Joseph had had to tell his story. Maryamor excused herself to check on the baby. He was awake and ready to be fed. As usual, suckling ended with the baby sound asleep. She wrapped him and went back to the roof with him. Torches had been lit during her absence. Her aunt insisted on holding the baby.

It was a happy time for all.

Joseph's uncle insisted that they stay after Maryamor's purification at least until after *Shabbat*. Joseph wanted to leave as soon as the ceremony was completed, but his uncle wouldn't hear of it. In a way, Joseph was happy because the break in the travel would give everyone time to relax.

The uncle soon suggested that the next day would be a busy one for all, so they should retire to get some sleep. Maryamor offered to help clear the food, but her aunt insisted she take the baby and go to their room.

Maryamor, Joseph and the baby nestled into the comfortable bed and were soon asleep.

Jerusalem

History doesn't report when Salem (Jerusalem) was founded but Salem is mentioned in Genesis, *"Melchizedek king of Salem brought forth bread and wine: and he was the priest of the most high God."* Genesis 14:18 History does report, however, that King David conquered the city in 1000 B.C., defeating the Canaanite tribe (the Jebusites) which occupied the city called Jebus at the time. King David named the city the capital of the Kingdom of Israel, and it was called the City of David. When King David's son, Solomon, was named King, he built the first temple (called Solomon's Temple). Solomon was king from 970 B.C. to 931 B.C. The Temple took seven years to build, and history doesn't report a date of completion.

Jerusalem prospered under the management of King Solomon and many of the 20 kings that followed him. Solomon's son, Rehonoam, replaced him, followed by Abihah, Asa, Jehosaphat, Jehoram, Ahaziah, Athaliah, Joash, Amaziah, Uzziah, Jotham, Ahaz, Josiah, Jehoahaz, Jehoiakim, Jehoiachin and Zedekiah. In 586 B.C., during Zedekiah's reign, Babylonian King Nebuchadnezzar's army conquered Jerusalem and totally destroyed the city, leveling it to the ground. He then took all of the people of Jerusalem to Babylon where they remained in exile for 70 years.

It was October, 539 B.C., when Persian King Cyrus the Great conquered Babylon, the capital of the Babylonian Empire. The Battle of Opis took place near the confluence of the Tigris and Euphrates Rivers some 59 miles north of modern Baghdad. King Cyrus allowed the people of the City of David to return to their homes and, under the direction of Zerubbabal and Joshua, they rebuilt the temple and the alter, which was known as the Second Temple. Nehemiah was appointed as governor of Judah by King Artaxerxes I. Nehemiah directed the rebuilding of the walls around the city. The second temple (called Zerubbabal's Temple) was built in 516 B.C. and was the center of Jerusalem throughout Jesus' life.

The Temple

Herodes Magnus, called Herod the Great, was appointed king over Israel in 37 B.C. He was not Jewish by birth. He was an Edomite, a descendant of Esau. His family had converted to the Jewish faith, so Herod lived as a Jew. He was king for 33 years, and, during his reign, Jerusalem experienced a major growth and transformation as did the temple and the Temple Mount.

The Temple of God was constructed at The Temple Mount, the highest point in Jerusalem. It was also known as *Har Habayit*, "the Mountain of the House of God". It was the focal point of the city. Herod's changes included turning the entire Temple Mount into a huge flat platform surrounded by a massive retaining wall. Herod's Palace was the centerpiece of the upper city where the wealthy aristocrats and priestly families lived. The upper city was east of the temple. There were many white marble mansions and palaces and wide avenues. South of the city, on a lower plateau, was the lower city. It included much of the ancient city, and it is where the poor lived. Small houses and narrow, unpaved streets characterized the lower city.

Gates were constructed to allow for organized entry and exit from the city and the temple. The Sheep Gate opened on the portico where merchants sold sheep and doves for sacrifice. Southwest of the lower city was The Zion Gate that led to the Jewish section of the city. The Dung Gate was the primary trash removal gate and led to the valley where the refuse of the city was burned. Its location was chosen because the prevailing winds would generally carry the smells away from the city. Depending on the source, there were between 12 and 20 gates in the walled city.

The important gate for Maryamor and Joseph was The Beautiful Gate, also called The Eastern Gate and The Women's Gate. It opened onto the Women's Court, the place where the ceremonial cleaning of Maryamor's impurity would be conducted. According to Jewish Law (Leviticus 12:2-8), for 40 days following Jesus' birth, Maryamor was considered to be unclean, *tumat yoledet*. Maryamor was to present "a lamb of the first year for a burnt offering, the lamb was to be presented to the priest at the door of the congregation. The lamb would be offered before the Lord and made as an atonement for her. And she shall be cleansed from her impurity." Leviticus 12:6 Two doves were also to be presented to the priest as a sin offering for the child.

Maryamor's Purification & Jesus' Recognition

Maryamor, Joseph, and the baby were up early the next morning, the morning of her purification. Joseph had carried the young lamb presented to her by the shepherd boy in Bethlehem. Maryamor and the baby, Joseph and the young lamb, the uncle and aunt were a festive parade through the dirt streets of the lower city to The Beautiful Gate of the temple, The Women's Gate. There were others already waiting there when they arrived. For Maryamor, it seemed like forever, but finally they were next.

Joseph presented the young lamb to the priest. He said his prayer and accepted the lamb. He asked for the doves to complete the ceremony. Joseph had brought no doves and neither had the uncle. The priest then said without doves he could not complete the sin offering. After a moment of silence, a pair of doves flew in and settled on Maryamor's shoulder. Their cooing punctuated the amazement of the priest who was speechless. After regaining his composure, he collected the doves and placed them in the cage with the others collected that morning. He completed his prayer and asked for the baby.

It was Jewish custom for the first-born male child to be presented at the synagogue as a gift to God. *"Every male that openeth the womb, shall be called holy to the Lord,"* so the baby Jesus was brought to Jerusalem to be presented to the Lord as the law directed.

Maryamor removed the cover from the baby's face and handed baby Jesus to the priest. The priest on duty that morning was an elderly priest named Simeon. Simeon took the baby and looked into his face. Tears began to fall from the old man's eyes. A few of the tears fell on the face of the baby and the baby smiled. Simeon smiled and looked to heaven and said in a soft but audible voice, *"Lord, now let your servant depart in peace, according to your word; for my eyes have seen your salvation which you have prepared in the presence of all people, a light for revelation to the Gentiles and for glory to your people Israel."* Simeon was not speaking to Maryamor and Joseph. It was as if he and the baby Jesus were in the presence of the Lord. Moments passed following the prayer.

Then Simeon spoke directly to Maryamor, *"This child is destined to cause the falling and rising of many in Israel, and to be a sign that will be spoken against, so that the thoughts of many hearts will be revealed. And, a sword will pierce your own soul, too."*

Simeon looked to heaven and said for all to hear, *"Lord, now let thy servant depart this world in peace, for mine eyes have seen the Messiah, thy salvation."* And with that, he handed the baby back to Maryamor, kissed her on the forehead and left the ceremonial area.

The family was silent. They all had seen everything that had happened, but none understood. They walked out of the Women's Court, still without speaking. On the Royal Porch, the Portico, they were approached by an old woman, Anna, daughter of Phanuel an Israelite of the tribe of Asher, a prophetess. "Thank you, Lord God. You have allowed me to see this babe who will be the Messiah we have been praying for. This child will be the redemption of Jerusalem. I have prayed daily here at the Temple for lo, these 84 years. My prayers have been answered; now I will tell all that I meet." Anna left the Royal Porch, telling everyone she saw that she had seen the Messiah.

Joseph, his aunt and uncle were left stunned by the events of the day. Speechless, the trio was left standing on the Royal Porch watching Anna as she left rejoicing, stopping everyone she met, telling them that she had seen the Messiah. Maryamor was smiling. The prediction of the angel was coming true. The baby was smiling too. One could only imagine what the little one was thinking.

Anna had already left through The Women's Gate before composure returned to Joseph and his family. The uncle was the first to speak, "What has just happened, Joseph?"

"I don't really know, but the angels that appeared to us and the shepherds in Bethlehem said he was a special child, the Messiah, and that has been confirmed today by a prophetess and a priest. Just think, the woman had been waiting and praying to see our baby for 84 years, just to see our child! 84 years!"

"Can you imagine," the uncle started, paused and repeated himself. "Can you imagine the priest saying, 'Lord, now let thy servant depart in peace, for mine eyes have seen the Messiah, thy salvation.' I wonder, could this babe be the promised Messiah?"

It was a rhetorical question, and no one attempted to answer him.

No one spoke on the short way back to the uncle's house. Maryamor hummed a lullaby to the baby. The baby was smiling. The rest were totally engrossed in their thoughts. Nothing was said about the unusual happenings at the temple when the group returned home. Maryamor assisted in the kitchen now that she was ceremonially clean. Joseph helped his uncle chop and stack wood. The men washed for dinner and the women carried plates and bowls to the table on the roof.

The uncle stood for prayer. "Holy Father, I ask Your blessings on this house and our visitors, our family. The events of this day are puzzling. If this baby is the promised by Isaiah, Jeremiah and the prophets of the Bible, then we rejoice. I thank you, Lord. Amen and Amen." After the meal, each found a comfortable pillow, and they sat and talked. Maryamor told of the visit of Gabriel and his promise. Joseph told of his visitation. Maryamor told of the unusual happenings with the doves and the animals at Bethlehem. Soon the sun was setting and provided an ever-changing painting in the western sky. *Shabbat* would begin at sunset.

The group retired to their sleeping rooms. Soon, they would revisit the Temple.

It was a happy group that walked to the temple. The men in their best robes and the women in their finest head scarves. They separated when they reached the "Portico," the women proceeding to The Women's Court and the men to the Court of the Israelites.

The service began with a blessing, which was followed by the Shema. The *Shema* is the oldest statement of our unequivocal belief in the one true God and one of the most sacred prayers in all Judaism. "*Shema Yisrael Adonai Eloheinu, Adonai echad. Barch shem k'vod malchuto, l'olam va'ed.*" "Hear O Israel, the LORD our God, the LORD is one. Blessed be His glorious name, whose kingdom is forever and ever." Other prayers and readings from the Torah followed, ending with *the Amidah*, a prayer consisting of nineteen blessings, said both aloud and silently.

After the service, the men participated in social discussions, and the women talked among themselves. There was much attention paid to the baby, but nothing was said about the happenings of the day before. Neither Anna nor Simeon were at the temple.

Joseph and his family spent a pleasant and relaxing day together.

The trip back to Bethlehem was a mirror of the trip to Jerusalem, with the exception that Joseph wasn't carrying the lamb. They were again made welcome in Emmaus and at the inn in Caesarea. Back in Bethlehem, the donkeys recognized home and quickly settled in the stable. It was late when they arrived at their uncle's inn, so Maryamor, Joseph and the baby went straight to their room. Sleep came quickly.

The sun rose on another hot, dry day in Bethlehem. It was Wednesday. The next day they would be preparing for the trip home. The baby was restless. The constant rocking of the donkey and being in his mother's arms had kept him quiet and settled during the trip to and from Jerusalem. Back in Bethlehem, nothing would settle him. Suckling, usually the best thing to quiet him, was short and did little to quiet him. Maryamor would hold him, and he would settle for a few minutes and then start crying. It was as if he knew something was about to happen. Maryamor didn't know what to do. Her aunt offered to rock him. That worked and he went to sleep.

Joseph helped his uncle with repairs to the inn. It was fair payment for the days at the inn and welcomed help for his uncle. The late afternoon was spent organizing things for the trip back to Nazareth. The food and a skin of good wine relaxed the adults. Even the baby was quiet. All finally went to bed. They needed a good night's sleep since Joseph had planned to return home on Thursday.

The family awoke to quite a commotion.

The Arrival of the Kings from the East

Joseph was awakened by a frantic knock at his room door. "You have visitors and you need to hurry." Joseph could tell by his uncle's voice that it was urgent. Joseph quickly slipped on his tunic, sandals and his robe and, with his uncle, walked to the front door of the inn. Joseph was at a total loss for words.

It was Melchior, a short heavy man wearing an ornate jeweled crown, who spoke first, "Are you Joseph, husband of Maryamor, mother of the new King of the Jews?"

"Yes." That was all Joseph was able to respond.

Balthazar, a tall black man with a heavy beard, next spoke up, "We have traveled from various places in the Parthian Empire to bring gifts to the new King."

Casper, dressed in more simple robes but with a magnificent golden crown, was the next to speak, "Each of us is a king. We are from different places but met in Jerusalem. We were asking King Herod where the new king was born. Our astronomers had each seen his star. So, we are here to present gifts and pay our respects."

Each of the kings was accompanied by a group of attendants. Melchior was accompanied by his astronomer, his chief priest, 12 mounted guards, 24 servants, 12 liverymen, and 7 storekeepers. Balthazar also brought his astronomer and chief priest, 10 mounted guards, 20 servants, 14 liverymen and 10 storekeepers. Casper also had his astronomer and 12 mounted guards, 20 servants, 10 liverymen and 10 storekeepers.

There were 169 people standing in front of the inn, not to mention 25 camels, as many horses and over 50 donkeys.

Joseph was speechless. So his uncle took charge. "Who is the leader of each entourage?" Lead guards of each group stepped forward. "Take everyone and the animals to the back of the inn. There will be plenty of water there. Gentlemen, if you, and your essential servants will join me on the roof, Joseph will get Maryamor and the baby."

There were enough cushions for all the kings to be seated. Joseph went back to the room to get Maryamor and the baby, and they joined the royalty on the roof. Maryamor was glowing when she walked onto the roof carrying the baby.

Casper was the first to speak as soon as Maryamor and the baby were settled. "I am Casper," he said. "I am king of a principality in Armenia, one of the kingdoms of the Parthian Empire. I am here to celebrate the new King of the Jews. My astronomer reported the star a month ago. My Chief Priest said he would be born in the City of David, so we went to Jerusalem, the City of David. King Herod knew nothing of a new king, but he did suggest that Bethlehem was where King David was born. I bring the new king this jar of the finest Frankincense. A perfume used by the kings of my country,"

"I am Balthazar, ruler of the Kingdom of Nineveh. I, too, am here to celebrate the birth of the King of the Jews. In my kingdom, Myrrh is highly valued, as it is a sweet perfume and is essential at the time of death. My astronomer also reported the star. My Chief Priest knew of an old reference that a new king would be born in the birthplace of the great King David. I, too, came to the City of David in Jerusalem. Casper and Melchior met me there. So, we came together to Bethlehem."

"I am the King Melchior from Persia. All of our kingdoms are in the Parthian Empire. I bring the new king this chest of gold pieces. Our wish is that he be told of our visit so that we can prosper together. Great leaders of great people need to league together. We celebrate his birth."

Each king held the baby and kissed his forehead.

Balthazar recounted their visit with King Herod and his demand that they return to Jerusalem to tell him of the young king and where he was. "As we traveled, an angelic being appeared to me and warned us not to return to Jerusalem. The vision told us to return to our kingdoms and not meet with King Herod. I fear King Herod will want to do harm to the baby."

The kings stood as one, indicating they were ready to start their journey home. For the second time, they each kissed the baby's forehead. Joseph and his uncle led the group to the back of the inn. The entire group quickly prepared for their travel. And, as quickly as they appeared, they were gone.

Joseph and his uncle went back up to the roof. Joseph thanked his uncle for allowing the group to rest behind the inn and for watering the animals. It was the uncle who began the conversation. "Joseph, the king was correct. If Herod believes the baby is a challenge to him, he will want to kill him. You are a good woodworker and a talented furniture maker. You should consider taking Maryamor and the baby outside of Herod's kingdom. I know one of the finest furniture makers in this part of the world, Simon bar Simon. He has a palace and workshop in Alexandria. He may be able to give you a place to stay and a place to work. You should consider it."

It was a few moments before Joseph spoke. "Alexandria is a long way from here but from what the king said, I believe you are correct."

"You are my nephew. We are family. I will provide food that will feed you for a part of the trip. You can take the donkey you used to go to Jerusalem, and you have the treasures given you by the kings. Use some of the gold but keep most of it hidden. I will also give you the names of some of the inns that you can use as you travel the Via Maris. It will be a rough trip, but you know the Lord will be with you, and He will keep the baby and you and Maryamor safe."

Joseph decided his uncle's advice was best. He stayed another day. The pair prepared the food and essentials for the long trip to Alexandria. It would be at least 30 days if they left from Bethlehem, but it would be longer if they were to go to Nazareth and leave from there.

The pair continued the discussion throughout the evening. Joseph wanted to go to Nazareth to collect some of his woodworking tools and make arrangements for the safety of his house and workshop.

Maryamor, Joseph and the baby left early the next day, Monday. They reached Nazareth before sundown and the beginning of *Shabbat*.

NAZARETH—HOME

They arrived at their home in Nazareth in time for Mary-amor to do a quick house cleaning before she bathed herself and the baby as required by *Havdalah* (Jewish religious law). Joseph also bathed after the animals were settled in their stalls. The young family settled in to celebrate their first *Shabbat* as a family in their own home. Joseph lit the candles just before sundown. Joseph welcomed *Shabbat* with the customary prayer. Joseph and Maryamor sang the song welcoming the *Shabbat* angels into the home and Joseph sang "Women of Valor," the song praising the new woman of the house.

The wine, served in wooden *kiddush* cups that Joseph had made, and the two loaves of *challa*, (representing the double portion of manna that fell on the day before *Sabbath* during the exodus), served on Joseph's wooden plates, were blessed and eaten. It was a very festive and symbolic time for the couple. Even the *kiddush* prayer took on special importance.

Before they drank the wine Joseph prayed, *"Blessed are You, the Lord our God, King of the Universe, Creator of the fruit of the vine. (Amen)* Before breaking the bread Joseph prayed, *"Blessed are You, Lord our God, King of the Universe, Who sanctified us with His commandments, and hoped for us, and with love and intent invested us with His sacred Sabbath, as a memorial to the deed of Creation. It is the first among the holy festivals, commemorating the exodus from Egypt. For You chose us, and sanctified us, out of all nations, and with love and intent You invested us with Your Holy Sabbath."*

Even though the *Shabbat* ceremony was invigorating, traveling all day and the ceremonial wine began to settle Maryamor and Joseph, and sleep began to approach. With the baby fed, the entire family settled in for a good night's sleep.

Nazareth was where both Maryamor and Joseph were from.

Nazareth, with a population of 400 people, was not much bigger than Bethlehem, but it did have a synagogue.

It was Sabbath day. A day set aside for rest, prayer and thanking God for blessings. The building could only hold about a hundred people, but there was room outside for all those who wanted to listen to the reading of the *Torah*. The synagogue was the focus of activities for the Jewish people of Nazareth. Family groups would gather early. It was the opportunity for everyone to hear about the good things that were happening. Observing the Sabbath required refraining from work and all talk of work. So, when Maryamor, Joseph, the baby and James arrived, there was good news to talk about. Maryamor and the baby were quickly surrounded by the women. Joseph and James were greeted by the old rabbi who had been the religious leader of the village for many years.

Almost all conversations were about the baby. There were some who didn't believe, some resentful, and some just plain envious of the attention Joseph was getting. But on the Sabbath, none of that could be expressed.

The celebration of the Sabbath is said to have begun on the seventh day of creation and is based on the reference in Genesis. *"And on the seventh day God ended his work which he had made; and he rested on the seventh day from all his work which he had made. And God blessed the seventh day, and sanctified it: because that in it he had rested from all his work which God created and made.*"

In Nazareth, on that day, the celebration was officially begun by the rabbi who sang a call to the people. And the people filled the synagogue. There were many who had to sit on the ground outside, but the windows and doors were open so all could hear. Soon, the *Torah* was unwrapped and placed on the beautiful custom-made stand that Joseph had built for the purpose. The rabbi began to read from Exodus about the deliverance of the Israelites from captivity in Egypt. Joseph couldn't help thinking about the journey he and his family were about to take. As the rabbi read the Mosaic Covenant, the covenant God made with Moses and all generations of Israelites to follow, Joseph personalized each word. It was God's covenant with him. God had chosen him and Maryamor to be the earthly parents of His son. The trip to Egypt would be a difficult one, but the reading assured Joseph that there would be five making the trip - Maryamor, Joseph, the baby Jesus, James, and God. The smile that the thought brought to Joseph's face remained for the entire day.

The *Shabbat* celebration ended Saturday evening as the sun was setting. Joseph was sitting on his roof. It was as if God had made the sunset a graphic representation of his feelings. The bright golden color symbolized his feeling of being God's chosen. The fiery red ball as the sun sank low on the horizon symbolized the fire that he felt as he was beginning a new chapter in his life. The transitions of blues symbolized the calmness of God love. And then the sky was black, no moon, a void. Three stars signaled the end of the Sabbath.

The Trip to Egypt

By the time the sun was peeking over the eastern mountains surrounding Nazareth, Joseph and James were awake, packing and preparing for the trip. It had been decided that James would accompany the family in order to provide additional security and to be an extra hand. A distant cousin of Joseph's lived in the adjoining house and had agreed to take care of his animals and watch after the house.

Joseph had hidden the frankincense, myrrh and some of the gold, the baby's gifts, in the house. Joseph took 50 of the gold coins, divided them into five piles, and wrapped and tied each. He had decided he would hide the packages on Maryamor, the baby and various places in the luggage. He and James also were carrying some money.

Joseph's tools, some food and other essentials were secured on the lead donkey. There was also a place for the baby when Maryamor tired of carrying him. Maryamor had decided she would walk alongside the lead donkey. Joseph walked beside the middle donkey loaded with food for the early part of the trip. James walked with the last donkey loaded with water and clothing.

The trip to Egypt would take at least 42 days and that, only if the small band could average seven hours each day. It would be a long, trying and dangerous trip. Joseph had made the decision to travel on the Jordan River Road from Nazareth to Jerusalem. It was well-traveled by Jewish pilgrims and allowed them to miss the dangerous parts of Samaria. It was the easiest part of the trip, and there were friends along the way to help if needed. It also offered more springs and villages.

The trip started with a simple prayer, "God, I ask that you send angels to protect your son and the rest of our family." It was Joseph's prayer that caused fear to well up in Maryamor.

It was almost more than a teenager could bear, but she remembered what Archangel Gabriel said when he first met Maryamor at the well in Nazareth, "Don't be afraid, Mary; God has shown His grace in you." Holding the baby Jesus close to her, she embraced her husband and said, "Husband, God has shown His grace on us. The angel called me Mary and that is what I want to be called. I know the same angel who told me of this baby will precede us to Egypt and keep all of us safe. My prayer is to the angel Gabriel, 'please keep us safe.'" With that said, Jesus, Mary, James, and Joseph set out for Egypt and the unknown.

The first day on the road was not an easy one. Everyone was on edge. Getting into the routine of the trip was harder than they expected. They decided to overnight on the road and no one got much sleep. By the end of day two, they had reached the Jericho Road. It paralleled the Jordan River. They headed south toward Jerusalem. On day four Joseph decided they would stay in an inn. They all got a full night's sleep. They fill the water jugs and fed the donkeys hay instead of the grass along the road.

The first Sabbath was to be celebrated starting the evening of day six while the group was traveling on the Jericho Road. Joseph had found a small meadow near the Jordan. They settled the donkeys in the afternoon. They were able to wash in the river and prepare for the beginning of the Sabbath. Joseph had prepared a shoulder bag that contained everything they needed to celebrate *Shabbat*. A candle was lighted and the *Kiddush* blessing was recited and each was able to take a swallow of wine from the wine skin. The troop slept peacefully. As she lay next to Joseph, she again whispered her prayer to Gabriel, "Oh Angel Gabriel, please protect us and keep us safe."

When they rose on Sabbath morning, Joseph again recited the *Kiddush* blessing, each had a swallow of wine and a small piece of unleavened bread, and they rested. When the sun was high, Joseph separated himself from the group to pray. Closing his prayer, he asked for forgiveness for breaking Sabbath. When he returned, he said it was time to resume their trip.

On day nine they reached Jerusalem. Joseph arrived at his uncle's house. There was much hugging, and then Joseph requested a night for the family and animals. Happily, the aunt took the baby from Mary, allowing her to bathe. The animals were fed and watered. James and Joseph filled all of the water jugs. Joseph filled his ceremonial wine skin and his uncle provided a second one. The aunt had bathed the baby, wrapped him in a clean soft woolen cloth, and given him some honey. Mary helped with the evening meal, which was served on the rooftop as before. They visited until sunset. The baby was the center of attraction for the women. At sunset, Joseph made his apologies but asked that they be allowed to go to their room. Sleep came quickly and so did the morning.

Breakfast was to be the last for a number of weeks so the aunt provided milk and honey, bread and cheese, some dried meat, dried figs and olives. Mary had suckled the baby while the men were preparing the donkeys. So it was on the road again to Ascalon. It would be a five-day trip, and most of it was across Samarian territory. Mary, again started the journey with her prayer to the Arch Angel Gabriel.

Not long after leaving Jerusalem, they entered a mountain range, one of the more treacherous parts of their trip. Nearing the end of the first day of the trip to Ascalon, the family was surrounded by a group of six thieves. As they approached, the leader asked Joseph where they were going. Mary noticed the baby stopped moving, sat up and was looking at the group. Joseph answered that they were headed for Ascalon.

"That's some dangerous country for two men and a woman." With that he opened his cloak to reveal a *pugio dagger* that was secured by a sash keeping his robe closed. One by one, the rest of the thieves showed a variety of weapons. One had an Egyptian scimitar, another a sicarii dagger.

The leader again spoke, "Traveling? You must have money. Give it to me and you will be allowed to continue."

The baby again stirred and leaned forward. Mary saw what looked like a smile on his small face. Joseph said he had no money. And with that the lead thief grabbed his dagger. As he pulled it out, he cut the sash and his robe fell open. He dropped the dagger and pulled the robe closed to cover himself. The scimitar wouldn't come out of it scabbard. The sicarii-wielding thief cut himself. Another thief tripped on his cloak and rolled off the path down an embankment. The other two thieves took in the spectacle happening in front of them, looked at each other and started laughing. Joseph suggested that this day was not a good day for thievery and moved on down the path. The baby snuggled back into Mary's arms and grabbed for a breast.

The group continued arriving safely at Ascalon about midday on Friday. Joseph picked an inn near the synagogue so that they could attend Shabbat. There was time for everyone to wash and for Mary to wash clothes. The animals were watered and fed and placed in the stall. Joseph had asked the innkeeper if he could have Kiddush on the roof at sundown. The innkeeper was happy to see a traveler who wanted to celebrate Sabbath and welcomed him to use the roof. Shortly before sundown Joseph, James and Mary, holding the baby Jesus, sat on cushions on the roof. Another couple was already there. Mary lit the candle and Joseph recited the prayers. The wine skin was passed around and included the other visitors.

The next morning Joseph and his family were at the synagogue. Joseph marveled at the reading from Hosea "... *Out of Egypt I will call My Son.*" Here they were in a synagogue, a 14-day trip from their home and at least 30 days from their destination, Alexandria, Egypt, and the rabbi was reading about their trip from the Scripture written hundreds of years before they started. That stayed with Joseph the entire day, even when they were preparing for the next day's trip—repacking clothing, refilling the wine skins, organizing the food and refilling the water jugs. It was remarkable. God already knew, and shared through Hosea, what they were going through.

They were up at sunrise. They finished packing the donkeys, settled up with the innkeeper, and headed for the Sea Side highway. For the next 15 days, the Mediterranean Sea would be on their right.

The morning sun had turned the water into a sea of diamonds. Every tiny ripple was a sparkling display. The trip to Alexandria followed the coastline all the way from Ascolon to Pelusium where the route turned inland and followed the

Nile River to Memphis where the group would cross the river. From Memphis, they planned to follow the caravan route north to Alexandria. Gaza was a one-day trip from Ascolon. The beautiful diamonds that covered the Mediterranean had melted into a beautiful blue sheet of glass. Small waves lapped at the shore. It was a magical sound that put the baby Jesus to sleep for much of the day. They spent the night in Gaza in an inn because they knew the next five days would find them sleeping on the road.

Day 16. Water bottles filled. Bread and honey purchased. Clothes washed and packed. Washed at the inn. With sunrise, three donkeys, two men, one woman, a baby, and their God started their journey again. Day 17. Day 18. Day 19. Each, much as the day before.

Mid-afternoon on day 20, they arrived at an oasis on the border of Egypt and Nabatea. There was only one well to refill the water jugs and let the donkeys have a long drink, but there was a number of trees to offer a retreat from the sun. Joseph decided that they would celebrate Sabbath there. It would be a good place to rest and complete the celebration.

Morning. Day 22. Rested. Donkeys loaded. The family was on the road again, almost halfway to Alexandria, Egypt. On the caravan trail, one day was pretty much like every other. Occasionally, a camel caravan would pass. Rarely would anyone stop to talk. Everyone was headed someplace. Day 23. Day 24. Day 25. Day 26.

Day 27. It was midday when they approached the walled city of Pelusium. There was an inn outside the city, and that is where Joseph elected to stay for the Sabbath. Even though the population of Pelusium was well over 1,000, there was no synagogue.

Author's Comments

Pelusium

Pelusium was a walled city built as early as 715 BCE. In 343 BCE, the city was captured by the Persians. In 346, Philophron was put in command of a garrison of 5,000 Greek mercenaries. The city was the site of numerous battles. It was returned to Egypt in 55 BCE by Mark Anthony. It was totally destroyed in 1118 CE by King Baldwin I of Jerusalem. The ruins of the grand amphitheater are still visible on Google maps.

PELUSIUM

Joseph arranged for a room. James unloaded the donkeys and took them to the stable. Joseph entered the city to purchase wine to fill the skins. They bathed and prepared for their fourth Sabbath on the road. They rested on the Sabbath and restocked food and water for their needs on Sunday and stayed one more night at the inn.

The trip to Memphis was made easier because one of the six Roman military roads in Egypt went from Pelusium to Memphis. They reached Memphis in five days. Memphis had one of the oldest synagogues in Egypt, dating from 246 BCE and dedicated to King Ptolemy III and his queen. Joseph found an inn near the synagogue. It was day 34 of their trip. It had been many long days, but they had traveled safely. The family celebrated that evening with the traditional prayers. Joseph added a personal prayer of thanks for the safe trip. They had made it to Egypt.

Once they had made arrangements to cross the Nile, the rest of their trip from Memphis to Alexandria was much easier. They lengthened their travel days and made it to the outskirts of Alexandria on the 41st day, so they were able to celebrate Sabbath on the ending of their six-week journey. As a result, the observance of that Sabbath was definitely a celebration.

Joseph had selected an inn near a synagogue. They

celebrated *Kiddush* in their room and went to sleep early. The next morning, they walked to the synagogue. Joseph was welcomed by the rabbi as Mary was by the women. The baby Jesus was the center of attention. He had smiles for all of the young girls, especially when Mary allowed them to hold him. There was no fretting as he was passed from one to another. Joseph said a silent prayer as he entered the synagogue, "O Lord, protect us here is the foreign land. Protect Your Son. Prosper us as we seek our place in Egypt, this land where the Passover started. Amen"

Joseph was welcomed at the synagogue. He told the rabbi that he was a *tekton* from Nazareth and was new here in Egypt. The rabbi welcomed him, and he was given a place among the craftsmen, an honored group. Then the rabbi read from the *Torah*.

And Moses said unto the people, Remember this day, in which ye came out from Egypt, out of the house of bondage; for by strength of hand the LORD *brought you out from this place: there shall no leavened bread be eaten. This day came ye out in the month Abib. And it shall be when the* LORD *shall bring thee into the land of the Canaanites, and the Hittites, and the Amorites, and the Hivites, and the Jebusites, which he sware unto thy fathers to give thee, a land flowing with milk and honey, that thou shalt keep this service in this month. Seven days thou shalt eat unleavened bread, and in the seventh day shall be a feast to the* LORD. *Unleavened bread shall be eaten seven days; and there shall no leavened bread be seen with thee, neither shall there be leaven seen with thee in all thy quarters. And thou shalt shew thy son in that day, saying, This is done because of that which the* LORD *did unto me when I came forth out of Egypt. And it shall be for a sign unto thee upon thine hand, and for a memorial between thine eyes, that the* LORD'S *law may be in thy mouth: for with a strong hand hath the* LORD *brought thee out of Egypt. Thou shalt therefore keep this ordinance in his season from year to year. And it shall be when the* LORD *shall bring thee into the land of the Canaanites, as he sware unto thee and to thy fathers, and shall give it thee, That thou shalt set apart unto the* LORD *all that openeth the matrix, and every firstling that cometh of a beast which thou hast; the males shall be the* LORD'S. *And every firstling of an ass thou shalt redeem with a lamb; and if thou wilt not redeem it, then thou shalt break his neck: and all the firstborn of man among thy children shalt thou redeem. And it shall be when thy son asketh thee in time to come, saying, What is this? that thou shalt say unto him, By strength of hand the* LORD *brought us out from Egypt, from the house of bondage."*

As Joseph left the synagogue, he again said a prayer, "Thank You, oh Lord, for this sign."

Joseph was again greeted by the rabbi as he left the synagogue. "I have someone I want you to meet." He introduced Joseph to Simon bar Simon whose reputation Joseph knew well. Since it was the Sabbath, they couldn't discuss work. So, Simon told Joseph to visit him on the morrow. That is how God arranged the meeting of Joseph and Simon.

JOSEPH & SIMON—FATHERS WORKING TOGETHER

Joseph and Simon met at Simon's workshop and display area on Canopia Road. Joseph arrived before Simon, allowing him time to look at some of Simon's work and the work of other craftsmen who worked there. The quality of Simon's work matched his reputation.

Joseph was prepared to present information on his work and the names of some of his clients. To his surprise, Simon already knew of Joseph's work and had one of Joseph's desks in his office. Simon showed Joseph around the workshop. There were ten craftsmen working.

"Your work is truly outstanding," Joseph was speaking to Simon but said loud enough for many of the workmen to hear.

As he looked around the workshop, he saw three of the new Roman hand saws. Egyptian hand saws were commonly used in Galilee and throughout the world. They were difficult to use because they were made of copper, a soft metal, and could only be pulled, so sawing wood was a slow, tedious process. The Roman saws were made of iron to make the blade stiffer so they could be pushed and pulled. Also, the teeth were set at opposing angles. It made the sawing faster and smoother. But they were too expensive for the average craftsman.

Craftsmen in Simon's shop, had their own tools, but there were some tools, used in making finer furniture, displayed on the walls for any of them to use when necessary. Joseph saw tools he had only heard about. There was a foot-powered lathe. The faster turning speed and the sharper chisels allowed the craftsmen to make smoother and finer turned work and made matching designs much easier. And, he noticed that each craftsman had a book at their workstand where drawings and measurements were recorded. There were records of tools used and comments to make duplicating a design easier. Joseph had never seen a work area so well organized.

There were at least a dozen apprentices. They were to learn from the masters but they were also there to cut the trees for the lumber used by the craftsmen. Something else new to Joseph.

Simon and Joseph returned to Simon's office.

"Are you ready to join me here, Joseph?" Simon had already made that decision. He then answered Joseph's next question before Joseph had a chance to ask. "There is a house right behind the workshop that would be available to you. It has its own well and stable. And, from the roof you can see the sea and the great Pharos Lighthouse."

Joseph agreed on the house and the payment. Joseph was introduced to Simon's lead craftsman.

Since both were new fathers, the conversation turned to their babies. Finally, they both agreed that they had the smartest children on earth. With the agreement on work arrangements, Joseph returned to the inn to tell Mary and James the good news. While Mary and James got all of their goods packed and loaded back on the donkeys, Joseph went to settle up with the innkeeper. Initially, Joseph had said he didn't know how long they would be there. Working with Simon, a man the innkeeper knew well, was well received.

Joseph paid for the night and pledged that he would build a piece of furniture for the synagogue and donate it in the innkeeper's name. So, everyone was happy when the foursome moved into the house behind the workshop.

The house that Simon was providing was typical of houses for craftsmen of the day. It was much like other houses in Alexandria and in Nazareth as well. The ground floor was a stable with a cooking area that allowing for a fire, cooking utensils and the bread oven. There was also room for storage of large containers for olive oil, wheat, olives, wine, legumes, fruits and vegetables in season. The storage room was secured to protect against mice. This house had it's own well so water would be easily accessible for the family and the animals. There was a rather large area in the walled-in yard with room for kids to play and room for a vegetable garden. The house was in the corner of the walled area. The floor of the second level living area was the ceiling of the covered area of the stable and the storage room. The sleeping area was on the second floor. There was a raised platform at one end of the room. The cushions and mats made sleeping quite comfortable. The roof was the ceiling of the rooms on the second floor. During the dry season and occasional dry days during the wet season, the kids would play on the roof, and that is where the family would eat their meals. The roof was also important as a work area—better light for spinning and weaving and a place for flax to dry.

The roof was accessible from the ground by ladders. On particularly hot days, shade was provided by an awning woven of goat's hair. Unlike most of the houses, Simon's house faced the sea, usually providing cooling breezes and beautiful views.

Joseph quickly became the *go to* craftsman at the workshop.

James stayed in Alexandria for another month before heading back to Nazareth. He knew it was a 40-day trip, but he knew work was piling up and needed to be handled. He borrowed one donkey, mostly for food and water and returned to Nazareth.

Mary quickly became an excellent housekeeper, thanks in part, to her experience as a member of the virgin group at the temple and with the help and advice of the older women at the synagogue. The baby Jesus grew strong and healthy and soon, far too soon for Mary, he was nearing the end of his first year. That fact was made obvious when an invitation arrived announcing a celebration of Judah's first birthday. Jesus was invited. Mary didn't know it, but Leah had decided it would be surprise celebration of Jesus' birthday, too.

Friends from the synagogue brought presents for both babies. They shared food and wine, songs, toasts, good wishes and prayers for the babies and God's plan for each.

The child Jesus grew and became strong in spirit and filled with wisdom and the grace of God. The child Judah grew strong, and the two became inseparable. From the earliest years, Jesus was wise in his actions and exhibited awareness beyond his years. Judah was smart. So they made a good team, even as young children.

Some 20 months later, James showed up in Alexandria with a report from Nazareth. King Herod the Great had heard that Mary and Joseph had presented their new son at the temple. The combination of the report by the Magi that a king was born and statements by the priest Simeon and the prophetess Anne, led Herod to calculate that this child king would have to be under two years of age. So, he sent soldiers to kill all male children two years and younger. Over

14,000 young children were killed. All throughout Galilee were heard the screams and crying of the mothers. The event became known as the Massacre of the Innocents.

James also reported that Herod the Great had died and his kingdom was divided among his sons. Herod Antipas was named Tetrarch of Galilee and Perea. He was as much of a tyrant as his father. So, James recommended that Joseph, Mary, and Jesus should remain in Egypt.

Author's Comments

Herodes Magnus—Herod the Great

Herod was born in 73 BCE in the town of Idumes (Edom in Hebrew) in southern Judea. His father, Antipater, was an Edomite whose ancestors had converted to Judaism. He was raised as a Jew, but his mother was not Jewish, making him only half Jewish. A concern through his lifetime. Antipater was trusted by Julius Caesar, so he named Herod provincial governor of Galilee when he was 25. Herod successfully led an army and captured Jerusalem for Mark Antony in 37 BCE, becoming sole ruler of Judea and naming himself king. The Roman Senate designated him "King of the Jews," changing the Hasmonean Kingdom into the Herodian Kingdom.

For much of his life, Herod suffered from serious mental problems. He was considered to have severe manic paranoia with personality disorder. At times he was a cruel tyrant. He murdered one of his ten wives and her brother, along with three of his sons, after falsely accusing them of having an affair. He also executed two more of his 14 sons for plotting to take his throne. A Roman author, Macrobius, claimed that Octavia, the fourth wife of Mark Anthony, once said, "It is better to be one of Herod's pigs than one of his sons."

Herod was intensely jealous and insecure. Evidence of

this is the Massacre of the Innocents. The visit of the Kings of Parthia had mentioned a new King of the Jews. In his paranoia, since he could not isolate this baby, he decided to kill every male child under the age of two. He oversaw the slaughter of over 14,000 young boys.

As with many people suffering personality disorders, Herod was as kind and good as he was evil. During a famine when many of the people were starving, Herod distributed food from his own "royal" supplies. On two occasions he actually cut taxes. He was a patron of the Olympic Games, providing large sums of money. He was even named President of the Games. He was best known for his building and architectural legacy. He built the ancient world's largest palace (Lower Herodium), the largest plaza (The Temple Mount) and the largest royal portico (The Temple Mount). He built additional palaces in Jericho and Caesarea and the Caesarian Port, which was one of the most sophisticated ports in the ancient world. He rebuilt the Second Temple at Jerusalem and the fortress at Herodion in Judea and the ones at Masada and Machaerus. He rebuilt Samaria and built the Tomb of the Patriarchs in Hebron, as well as theaters in Jerusalem.

However, his health deteriorated much of the end of his reign. He suffered from depression and paranoia during his adult life. Historians report that his final days were filled with excruciating pain. He suffered from chronic kidney disease, painful intestinal problems, convulsions, intense itching and maggot-infested gangrene of the genitalia probably caused by gonorrhea.

Herod died in Jericho in 4 BCE at age 69 with what historian Josephus called an "excruciatingly painful and putrefying illness."

Education

The Jewish nation is traditionally the most literate nation on earth. Jewish people were known as "People of the Book." Hebrew was the first formal alphabet. As far back as 1446 BCE, Moses mandated fathers to read to their sons so their sons could repeat the process for their children. The same was true with reading and writing.

"And these words which I command you today shall be in your heart. You shall teach them diligently to your children, and shall talk of them when you sit in your house, when you walk by the way, when you lie down, and when you rise up." It was also a Jewish custom to teach their male children a trade or craft. There was an old Jewish saying, "If a man does not teach his son a trade, he teaches him to be a robber."

Jewish children were taught to speak and write both Hebrew and Greek at a young age. Elementary school was considered compulsory as early as 75 BCE.

Joseph's recognition as a *Tekton,* by definition, identified him as a craftsman with some education and since he was often called a *naggar* (a very learned man, highly literate in the *Torah*), he would have been ideal to start the learning process for both children.

START OF SCHOOLING

From the earliest years of his childhood, the baby Jesus showed unusual intelligence. Even though Joseph and Mary spoke Aramaic, Joseph read to the baby in Hebrew. Very soon after his second birthday, he started repeating the words that Joseph would read to him. The baby Jesus would sit quietly when Joseph was reciting from the *Torah*. Simon asked Joseph if he would add Judah to his readings. Judah began picking up and repeating words just as the young Jesus was doing.

Education in Alexandria was the best in the world, so Jesus and Judah had access to some of the best teachers and the world's finest libraries. Each of the synagogues offered schooling for children. Jesus and Judah started attending school when they were four years old. The children would sit on the benches that lined the walls. The younger children would be taught from the *Mikra,* stories of the Bible. They would listen for a short while and then start to play. Jesus and Judah were accustomed to sitting and hearing Joseph read and they did the same at school. Within a few weeks Jesus and Judah were moved up to study with the older children who were studying the *Mishnah,* an authoritative collection of the material that made up the oral tradition of Jewish law, the *Talmud.*

It was during this time that Mary gave birth to her second son. They called his name James in honor of Joseph's other son who had been so helpful to them.

At age five, Joseph took Jesus and Judas to Zacharias, the top teacher at the synagogue and said, "Take these children and teach them their letters." Two days later, Zacharias sent word to Joseph by Jesus that he wanted to talk with him. When they met, he said, "You brought me this boy to teach him his letters. He already knows them and he knows how to read."

Joseph kept Jesus at home until he could decide what he should do.

†††

Jewish children played games in the open streets or on the flat roofs of their homes. They imitated adults, made pipes and whistles out of reeds, practiced with their slings and stones, and everyone played with pebbles. GAP was one of the most popular games. Twelve pebbles were thrown into the air. The object of the game was to see how many you could catch on the back of your hand.

One day when Jesus was at home, Mary went up to the roof to see what he was doing. She was surprised to see that he was sitting on the retaining wall facing the sea. She asked him what he was doing.

He said, "I'm marveling at the world."

Joseph approached Simon the next time he was at the shop. "Our sons are much more advanced than the children at synagogue school. What can we do?"

Simon was amazed and pleased that Judah had been doing so well in his schooling. His answer to Joseph was that he would contact his friend, Simon ben Hillel.

"Gamaliel is the son of my friend, Simon. He is a noted teacher at the school of Hillel that his grandfather started and I think he should meet with the boys. He can recommend what we should do."

Joseph told Simon that he was going to keep Jesus at home until Gamaliel was able to come to Alexandria. Jesus worked at Joseph side, learning to be a woodworker. With that, too, he learned quickly to hand Joseph's tools that he requested.

Author's Comments

Gamaliel

Gamaliel was born c.23 BCE, son of Simon ben Hillel and grandson of Hillel the Elder who was the founder of the Hillel school, one of the two recognized schools of thought in the first century BCE and CE. Hillel school took a more liberal view of the Old Testament. Gamaliel was one of the most famous men of his time. The *Talmud* called Gamaliel *Rabban* "our master."

He was renowned as a Doctor of Jewish Law. He was a Pharisee and of the House of David, as was Jesus. He was president of the Sanhedrin when Jesus was brought before him by Annas (the former High Priest) and then before Caiaphas (Annas' son and High Priest at the time). He was charged with saying he was the Son of the Most High (God); that would be considered blasphemy under Jewish law. He was also charged with sedition under Roman law for being called King of the Jews.

Gamaliel and his knowledge of both Jewish and Roman law is possibly the reason Jesus was sent to Pontius Pilate, the fifth governor of Judea under Roman rule. He would have expected that Pilate would simply punish Jesus and release him. That is what Pilate offered to do. Ecclesiastical tradition says that Gamaliel was a Christian baptized by both Peter and John. He died in 52 CE, thought to be about 78 years old.

SCHOOLING WITH GAMALIEL

Simon sent word to Cairo where Gamaliel was supposed to be. His servant left Alexandria on a fast camel and was at Gamaliel's school the next day. The servant was instructed to tell Simon that he agreed to his request and that he would be in Alexandria the beginning of the next week.

On the next Sunday, Gamaliel arrived at Simon's palace. Mary, Joseph, and Jesus were invited to an evening meal. After the meal, Simon asked Joseph to tell Gamaliel what had happened at synagogue school.

"I took the boys to synagogue for their schooling. They were placed with the younger children. Within days they were moved to a class with the older children. They both knew their letters and could recite the lessons along with the rabbi. I asked for help and Zacharias, one of the top teachers at the synagogue, was assigned to teach the boys. Two day later, Zacharias sent word by Jesus that he wanted to talk with me. When we met the teacher, he said, "You brought me this boy to teach him. He already knows how to read. I took your son as a disciple. He is six years old. I have no idea what to do with him. He is not like any of the other children. Please take him to your house."

Gamaliel asked to meet with the boys. They met at the workshop the next morning. The boys were just six years old.

Gamaliel expected typical young boys who wanted to play more than talk to an adult. He was wrong. They discussed the stories of the Bible, the *Mishnah,* which most children usually start reading when they are ten years old. Gamaliel decided to push them. They understood the commandments and what they meant and had started studying the *Talmud.* They understood his questions and answered them. He was amazed. Jesus asked questions exhibiting knowledge well beyond his years. Talking to Jesus was like talking to a boy-man. Judah also answered questions, but it was Jesus who was asking the questions.

Gamaliel ended the meeting and walked to the door with the children. Just as quickly as the boys had been answering and asking questions as adults, they were playing tag like children.

Simon was working in the workshop, as was Joseph. When the boys left, Gamaliel told Simon he wanted to meet with him and Joseph. "You have two very special children here," he started. "Judah has learned well, Simon, and you should be very proud of him. Joseph, Jesus has knowledge well beyond his age. I am certain you have been reading to him and teaching him as well. When we were talking, Jesus was asking questions, insightful, well thought out questions. I felt I was talking to adults. The minute they were outside, they instantly became children playing tag. I have never seen anything like this. I can understand why their teachers couldn't teach them. There is one person here in Alexandria who, I think, could actually teach them, and he may be willing to work with them. Philo Judaeus. I know him and I will speak to him for you.

Gamaliel met with Philo that afternoon and, with Gamaliel's recommendations, he accepted both Jesus and Judah the next day.

Author's Comments

Philo

Julius Philo, also called Philo Judaeus (Philo the Jew), was born c. 20 BCE in Alexandria. He was an honored student of the Stoic philosopher and mathematician, Dionysius of Cyrene. Philo did not invent allegorical interpretation, but he was one of the first to use allegory for understanding scripture. Philo's philosophy, allegorical interpretation, represented the apex of Jewish-Hellenistic attempts to amalgamate the teaching of Plato and Moses into one school of thought. His teaching was influenced by Aristotle, Pythagoras and stoic ethics. His doctrines were based on the Hebrew Bible, which he considered to be the source of all truth. He utilized the Septuagint, a Greek translation of the Hebrew Bible. He taught that the Holy Word was presented directly and sometimes by a prophet, especially Moses.

Philo was one of the first to use allegory or parables to harmonize Jewish scripture with Greek philosophy. His teaching methods followed both the Jewish exegesis (critical interpretation of Scripture) and the stoic philosophy. Philo is best known for his allegorical rather than literal interpretation of the Hebrew Bible and probably was influential in Jesus' use parables in His teaching. Philo was greatly influenced by the "Book of Solomon," also called the "Book of Wisdom."

Philo was possibly the most important representative of Jewish Alexandrianism. His philosophy was a foundation stone of Christianity and the church's interpretation of the Old Testament. Philo died c.50 CE at 75.

THE BOY JESUS

I t became obvious that the boy Jesus had the powers that the man Jesus would exhibit.

Following the Sabbath service, Jesus and a few of his friends were playing in the yard behind his house. One of his friends was the son of the rabbi. Jesus had made 12 doves out of clay and was standing them up in a line. The rabbi's son at age nine was two years older than Jesus. The child went to Joseph and complained that what Jesus was doing was profaning the Sabbath. Joseph returned to where the children were playing and asked Jesus if he knew what he was doing was considered work and against Sabbath rules.

Jesus looked up at Joseph and back at the clay birds and said, "Fly away," and they did. Jesus again looked up at his Joseph and said, "Leviticus says that doves should be offerings to God." Joseph marveled at what he had seen and what he had heard.

That evening Joseph told Jesus he wanted to talk to him on the roof after sundown. Joseph lit a lantern and they sat together on cushions. "Son, we have to talk. You know that the Archangel Gabriel told me that you were to be the son of God. I saw today that you have great powers. Having them is one thing, but you need to recognize that most people don't have these powers and they don't understand why you should have them. When you get older, I know they will be important to you and you will know how and where to use them. I need you to promise that you will only use your powers when you are here, in the house, with no one except your mother and me around. Do you understand?"

"I understand what you said but I don't understand why."

"Son, your powers challenge other people. Just today, one of the men at synagogue complained to me about you, 'Every word he says has an immediate effect. You must teach your child to bless and not to curse' that is why it is important. We must live in peace."

"You are my father here, so I will respect what you say."

He continued to grow in body and spirit. He attended his schooling with Philo. He helped his mother with chores around the house. He planted corn with Joseph, and their small garden produced many times what they needed, allowing them to give the excess to the poor. He worked with his father in the workshop. Judah was his friend and they spent time together playing. They had friends at synagogue but, since they were being schooled by Philo, there was little time for play with their other friends.

Every Friday he joined in the preparation for Sabbath. He and Joseph went to synagogue service and he looked forward to celebrating the festivals of the Jewish year. It was through his participation in the festivals and their meaning and the preparation at home that he learned what it meant to know God and not just use the power.

THE PLEDGE BROKEN & THE PROMISE RECEIVED

Jesus and Judah often helped with needs at the workshop. One of these was gathering wood, which meant cutting trees and dragging them back to the shop. To Jesus and Judah this was fun. They made a game of it. They would have a competition to see who could cut a tree with the fewest number of swings of the ax. This was a regular game for them.

Judah always lost. Judah decided that on their next trip to the forest he was going to win. He sharpened his ax. The pair went to the forest together. There was the usual banter on the way to the forest—who would cut the biggest tree, who would use the fewest swings, who would be the champion that day.

Judah found his tree. He took the first swing cutting a big gash in the tree. His second swing removed a big chunk. Another swing and another big gash. Then the ax slipped and the blade hit his right leg. The painful cut had cracked a bone and cut an artery. Jesus knew he had promised Joseph that he would only use his power at the house, but this was his friend and he would surely die. Jesus touched his leg. The blood stopped. The bone reconnected. The pain stopped. Judah stood as well as he did before he left home. He was amazed. Jesus actually saved his life. Jesus was happy he was able to save his friend but afraid because he had broken his pledge to Joseph.

"You must never say anything about this to anyone. You must promise."

Judah was thanking Jesus over and over. "You saved my life, Jesus. Saved my life. This is my solemn promise to you; if you ever need me to do anything for you, save your life, it is yours. Just ask. Even to my life. My promise to you forever, my friend."

The boys finished chopping down the trees and dragging them back to the workshop.

Nothing more was said about the ax incident but there was less competition between the boys.

SCHOOLING WITH PHILO & THE IMPORTANCE OF ALLEGORY

Philo lived on Canopic Road between the workshop and the famous Library of Alexandria. The boys would walk there three days a week and work at the woodshop three days. Judah would occasionally stay at Jesus' home but would mostly stay with his mother at their palace over looking the great harbor.

One day a week would be spent at the Library. That was Jesus' favorite part of schooling. There, within his reach or with some help, was the greatest collection of written works in the world. He could study the writings of Aristotle from his own hand. The Library was founded in 306 BCE by Ptolemy II. By the time Jesus and Judah were there, the Library held well over 100,000 scrolls.

Children were not generally allowed in the library, much less allowed to use the scrolls. But since the children were Philo's students, they were allowed entrance when they were with him. Because of the care with which the boys handled the scrolls, soon they were welcomed at any time they wanted. Jesus had access to books about many religions. In addition to virtually all of the great Greek dramas and poetry, critical writing on law, politics, mathematics, natural science, medicine, history, anything he could want, was cataloged and easy to find. This system designed by Greek poet and scholar, Callimachus, and became the standard for libraries that followed.

Philo taught the boys to speak, read and write Hebrew, Greek, Aramaic, Copic, and Latin.

For the next four years, Jesus was taught two days a week by Philo. He spent one day in the library and three days in the workshop with Joseph. It wasn't long before he was making furniture of his own design. His pieces were well constructed and on a par with Joseph's or any of the other *Tekton* in the workshop. Joseph was proud of Jesus and his accomplishments.

Philo taught the boys the importance of using allegory in providing a means for the uneducated and the closed minded to understand the principles of the Bible. Allegory brings out the "deeper meaning" of religious writings. For one class, Philo had taken the boys to a stable. They were sitting on piles of hay. The sheep and lambs were grazing near them. The boys were petting the lambs. Judah picked up one of the lambs and held it while they settled in for their lesson. Philo started by asking the boys for their definition of allegory. Judah was the first to start the discussion.

"Allegory is a story that has two meanings—one you see on the surface and one you see after you think about it."

"That is a good way to describe an allegory, Judah." Judah was smiling since he had correctly answered the teacher's question. "Tell me how the story in Second Samuel is an allegory and what it means."

"In Second Samuel, the prophet Nathan was told by God to talk to King David about his sins concerning Bathsheba and Uriah. It was a potentially dangerous assignment." Judah thought for a few minutes and began quoting the story from the Bible. "'*There were two men in one city; the one rich, and the other poor. The rich man had exceeding many flocks and herds: But the poor man had nothing, save one little ewe lamb, which he had bought and nourished up: and it grew up together with him, and with his children; it did eat of his own meat, and drank of his own cup, and lay in his bosom, and was unto him as a daughter. And there came a traveler unto the rich man, and he spared to take of his own flock and of his own herd, to dress for the wayfaring man that was come unto him; but took the poor man's lamb, and dressed it for the man that was come to him. And David's anger was greatly kindled against the rich man; and he said to Nathan, as the* LORD *liveth, the man that hath done this thing shall surely die:*

And he shall restore the lamb fourfold, because he did this thing, and because he had no pity. And Nathan said to David, Thou art the man.'"

"And how is that an allegory, Judah?"

"The passage goes on to say, '*Thus saith the* LORD *God of Israel, I anointed thee king over Israel, and I delivered thee out of the hand of Saul; And I gave thee thy master's house, and thy master's wives into thy bosom, and gave thee the house of Israel and of Judah; and if that had been too little, I would moreover have given unto thee such and such things. Wherefore hast thou despised the commandment of the* LORD, *to do evil in his sight? Thou hast killed Uriah the Hittite with the sword, and hast taken his wife to be thy wife, and hast slain him with the sword of the children of Ammon. Now therefore the sword shall never depart from thine house; because thou hast despised me, and hast taken the wife of Uriah the Hittite to be thy wife. Thus saith the* LORD, *Behold, I will raise up evil against thee out of thine own house, and I will take thy wives before thine eyes, and give them unto thy neighbour, and he shall lie with thy wives in the sight of this sun. For thou didst it secretly: but I will do this thing before all Israel, and before the sun. And David said unto Nathan, I have sinned against the* LORD. *And Nathan said unto David, The* LORD *also hath put away thy sin; thou shalt not die.'"*

Judah said, "The allegory here is clear. David was the rich man. Uriah was the poor man and Bathsheba was the lamb. Clearly the Lord is using Nathan's story to show King David he has sinned and, further, is letting the King prescribe what would be his penalty without omniscience and love of the Lord."

Philo complimented Judah, "Yes, that is clearly the allegory presented here." He then looked at Jesus and asked him if he agreed, as if he knew that Jesus would find a deeper interpretation. Jesus sat quietly for a few minutes as if collecting, prioritizing and evaluating his response.

"The beauty of this allegory is the many levels on which it speaks to the reader. That is why it is important. Judah has clearly presented one level. The points of the allegory on the first level are simple. We have a rich man stealing a lamb from a poor man to provide for a wayfarer. But, since it is an allegory, there are other points to be examined. King David saw Bathsheba and lusted after her while her husband was away serving at the battlefield. He either raped her, or she desired the affection of the King. She became pregnant, providing for the adultery to be made public. King David made arrangements for Uriah to be sent into a battle where he would surely be killed. He was killed and David then married Bathsheba to cover a compounding of sins. Since the story is a good allegory, it has a number of deeper meanings that are not so clear-cut. At various times, it seems to me that the characters actually swap places.

"Consider Bathsheba's situation. An adulterous affair results in pregnancy. Bathsheba goes to David and asks for David to recall her husband from the battle so that the pregnancy could be attributed to him. David doesn't want to risk being implicated, putting Bathsheba in a desperate situation. She is an adulteress for which she could be stoned to death. David is still the rich man, Uriah is the poor man, and Bathsheba is still the lamb.

"Consider the wayfarer. He is essential to the story but not to the deeper meanings so far. When David considered helping Bathsheba because he wanted her as his wife and because the baby would be his son, it changed the allegorical meaning. David is still the rich man. Bathsheba is the poor man. Then Bathsheba's baby is the wayfarer. And, Uriah is the lamb.

"And when David decided to send Uriah into a battle where he would certainly be killed, it becomes a story of murder and changes the roles. David is still the rich man. The poor man is Uriah's wife ,in this case, Bathsheba. The wayfarer is David's unborn child. Bathsheba's husband, Uriah, is the lamb.

"That's the way I see it. That is why I said it is a good example of an allegory."

Philo sat dumbfounded. He was listening to his student teaching him. Here was a nine-year-old boy telling him more about the meaning of a section of the Bible than he knew. His belief that he had taken two very special children as students was confirmed on that day.

Jesus understood that he had learned a valuable lesson sitting in the stable that day. Allegory could be valuable in the rest of his life as a teacher. Parables would be his way of teaching.

The Son of God

Philo announced that he would be discussing God and the Son of God at the next class meeting. Mary and Joseph had told the child Jesus that he could never tell people he was the Son of God. Mary had told him that people would not understand. She was his mother and had given birth to him but that his father was God. Joseph had made it clear to Jesus, when he had given life to the clay doves, that even though there was nothing wrong with his powers, other people didn't have such power and therefore would not understand why he had them. He had promised only to use his power at their house and with no one there except his mother and Joseph.

When Jesus returned home, he told his mother about the next class subject. Mary told Jesus that she and Joseph would talk with him after the evening meal. When Joseph finished his projects at work and returned home, Mary told him of Jesus' announcement. It was the beginning of sunset. Jesus, Mary, and Joseph were sitting together on cushions on the roof. The sunset was a painter's palette of colors. Joseph asked Jesus the first question.

"My son, look at the sunset. How would you describe it?"

"What do you mean? It is a sunset. How would I put that into words? Its colors aren't something you can touch or hold."

Jesus couldn't pick words that would adequately describe the beauty of the sunset. He had often sat on the same roof at sunset and marveled at the beauty of the blending of the colors. Each instant was different. He understood that the exact color blend would never be duplicated. Each instant was unique.

"You expressed the answer to my question. Just as God made the ever-changing sunset, He did not give humans the means to explain it." For a few moments all three looked at the beautiful sunset. The darker colors were getting darker, adding emphasis to the brighter colors.

"Your mother tells me that your teacher, Philo, will be teaching you about God and the Son of God. You know that angels told your mother and me that you are the Son of God. Mary is your mother but God is your father. There will be a time when you will make your divine paternity known but this in not the time. You must promise your mother and me and your Father, God, that you will not reveal it until you are told by God or one of the divine angels that the time is right. Do you understand?" Jesus looked at Joseph and then at Mary. It was obvious he didn't understand.

"Why?"

"Just as you don't understand why you can't reveal you are the Son of God, everyone around you won't understand how you could be the Son of God. They all think I am your father. And, I am happy with that. But, it's just not the right time for you to say you are the Son of God. They just won't understand. You remember when you made the clay doves and you told them to fly and they did. You said to me that in the *Torah* in Leviticus it says the doves should be an offering to God. Your friends didn't understand how you gave them life because it was something they couldn't do. God will tell you when it is the right time to claim Him as your father and reveal all of your power. Until then, it must remain our secret. Your teacher Philo mustn't know. Your friend Judah mustn't know. No one should know."

Jesus was looking at Joseph as he was talking. "I still don't understand, but I respect you and my mother, so I will honor your request."

All three watched the final colors shift as darkness finally reclaimed the beauty of the sunset.

The Angel Gabriel appeared to Jesus behind sleep that night. It was the first time an angel appeared to Jesus. The angel glowed. He was standing with arms outstretched surrounded by white fluffy clouds. His voice came from inside him because his mouth wasn't moving. "Be not afraid, most holy one." The dozen doves that Jesus made of clay landed on his outstretched arms. "You are the Son of God. I am to be the one to meet with you when the time is right for the world to know. You have a big job, but God is with you and I am with you. I will be guiding Joseph and your mother as they will be guiding you. They will speak my words. Please honor them and your Father and me." With that the doves flew away and Gabriel vanished into the light that surrounded him.

The next day was work at the workshop. Jesus finished a marvelous lectern with holders for the *Torah* scroll. Joseph took it to the house. It would be his gift to the synagogue. He had been thinking about the commitment he made to God when he first arrived in Egypt. He thanked God again for the rabbi who introduced him to Simon. The lectern would be delivered Friday morning so it could be in place for Sabbath.

The next day was class with Philo. Jesus and Judah sat on cushions and Philo walked around them as he spoke.

"God," Philo paused. "How do you describe God? How do you describe a sunset? How do you comprehend God?" Jesus marveled that both Philo and Joseph were using a sunset as an example for describing God.

"People with great wisdom have been trying to comprehend God for many years. One of these men is Abraham. He spent much time considering God, especially 'What is He?' Finally Abraham said, 'I can not comprehend God'. It was only when he completely renounced himself that he learned to comprehend the living God. Abraham realized that God was air and light. He called air the breath of God because it is air which is the most life giving of all things. He called God light because that which is perceptible by intellect is far more brilliant and splendid when seen in light.

"What kind of place can one occupy in which God is not? Moses testified, '*Know therefore this day, and consider it in thine heart, that the Lord he is God in heaven above, and upon the earth beneath: there is none else.*'

"Some may inquire why man was the last work in the creation of the world. The Creator and Father created man after everything else as the scripture informs us. Accordingly, God created man to partake of kinship with himself. This is the doctrine of Moses, not mine.

Philo differentiated between the existence of God, which can be demonstrated, and the nature of God, which humans cannot understand. God's essence is beyond human experience or cognition. "For God is not only devoid of peculiar qualities, but He is, likewise, not of any form that man understands. Because of that, we can perceive God's existence, though we cannot fathom His essence."

"God considered Logos as an external generation. It exists and is considered God's first-born."

Philo continued his description of his Son of God but Jesus wasn't really listening. *The son of God has all of the power of the Father.* That statement brought Jesus back to Philo's discussion. Jesus had lots of questions, but they would all start with the expression, 'I am the Son of God,' and he had pledged that he would not reveal that to anyone at this time.

And with that, Philo dismissed the boys for the day. Jesus was unusually quiet as the pair walked back to the workshop. There were so many questions and so few answers.

The two split. Judah went on to the family palace two short blocks from the workshop and Jesus went inside. He did his chores but had very little to say. The family ate the evening meal and, since it was Friday, they went up to the roof to prepare for Sabbath. Jesus spent all of his time looking at the sunset. When the three stars appeared, he voiced each of the prayers and participated in all of the ceremonies. He had much on his mind.

When the last candle was extinguished, his mother asked the question, "Well, how was class today?"

"I am not ready to talk about it, if you don't mind. I need to do some more thinking." And with that, he went to bed.

Gabriel was in his dreams again that night. He was sitting on the wall of the roof with a beautiful sunset in the background.

"Most Holy One. You are still young in your human experience. Today you learned that humans are egotistical beings.

You heard your teacher talk about the 'first Son of God.' I know the human side of you wanted to tell him he was wrong, that the 'first Son of God' was sitting in the room with him. You did right in saying nothing. It is true that you have access to all of your spiritual powers, but you need the experience that comes with age. I know you don't understand that right now but it is true. Your earthly father, Joseph, is your best guide.

"Your heavenly Father is very proud of you and it is He who suggests you follow the advice of your earthly father. I continually watch over you, and if you have a problem that Joseph can't help you with, you can contact me by mentally calling me and telling me the problem before you go to bad. I will appear to you as I am now. You have Joseph when you need him, and you always have your Holy Father God and me watching over you. For now, it is best for you and for your spiritual mission that no one know of your powers and your paternity. Just continue being a very smart child. You will soon be at the temple celebrating Passover. Then you will be an adult. Then you can begin to prepare for your mission. Until then, enjoy knowing that you are very special and that you will make a difference. Mary, Joseph, God and I love you." And, with that, Gabriel disappeared, but the sunset remained for a few minutes. Then it faded.

Jesus awoke on Sabbath morning. Refreshed. Happy. And, importantly, centered. Jesus went to synagogue with Mary and Joseph. He told Joseph he wanted to listen to the rabbi.

"Now therefore arise, go over the Jordan, thou, and all this people, unto the land which I do give to them, even to the children of Israel. Every place that the sole of your foot shall tread upon, that have I given unto you, as I said unto Moses. There

shall not any man be able to stand before thee all the days of thy life: as I was with Moses, so I will be with thee: I will not fail thee, nor forsake thee. Be strong and of a good courage. Have not I commanded thee? Be strong and of a good courage; be not afraid, neither be thou dismayed: for the LORD *thy God is with thee whithersoever thou goest."*

It was as if the rabbi were talking just to him. The reading from the *Torah* made Jesus smile. It was one more confirmation that he had nothing to question and nothing to fear.

Jesus and Judah remained the best of friends. Neither mentioned the miracle when Jesus saved Judah's life. It was during this time that Mary gave birth to her third son, Jude.

EGYPT TO JERUSALEM

The next two years passed with few issues. Jesus continued with Philo until he decided both boys were prepared to be adults in the synagogue and the world. Jesus continued improving both his furniture-making skills and his designs. His work was in demand, a fact that made Joseph very happy. In their world, a teacher was judged by the success of his student. As Joseph and his family were preparing to celebrate *Hanukkah*, he realized that they would need to be in Jerusalem by the middle of Nissan for Passover. Just 100 days away. There would be a 40-day trip, so the family had around two months to prepare to leave Alexandria. This had been their home for 12 years. For Joseph, that was hard to believe. The trip was important since Jesus would be 12 and would be recognized as an adult. He would be allowed to sit with the men at synagogue.

At the same time, James in Nazareth was visited by an angel telling him it was time to make the trip to Egypt. James knew that one purpose of the return trip would be to go with Joseph, Mary and Jesus to the temple in Jerusalem for Jesus to officially enter manhood. James wanted to be there for his brother, regardless of blood relationship.

He packed two donkeys on *Tevet* 1 and started on his way to Alexandria. He knew it meant traveling during the wet season, but that wouldn't slow him too much. Since he would be traveling alone, he would be able to make good time. He traveled from first light to last light. It was slow traveling, however, because of the wet conditions, so it took James 47 days. He arrived on *Shvat* 17.

ALEXANDRIA

They would be traveling with a group from the synagogue. The rabbi set the time to leave Alexandria on *Adar 2*. That would give the group at least 45 days to make it to Jerusalem. They should get there before then, but it was the end of the wet season and no one could predict the weather. Passover would start on *Nisan* 15.

Everyone was happy to see James. Jesus was still a baby when he went back to Nazareth. Now he was 12, almost a man in the eyes of the synagogue, but he was already a man in his own eyes. Jesus was happy to wash the donkeys. It was a dirty job but that is what a man does. He got them settled in the stable area and fixed each of them a pile of fresh hay. Then he got a bucket of clean water from the well and poured it over his head to clean himself because that's what a child does.

James cleaned up and changed clothes. Mary had provided him a toga and a robe from his father. Joseph was in the dry cooking area of the lower level watching Jesus wash the donkeys. He had already poured a mug of wine for James and himself and a small mug for Jesus. Joseph had brought dry clothes for Jesus. James had arrived when Jesus was preparing the hay for the donkeys, so he saw his impromptu shower. He and Joseph were laughing as Jesus changed into his dry clothes. It was a special family moment, a special man's moment.

The men spent the next hour discussing business and events in Nazareth. James had been managing the family business. He had started selling furniture and taking orders in Sepphoris. Joseph complimented James and they discussed enlarging their space in the market. Jesus was excited. Since he would be recognized as a man, he could have his furniture there for sale and help manage the business.

Mary announced that the evening meal was ready. Mary, Joseph, James, Jesus, James, and Jude were together. Joseph thanked God for a safe trip for James, for the success in Nazareth, for the Passover the family would soon be celebrating as a family and for the special event of Jesus' manhood. Following the meal, James went to bed. Since there was a break in the weather, Jesus went to the roof to watch the sunset. No artist could paint the actual beauty of the real sunset. Jesus thanked God as he did every night.

It was morning. James joined Joseph and Jesus at the workshop. James was impressed at the size of the business and with the skill that Jesus had developed. Simon had announced that he would close the shop on *Shevat* 28, giving all the Jewish workers time to get prepared for the trip to Jerusalem.

The group gathered at the synagogue the morning of *Adar* 2. The rabbi prayed a blessing on the group of between 60 and 70 people. No one was more excited than Jesus and Judas.

Mary, Joseph, James, James the younger, Jude and Jesus would stay with Joseph's uncle. Leah, Simon and Judah would stay at their palace in Jerusalem.

The group, led by the rabbi, set out for Jerusalem.

The trip was without problems. The travel allowed everyone

to enjoy each other more than they were able to in Alexandria. There was no work and fewer responsibilities. This was a special Passover.

It was a grand time for Jesus and his best friend Judah. This was the time they would be recognized as men by the synagogue. They would be allowed to sit in the Court of the Israelites. This was a joyous time for Joseph and Simon, a time of pride that their sons were now men. The *Talmud* says that when a boy reaches the age of responsibility, he is recognized by the community as a man.

Leah and Simon met Mary and Joseph at Joseph's uncle's house. Together they went to the synagogue for the service and ceremony. Leah and Mary sat with the women and children. Simon and Judah and Joseph and Jesus sat near the front to make it easier for the boys to complete the ceremony. The service was opened with reciting of the *Kaddish*. Since Simon was important to the rabbi, he and Judah were invited to the *bimah* to speak. It was customary for the man to announce his presence. He would then recite the *shema* prayer. At that time the new man is welcome to make a speech if he would like. Then the father would have a ceremonial response.

Simon and Judah went forward. Judah was nervous. "Today, I am a man. *Hear, O Israel: The* LORD *our God is one* LORD. Thank you." Judah had already told his father that he wasn't going to make a speech. Then Simon said, "Thank you, LORD, for removing my son from my responsibility. He is now a man." The men stood in recognition and welcome of Judah into the congregation.

Then Joseph and Jesus stepped forward. Jesus pronounced, "Today, I am a man. *Hear, O Israel: The* LORD *our God is one* LORD: *And thou shalt love the* LORD *thy God with all thine heart, and with all thy soul, and with all thy might. And these words, which I command thee this day, shall be in thine heart: And thou shalt teach them diligently unto thy children, and shalt talk of them when thou sittest in thine house, and when thou walkest by the way, and when thou liest down, and when thou risest up.*

"Today, I am a man. I thank God for a father like Joseph. He has taught me well. On being a man, the *Torah* says in Genesis...

"And God said, Let us make man in our image, after our likeness: and let them have dominion over the fish of the sea, and over the fowl of the air, and over the cattle, and over all the earth, and over every creeping thing that creepeth upon the earth.

"In the Psalms we are told...

"Blessed is the man that walketh not in the counsel of the ungodly, nor standeth in the way of sinners, nor sitteth in the seat of the scornful. But his delight is in the law of the Lord; and in his law doth he meditate day and night. And he shall be like a tree planted by the rivers of water, that bringeth forth his fruit in his season; his leaf also shall not wither; and whatsoever he doeth shall prosper. The ungodly are not so: but are like the chaff which the wind driveth away. Therefore the ungodly shall not stand in the judgment, nor sinners in the congregation of the righteous. For the LORD *knoweth the way of the righteous: but the way of the ungodly shall perish.*

"I have learned much in my training and in the words of the *Torah*. In Proverbs, King Solomon said words that are also important to me: *Iron sharpeneth iron; so a man sharpeneth the countenance of his friend.*

"Today I am a man with the help of my father, my teacher, the congregation and my friend."

Joseph stepped forward, "I am proud to say my son is

a man. Thank you, LORD, for removing my son from my responsibility."

The men stood again, in recognition. Many marveled at Jesus' ability to quote from the Torah without reading from the text.

Simon and Judah and Joseph and Jesus returned to their seats. James hugged Jesus to show how proud he was of his brother. There was no way that Mary could hide how proud she was of her son. Her smile was from ear to ear and there was a sparkle in her eyes.

After the service, the rabbi and two of the elders stopped Joseph and asked about Jesus' schooling. They were impressed when Joseph said Jesus and Judah were private students of Philo Judaeus in Alexandria for five years. The rabbi said he was pleased at the references from the *Torah* that Jesus had chosen and with the preciseness of his quoting the passages. "You must have been working with him on his speech."

"Thank you for your compliments, but I'm sure he made that up as he was standing there. He is very familiar with the scripture and can quote it whenever he wishes." It was with great pride that Joseph accepted the rabbi's comments. One of the elders said he and a number of the teachers at the synagogue met each day for discussion and they would like Jesus and Judah to join them. Joseph said he would tell the boys of the offer.

Simon had invited Joseph's family and all of the group that had come from Alexandria to his palace for a meal to celebrate Judah and Jesus' manhood. During the social time following the meal, Joseph discussed the elder's offer and Simon agreed that it would be good exposure for the boys. Judah wanted Jesus to stay with him at the palace. Joseph said that would be good but the family would have only one more night with the uncle so Jesus would have to stay with his family the next night because they would be joining the group that would be returning to Nazareth.

In the Synagogue

The next day, the elders and teachers met at the synagogue midmorning. Jesus and Judah were there, sitting at the feet of the teachers. One of the elders began the discussion group with readings in Exodus concerning the departure of the Israelites from Egypt.

"I will be reading from Exodus. *And it came to pass, that at midnight the Lord smote all the first born in the land of Egypt, from the first born of Pharaoh that sat on his throne unto the first born of the captive that was in the dungeon; and all of the first born cattle. And Pharaoh rose up in the night, and all his servants, and all Egyptians; and there was a great cry in Egypt; for there was not a house where there was not one dead. And he called Moses and Aaron by night, and said, Rise up, and get you forth from among my people, both ye and the children of Israel; and go, serve the* LORD *as you have said. Also take your flocks and your herds, as ye have said, and be gone; and bless me also. And the Egyptians were urgent upon the people, that they might send them out of the land in haste; for they said, We be all dead men. And the people took their dough before it was leavened, their kneading troughs being bound up in their clothes upon their shoulders. And the* LORD *gave the people favor in the sight if the Egyptians, so they lent them such things as they required. And the children of Israel journeyed from Rameses to Succoth, about six hundred thousand on foot were men, besides children. And the mixed multitude went up with them; and flocks, and herds, even very much cattle."* And such is the reading of the *Torah*.

"It is appropriate that we discuss this reading in Exodus during this season of Passover. It reminds us of the death angel passing over the houses splashed with the blood of the sacrificial lamb. It is this historical event that we honor when we celebrate Passover."

Various ones of the teachers expounded on the importance of the events, the reasons, the capture, the four hundred and thirty years of slavery and bondage and the parting of the Red Sea. Judah and Jesus sat there, listening, taking in the wisdom and opinions of the leaders of the synagogue.

"Let us not forget the size of the army of our people that left Egypt." It was the young Jesus who spoke. "There were 600,000 men, along with women, children and animals. 600,000 men. More than the total number of people living here in Jerusalem."

"Who said that?"

"I did, sir." Since Jesus was small and only one of the group, he wasn't obvious.

"And what is your point, young one."

"The *Torah* would have us believe that almost a million people, plus as many or more animals crossed through the Red Sea. And it was in one night, in 6 short hours."

"It was a miracle. God performed a miracle, just as he did with the plagues."

"Is it possible that the story is an allegory, to make a point. I don't know what actually happened, but I know that God provided a way for all of the Israelites to leave Egypt heading for the promised land. Isn't that what's important?"

Judah chimed in, "Philo taught us that there were many allegories in the *Torah*. He taught us that we could question the actual story as long as we didn't question the meaning or the outcome. Philo Judases was our teacher." Judah was speaking with great pride that he, too, was being noticed.

"Do you two children expect us to believe you were students of the great teacher, Philo Judases?" The teacher stood up when he directed the question to Judah and Jesus. Standing, he towered over them.

It was Jesus who answered him. "Sir, we are now men, not children. And, yes, Philo was our teacher for the last five years."

"What is this nonsense about allegories in the *Torah*?"

Jesus explained Philo's idea that there were allegories in the *Torah*. He explained the story about King David he had used in class. As he started on the next example the teacher called an end to the session but asked that Jesus and Judah return on the next day to resume the discussion.

Jesus went to his uncle's house and helped pack and get ready for the trip to Nazareth.

The next day, Joseph and James left with the donkeys and the men headed for Nazareth. Mary, with the younger James and Jude, connected with some of the women she had grown up with and they headed to Nazareth. The children were always running in groups, playing and occasionally with one of the many other family groups. Mary thought Jesus was with Joseph and James and the rest of the men. Joseph thought Jesus was with Mary and the rest of the children. So, the group traveled a full day without Jesus. It wasn't until the group stopped to prepare for the overnight that they discovered Jesus wasn't with them. Joseph was worried.

Mary was distraught. They searched and couldn't find him. James suggested that he was probably in Jerusalem and they should return to Jerusalem at sunrise. They agreed. Mary got little sleep. Joseph, James, Mary and the other two children left at first light, going back to Jerusalem.

Jesus and Judah went back to the synagogue because they had been asked to rejoin the group. Jesus had amazed some of them. He had angered some of them. But, he had truly impressed the elder, and it was he who asked the boys to come back.

The elder stood before the group. "Jesus had started another example of an allegory in the *Torah*. If you will, Jesus, I would like for you to read today's reading so that it will be appropriate to your story. Will you do that?"

"I will be happy to do the reading, but I will recite it from here." Jesus stood and began to speak, "*And the* LORD *sent Nathan unto David. And he came unto him, and said unto him 'There were two men in one city; the one rich, and the other poor. The rich man had exceeding many flocks and herds: But the poor man had nothing, save one little ewe lamb, which he had bought and nourished up: and it grew up together with him, and with his children; it did eat of his own meat, and drank of his own cup, and lay in his bosom, and was unto him as a daughter.*

And there came a traveler unto the rich man, and he spared to take of his own flock and of his own herd, to dress for the wayfaring man that was come unto him; but took the poor man's lamb, and dressed it for the man that was come to him.

And David's anger was greatly kindled against the rich man; and he said to Nathan, as the LORD *liveth, the man that hath done this thing shall surely die:*

And he shall restore the lamb fourfold, because he did this thing, and because he had no pity. And Nathan said to David, Thou art the man.'

"The passage goes on to say, "*Thus saith the* LORD *God of Israel, I anointed thee king over Israel, and I delivered thee out of the hand of Saul; And I gave thee thy master's house, and thy master's wives into thy bosom, and gave thee the house of Israel and of Judah; and if that had been too little, I would moreover have given unto thee such and such things.*

Wherefore hast thou despised the commandment of the LORD, *to do evil in his sight? thou hast killed Uriah the Hittite with the sword, and hast taken his wife to be thy wife, and hast slain him with the sword of the children of Ammon.*

Now therefore the sword shall never depart from thine house; because thou hast despised me, and hast taken the wife of Uriah the Hittite to be thy wife.

Thus saith the LORD, *Behold, I will raise up evil against thee out of thine own house, and I will take thy wives before thine eyes, and give them unto thy neighbour, and he shall lie with thy wives in the sight of this sun.*

For thou didst it secretly: but I will do this thing before all Israel, and before the sun. And David said unto Nathan, I have sinned against the LORD. *And Nathan said unto David, The* LORD *also hath put away thy sin; thou shalt not die.'*

Jesus again amazed them as he was able to quote the *Torah* perfectly. Few of the priests, rabbis or elders could do that.

"Judah, will you define allegory as you did for our teacher, Philo?" Judah was pleased that he was included.

The two young men pretty much recreated the presentation that they had made on that day in Alexandria. As they finished, Jesus said. "Philo mentioned other allegories that we can discuss but, if you will allow me, I have some questions. I was here with my mother. It was a special day for my family as I was recognized as a man and yet we were not together as a family. Why should the mothers of Israel be segregated from the men during services? Since the temple is dedicated to the worship of the Father in heaven, is it consistent with that worship to permit the presence of those who engage in secular bartering within the temple grounds? If God is a father that loves children and all living things, why all of this slaughter of animals to gain divine favor? Have the teachings of Moses been misunderstood?"

There was silence in the temple. Those listening were looking at each other and at the elders and teachers. To most of them, they were impudent questions even though they all wanted to hear the answer from the elder conducting the session.

He stood, looked at Jesus said to him. "Well, young man. You have amazed and educated many of us. Your questions are challenging and I wish to discuss them with the rabbi. If you will join us tomorrow we will discuss them further." And, with that he left the area. The rest left in silence. Judah said to Jesus as they were leaving, "It looked like you made him mad."

They left the building heading for Simon's palace.

At the evening meal, Leah asked Jesus if his mother knew where he was. He told her that he hadn't told his family but they should have expected that he would be at the temple learning all he could. After all he was a man now.

It was late when Jesus' family arrived at the uncle's house. He convinced them that they would be wasting their time looking for Jesus that night. But they were up early. As they were on their way to the temple, Jesus and Judah were approaching the temple from the other direction. It took some time for the two groups to meet. Eventually, they met where the elders conducted their classes.

Mary had contained her fear long enough. When she saw Jesus and Judah, she was so relieved. She ran to Jesus, crying, and grabbed him, holding him tightly, sobbing uncontrollably.

"Mother, what's wrong?"

It was Joseph who answered. "Son, we were worried. Your mother was distraught. We were looking for you everywhere. Why did you leave the group, and why didn't you tell your mother or me? We thought something terrible happened to you."

"I don't understand, father. I thought you would know that I wanted to be in the temple. I need to be about my Father's work. After all, I am a man now. I can take care of myself."

"Son, you are still our responsibility. I don't want you to ever cause your mother the distress of not knowing where you are. Do you understand?"

A part of Jesus wanted to say that his responsibility was to his heavenly Father and not to the earthly people. But, he knew that Joseph was right. He knew that among the commandments was, "honor your father and mother." He knew he was to abide by them. He disengaged from his mother and looked at Joseph, eye to eye, and said, "I have dishonored you and my mother. I commit to you that I will not let that happen again." With that said, both his mother and Joseph hugged him. Jesus went to Judah and said, "I will be leaving with my family. I will miss being at the elder's session today, but we will be leaving for Nazareth. I assume I will see you next Passover but I want you to remember your commitment. I know I will be needing you."

Judah whispered, "My life if you need it." The two embraced,

Jesus quickly turned, took his mother's hand, and he and his family started their trip to their first family home in Nazareth.

The trail Joseph decided to take took the family due east to the Jericho Road next to the Jordan River. They headed North toward Jericho. The road was narrow and there was only room for two people to walk side-by-side. If you were leading a donkey, no one could walk with you. So the family was spread out in a single line for this part of the trip. That was fine with Jesus. He had a lot of thoughts on his mind and he needed to sort them out. They had been on the Jericho Road for about an hour when Jesus stopped. There was a bend in the river. Jesus told Joseph that he needed to go down to the river to pray. The family moved off the road and Jesus walked down a slight embankment to a large rock at the riverside. Jesus needed some time with his heavenly Father. He had been dealing with the events at the synagogue that morning. Jesus had a dilemma. How could he "honor" two fathers, especially if what they wanted was at odds with each other? His earthly family was watching as he and his heavenly Father were talking. Suddenly, there was a big smile on his face and he said, "Amen," aloud. "It's that easy," he said to no one in particular.

He walked up the slope to where his family was standing with the donkeys. He looked at his mother and his father, "This is truly a holy place. God is here."

His mother asked what had happened but he would only smile. On his deathbed, Joseph had asked him what happened on the Jericho Road that day. Jesus finally told him that God had said until he tells me that I am to do His work, I am to honor you. So I have tried to do that, honor you and be a good son.

"You have, son. You have."

The rest of the trip was a pleasant, happy time for Joseph and his brood.

Nazareth

The early settlement of Nazareth took place in 2,200 BCE. It is located in the Northern District of Israel in what is called the Lower Galilee region. It is a relatively small town of 400 people. Nazareth had a synagogue and a spring-fed well in the center of town and a bathhouse next to the flowing water of the spring. That is important for the people to honor requirements of the synagogue—*mikva* for women—observant married Jewish women are required to dip in moving water once a month, seven days after the end of their menstrual cycle—and men were required to bathe before starting the *Shabbat* ceremony.

Nazareth was located in a sort of bowl, surrounded by mountains. Just south of the town, on the other side of the mountains, was the Jezreel Valley. Much of the important history of God's chosen people had taken place there. The old men of the synagogue were always ready to entertain a young man with stories of King Josiah, King Saul, King Ahab and their exploits. And Judge Gideon, also called Jeruabbaal.

On the other side of the Jezreel Valley was Megido, an ancient city that was an important Canaanite city state when Joshua led the Israelites into the Promised Land. It also became a Royal City for the Kingdom of Israel. More to the west was Mt. Tabor. Not too much farther south was a part Via Maris, the international road that connected Egypt with Mesopotamia. That road was the route Joseph used to go to Alexandria. And, to the north was the Roman Road from Tiberius to the port at Acre, the road that went through the center of Sepphoris. Nazareth was centrally located so that people from different parts of the world passed through the town on their travels.

There is archaeological evidence that Nazareth was occupied by Assyrians, Babylonians, Persians and Greeks, as well as Romans.

Mary and Joseph were both from Nazareth, and Jesus was listed as being from there. *"He shall be called a Nazarene."* Matthew 2:23

Growing up in Nazareth

Nazareth was a nice enough place for Jesus to grow up. Nazareth was surrounded by mountains, so Jesus and his family were protected from notoriety. Jesus' Jericho Road visit with God helped him curb his desire to use his powers without any encouragement from Joseph. Nazareth was also a good place for Jesus to augment his education. Visiting teachers would conduct their classes at the synagogue where Nazareth's best collection of books was kept. So, the synagogue is where you would find Jesus on most Sabbaths.

Jesus would eventually meet and get to know everyone in town. When he wasn't in synagogue or helping his mother, he was working with Joseph in the workshop and using his woodworking skills.

In these developing years, Jesus was observing people. Learning what made them alike and what made them different. So, Nazareth offered Jesus an excellent place to grow inside and to grow outside as well. Because it was a great place to observe.

It was early evening when the family reached Nazareth. James and Jesus washed the donkeys and made a quick visit to the baths. It was Friday and almost time for Sabbath ceremonies to begin. There was wine in the storage area when James left for Egypt. The wife of one of James' friends provided some freshly baked *challah*. James and Jesus arrived home before the beginning of Sabbath at sunset. All six gathered on the roof. Joseph lit the candles and said the Sabbath prayers but added one of his own at the end... "Oh Holy God, thank you for returning us to our home. We are truly blessed and we honor you as our heavenly Father. AMEN." Jesus couldn't help smiling at Joseph's prayer.

With the *Birkat Hamazon* closing prayer completed, James and Jesus and young James retired to their beds. Joseph cleaned the *Shabbat* opening ceremony area and Mary cleared the food. With the Sabbath service only a few hours away, everyone was asleep.

Since Joseph had been missing Sabbath service in Nazareth for a little over 12 years, he asked to read at the service. It was like a welcome home.

Mary was home. Word had quickly gotten around the town that she would be at synagogue on Sabbath. All of her friends and relatives were at the Sabbath service. Jesus had been a small baby the last time Mary was in her hometown. So, she was totally occupied following the service. The same was true of Joseph. Jesus had never met any of his cousins, so James accepted the responsibility of introductions. It was four hours before Joseph, James, Mary, Jesus, young James and Jude could return home, but since it was the Sabbath, they couldn't do any work, so spending time with family and friends was very satisfying.

Sabbath ended at sunset and James, Joseph and Jesus unpacked items they would need at the workshop.

Joseph, James and Jesus met on the roof by candlelight to plan their upcoming day. Joseph said the first thing he wanted to do was to find out what the cousins were working on.

James said that was on the top of his list as well. "I want them to know we appreciate their work and I want the transition to be smooth. If we can, I would like to keep them working if they are doing good work," Joseph wanted to make that point clear to James. Then he added, "Your brother here has been doing some excellent work so I want to make sure we have a place for him to work." Jesus smiled. With that Joseph ended the meeting.

Mary was the first one up. She had prepared dough for bread while the men were having their meeting. She had already baked fresh bread. Joseph and James were up early, too. They already had a mug of wine poured and were waiting for the bread and some dried figs. Jesus arrived as Mary delivered the bread. At sunup, the men moved to the woodworking shop at the back of the property. They weren't there very long before the cousins arrived. After suitable greetings and introductions, the next couple of hours were spent catching up with what was happening with the business. The cousins were journeyman craftsmen, so the business had moved from furniture to yokes, wooden farming implements and tables and benches. The business was still profitable but adding three more people would require an influx of new business. Joseph wanted to keep the cousins because they had kept the business going and maintained the house for the 12 years he was away and because they were, after all, family. Some of the old customers would return, Joseph knew that, since they now knew that Joseph and James had returned. Joseph and Jesus were accustomed to making higher quality furniture than the people in Nazareth were accustomed to buying, so one of the first objectives would be to build clientele for the higher quality, higher priced furniture.

Joseph decided that it would be best for the business to allow James and the cousins to continue work on the business that they had. He and Jesus would visit with his friends to let them know that he would be in the shop and would appreciate any work they could bring his way.

They also stopped by the synagogue to talk to the rabbi. He told Joseph that he should consider selling his furniture in Sepphoris. He mentioned a big market that was on a primary road from the town of Tiberias and the port of Acre. Lots of international people use that road and many of them stop at the market. Joseph remembered James talking about it.

Sepphoris

Sepphoris was first settled in c. 5,000 BCE. In 47 BCE, Herod the Great conquered the city and made it his capital in Galilee. In the time of the early Roman period when Jesus was in Nazareth, the population of Sepphoris was around 3,500. It was located north and west of Nazareth some 3.5 miles, about a one-hour walk at a brisk pace.

During the early Roman period, a number of great Roman roads were constructed. One of the most important roads in the Roman Empire was Cardo. Cardo ran from Tiberias on the Sea of Galilee to the port of Acre on the Mediterranean Sea. It was the route for goods from the Orient to reach Rome, and all of Europe, for that matter. Cardo divided the city from east to west. It was intersected in the center of Sepphoris by Decumanus, the road that ran from north to south.

Located at the intersection of Cardo and Decumanus was the Sepphoris City Market. It was the primary market for Sepphoris and all of Galilee. It was a large public building, 131 ft x 196 ft, almost the size of a football field. This was where James had arranged for a place to sell their furniture.

The *Talmud* listed 18 synagogues in Sepphoris.

SEPPHORIS

The sun was setting. The western sky was an artist's palette turned sideways. The family had finished the evening meal. Overhead a meteor shower was turning the sky into a lightning bug dance. The single candle cast dramatic shadows on the faces of the three men. Each seemed to be lost in his own thoughts. Joseph was the first to break the silence. "It was good to see my old customers. I am certain we will be getting more business from them soon. James, based on what we heard from the rabbi, your decision to take some space in the market in Sepphoris was a good one."

"Based on what I saw in the workshop in Alexandria, Sepphoris will be a good market for your furniture and the work of young Jesus." James reached over and punched Jesus on the arm. Joseph noticed the brotherly action and smiled.

"Soon I will want to visit the market."

"There's one other thing I would like you to consider, Father." James paused as if looking for the right words. "With all kinds of business growing in Sepphoris, there is a demand for houses that better reflect the position of the merchants. Nicer houses. Maybe not palaces but nicer than what they have now. We should look into what it would take to start building houses."

"We have been back in Nazareth not even a week and you

are taking over my business." Joseph realized his quick answer was demeaning James' idea. So, he paused, lowered the tone of his voice. "I will need some time. Some time to think. I need to look into this idea of building houses." Another pause. "Yes, some time." With Joseph's words, silence reclaimed control of the rooftop. The silence allowed all three to look up into the amazing light show as the meteors streaked across the sky.

"Father, I think James has a good idea. We can use what we learned and what we saw in Alexandria. Judah's house had walls that divided the inside into rooms," he paused. "We should be using what we learned." Jesus had been looking at the meteor show as he was talking. When he looked at Joseph he saw the confusion on his face. The outward expression of what was going on inside him. Joseph's plan was to return to Nazareth and take up where he had left off...with a small but quality woodworking shop. Now his two sons were looking into the future. Joseph was confused. He didn't know if he should be proud of the movement of both of his sons into manhood or angry that they were already beginning to move him out of his business.

A sudden puff of wind extinguished the light source. Almost as if God had decided that the family business meeting was moving into an area that should be left unsaid. As if the meeting should be over. Adjourning to their rooms, James and Jesus were quickly asleep on their pallets. Joseph slipped into his bed next to Mary. Sleep also came to him but only after his prayer for guidance.

Life in Nazareth began to fall into a routine. The business quickly started to grow and even with the cousins working with Joseph, James and Jesus, they were quickly fully occupied just in keeping up with the business and had little time to think about the next steps. The Sabbaths allowed time to think, but even thinking about work wasn't something they were supposed to be doing on Sabbath.

Two days each week, James would strap the ordered furniture on donkeys and head for Sepphoris and the great market. He paid the vendor next to his space to manage it when he wasn't there. He would take orders and sell some of the furniture that Jesus was making. It only took Jesus four weeks to convince Joseph that he should accompany James on his trips to Sepphoris. Jesus turned out to be an excellent salesman. He was quiet, soft spoken and yet persistent. Since he was the craftsman, he could explain the benefits of each piece and point out the reason why it was a good piece at a good price.

While Jesus was working in the market, he was still observing. He was watching the customers and the other vendors. He saw how people from different parts of the world bought and sold differently. He saw vendors that lied about their products in order to sell defective merchandise. He saw gentle, meek people who were often pushed aside. He often saw arguments break out and he saw the people who would go out of their way to make peace. He saw the poor people, poor in goods and in spirit and how they were ignored in this large city. He saw the hungry and the ones who showed them mercy. He saw those who were mourning the loss of family members and the ones who tried to comfort them. He saw all this and more and kept it in his heart, knowing he would call on those images in the future.

Twin Girls

Life in Nazareth was good to both Joseph and his family. Eight months passed very quickly. Keeping up with the work in the workshop, weekly visits to Sepphoris for James, and the weekly celebration of Sabbath filled Jesus' life and kept him busy. The news that Mary was pregnant was happily received by the entire family. Jesus had just turned 14. James was 10 and Jude was four. Jesus was looking forward to having a new brother or sister.

When Mary's time was fulfilled she gave birth to twin girls. They were named Salome and Miriam. Jesus may not have been looking forward to having a sister, but now he had two sisters. Joseph's little house was somewhat crowded when they had arrived from Egypt. But, now with two more children, something would have to be done.

It was time for another meeting of the men. Joseph called the meeting at the end of Sabbath. The three men, along with young James, gathered at sunset on the roof. After drinking mugs of wine, reciting the *havdalah* and extinguishing the Shabbat candle, the men said AMEN in unison.

Another candle was lit signaling the beginning of the meeting. One subject for a decision and one for discussion.

Joseph started the discussion. "Our house is too small. We need to expand it. Jesus, this will give us a chance to explore the possibility of building houses in Sepphoris. James, we need to start planning some time for ourselves. You need a private room. We need to consider building three additional rooms and adding a wall in our sleeping area. Do you agree?"

James said he really didn't need a private room but it would be nice. Jesus said the boys could sleep with him. But all agreed that the additional space was necessary.

"This will give us the opportunity to consider the idea of building houses in Sepphoris. James, do you know who is building houses there now?"

JUDAH IN JERUSALEM

As Jesus was growing in Nazareth, Judah was growing in his father's business in Jerusalem. Judah's skills in woodworking were lacking, but business was where he flourished. He quickly developed an understanding of pricing and Philo's lessons on organization were paying off in his scheduling ability. By his 14th birthday, he was managing the Jerusalem shop, which had quickly become the top profit producer of all Simon's businesses.

Judah also was adept politically. He was working closely with his great uncle who served on the Sanhedrin. His education in the *Torah*, the Prophets and the *Talmud* made him a good researcher to help his great uncle. He had also become active in the synagogue in Jerusalem. Occasionally, he was reading at the *Shabbat* service. Because of his interest in the *Halakha* and thanks to the education from Philo, Judah was appointed to the lay committee that assisted the rabbi in the application of the law. This committee functioned like a court when there were questions. Judah was the youngest member, but his sage advice made him someone the older members could rely on. Because of his family wealth, Judah wasn't required to work in his father's workshop. He only managed it.

Judah saw Jesus at the next Passover but neither had much

time to visit with the other. Both had demands on their time and both had adult responsibilities. They did meet at the synagogue after service on the Sabbath. Jesus mentioned the twins and starting the home expansion. Judah told Jesus about his new position at the synagogue and about meeting a guy whose ideas reminded him of Philo. Both appeared to be doing well so the conversation was short.

Judah did mention that his father wanted him to move to Alexandria because the workshop hadn't been profitable since Joseph and Jesus left for Nazareth. There was an agreement that they would stay in closer touch. Their different stations in life were more obvious than they had been, previously.

"If ever you need me," it was Judah's parting statement.

Judah watched as Jesus' brothers ran up to him, grabbed his hands and started pulling him toward Joseph and his uncle, "It's time to eat."

The picture made Judah think about the idea of marriage. Actually, not marriage as much as the enjoyment brought by children. But, he was way too busy to start thinking about a wife.

Judah watched until Jesus and his family were out of sight. It was a few minutes walk to the family palace. He paused outside their grand house in Jerusalem. He had always thought it was far too gaudy, but it communicated what his father wanted the people in Jerusalem to know. The palace in Alexandria was much more to his liking. The roof garden had a view of the sea and the famous Pharos Lighthouse. Nothing in his experience equaled sunset over the Great Sea and the marvelous lighthouse. That thought started him thinking about the benefits of living in Alexandria. He missed evenings looking at the sunset over the water. He missed his conversations with Philo. Maybe that was the place he needed to be.

The next time he saw his old friend, Jesus, was five years later. A few months after Passover, Judah moved to Alexandria. For the next five years, he celebrated Passover in Alexandria due to the long trip to Jerusalem.

Not long after Judah came back to Alexandria, Philo contacted him. He said he had an important visitor from Judea and he would like Judah to meet him. When Judah arrived at Philo's palace, he was introduced to Judas of Gamala (also called Judas of Galilee). Very quickly the conversation shifted from the weather and the niceties of meeting someone for the first time to the tax reforms that the Roman Emperor was proposing for Judea. Judas said the tax was wrong. The taxes when Herod Archelaus was King were high enough and now, since Rome wanted to take over, there would be more taxes. He mentioned that there was a group that had formed whose members were opposed to any attempt to have Judea under the control of Rome. He said they were adamant in their opposition. He said that he and the rest of the Zealots were ready to fight if they had to. He had become very animated and emotional.

"We are not going to just sit idly by and let the idolatrous Romans take over and impose unfair taxes on God's chosen people." Judas was standing, adding emphasis to what he was saying. He stayed on his feet but wasn't talking, waiting to see what Judah would say.

"I agree that Rome has imposed more taxes everywhere they have ruled, but what can we do? They have their legions everywhere. You say you and the Zealots. Aren't the Zealots just a wild group of uneducated ruffians? I hear they all carry daggers, and I have heard they actually believe in killing our own people who don't agree with them."

"One moment, Judah. Before you say the Zealots are uneducated, you should remember you are in my, house and the fact that I am showing interest should negate your statement." When Philo finished, there was a moment of silence.

"Yes, you are right." Judah paused. "I spoke too quickly, but that is what people say about the Zealots. And, they say that about you, Judas of Galilee."

Judas had returned to his seat but he again spoke up, "We are God's chosen people. We have been given laws to live by. The *Torah*, The Prophets and the *Talmud* are what we live by them. That is what makes us different. The people of Judea don't believe in domination by a government that is Godless. We believe in the Law of Moses, and we live by it." Judas was standing again, "and we believe that—I believe that—if you aren't committed to following the Law, then you should be killed."

"Okay, Judas, calm down and sit down." Philo then turned to Judah, "You are one of my honored students. You know that our people have divided themselves into three political groups. Your father is a Sadducee. The Sadducees believe that we should live by Moses' Law and most do, but because of their success in business they have softened on the requirements. The Pharisees believe that it was God's will that we live in the world where we were placed, sort of a live and let live philosophy. The Zealots and the Essenes believe essentially the same things about the law, but the Essenes simply ran away from the fight. That is why they have their commune near Qumran. The Zealots believe this is our country. It was the land given to our people many generations ago by God, and they believe that we should fight for it." Now Philo was standing and getting animated. "We believe the time has come to stand up for what we believe. We believe the Messiah will be coming soon and He will be our liberator. He will lead our people against the Roman government tyranny and the legions that have occupied our land. God will make us free. And, Judah bar Simon, we will be here to battle with Him." Philo returned to his seat before he continued. "The 'dagger-bearers' or Sicarii as they are called, are the beginning of the Messiah army. The Holy Legion."

Judah sat in silence.

Judah had been sitting, listening to Philo. After a few moments of silence he spoke, "Judah, my father is Hezekiah. He was given the name of one of the great Kings of Israel that is in our lineage. King Hezekiah was a pious man who united Judea in the Law of God as presented to Moses. He taught our people to live by the *Torah*. He restored daily services in synagogues. He brought back pride in being the people of Israel. He reversed the godlessness of his father, King Ahaz. He reinstated the true worship of God. He cleaned the Temple, restoring it to its former glory. He reorganized the army and restored the fortifications. He was a warrior king as well. He defeated the army of the Philistines and restored pride in our people. This was the heritage of my father and my family. So, this is in my blood."

Philo was again sitting calmly. "Judah, I remember your interests as a student were not too dissimilar to what you have heard today. Not all Zealots are 'daggarmen,' but we are all dedicated to the Israel that God showed to Moses. You and I can talk at a later time, if you like but, since Judas was here, I wanted you to meet him. I had already told him of you and your friend, Jesus."

And with that, Philo ended the meeting.

From what Judah had heard, he was intrigued about the Zealots. As he walked back to the family palace, he decided that he would take some time to meet with Philo to talk about the Zealots, but he would also visit the Great Library to see what had been written about the movement.

He found very little in the Library. There were short write-ups on Judas of Gamala, some positive, some negative. Judah decided his best source would be Philo.

Author's Comments

Zealots

The organized group called the Zealots started around 6 CE. Judas of Gamala (called Judas of Galilee) is listed as the originator. They started as a protest against the takeover of Judea Province by the Roman Empire and proposed tax reforms. The Zealot movement quickly became more than just a political movement because it was made up of Judeans who were fanatical about their worship. They were violently opposed to the godless Roman Empire collecting more and more taxes.

The Zealots drew their commission from the Maccabean takeover of Judea and the establishment of the Hasmonean dynasty some 200 years before and the Maccabeans took their commission from the *Torah*. Judea was located between the Ptolemaic Kingdom of Egypt and the Seleucid (Syrian) Empire. Upon the death of Alexander the Great in 323 BCE, Judea came under the control of Egypt. Judea was conquered by the Seleucids in 200 BCE. They ruled Judea for some 34 years until the Maccabees, a small group of Jewish rebel warriors defeated the Seleucidian army. Judea was ruled by the Hasmonean dynasty until 37 BCE when Herod the Great became King of Israel. Within a few short years Zealots began their relentless effort to keep Judea free from the domination of idolatrous Rome. They were especially relentless in their efforts against Herod until the famous siege of Masada. The length of the siege isn't agreed upon but it was from a few weeks to seven months. At the end, there were 960 Zealots left. When the Roman Legions breeched the wall, they were all found dead. The Zealots killed each other rather than be under Roman domination.

Although there were four philosophical groups among the Jews of this time, each group recognized the *Torah* as the basis of their religion. However, each philosophy looked at worship differently.

The most important trait of the Zealots was their passion for liberty. They were the defenders of the Law and of national life. They believed that God's chosen people must act on the behalf of God or the Lord would punish the whole nation. Most Zealots were, as their name would indicate, filled with passion and intensity. They were passionate about their God and their nation. A sub group of the Zealots, Sicarii, would kill others of their people who were not living by Moses' Law. That reputation found its way into the description of the entire Zealot group.

The Sadducees lived the good life and sought power in high places. They were composed of priests, aristocrats and the military. They were less dedicated to the entire Law. They believed that human beings had complete free will. They dismissed the idea of a soul living after death. They rejected the Oral Law (the *Talmud*) and focused on Temple Worship.

The Pharisees believed that it was God's will that they live in the world in which God had placed them. They were to remain pure. They believed in a combination of fate and free will. They believed in the afterlife and in punishment for evil in the afterlife. They believed in the complete Law, the *Torah*, Prophets, and the *Talmud*.

The Essenes were the pious people. It is even said that their names was derived from a Syriac word meaning pious. They voluntarily lived in poverty. They practiced water purification rituals. They were opposed to the current corruption of the Temple in Jerusalem. John the Baptist was said to be an Essene, and that was the origin of his belief in Baptism.

The Zealots believed that the Messiah would come as a military leader who would liberate the chosen people from Roman rule. There were many Zealot sympathizers who would not openly list themselves as members.

Judah in Alexandria

J udah enjoyed living back in Alexandria. It felt more like home than the family palace in Jerusalem. He had friends in Alexandria. There was always something to do. There were dozens of theaters and, on any given day, he could choose a play by Sophocles, Aeschylus or Euripides. Major events were held at the Great Theater on Hospital Hill.

Everywhere you looked, there was fantastic architecture. Egypt had a variety of gods and the temples built to honor these gods were unbelievable structures. Near the Great Theater was The Poseidon, the great Temple of the Sea God. On the west side of Alexandria was the Temple of Saturn. From his rooftop garden, Judah would spend hours looking at one of the seven wonders of the ancient world, The Great Lighthouse on Pharos Island was 453 feet high. The Lighthouse would help guide sailors and merchant seamen to the Sea Port of Alexandria.

There were lectures by many of the great minds of the time. And, occasionally he would be able to hear his friend and teacher, Philo.

Following his meeting with Judas of Gamala, Judas spent some time at the Great Library, researching the Zealots. There was very little written about the them but there was some information about the Maccabeans and their importance to the freedom the people of Judea have. He discovered what their beliefs were that confirmed much of what Judas of Gamala had said. There was a lot for Judah to think about.

Judah was active in the Alexandria Basilica Synagogue. For a young man, he enjoyed a place of honor among the old men.

On the eve of his 17th birthday, Judah was asked by the rabbi to meet with him after the service. That wasn't uncommon, especially when the rabbi had a question about the *Talmud* and its application. They met on the portico outside the main building.

"Judah, you are like a son to me. You will be 17 years old this week. You have been a man in the eyes of the synagogue for five years. You have honored your God and have been a special part of this congregation. You have honored your father, Simon, and your mother, Leah, in all that you have done. You have been a good citizen to your chosen city." The rabbi paused. "Don't you think it is time for you to be thinking about choosing a wife? Although God did not prescribe when a man should be married, the congregation expects when men are 18, they should be following God's directive as given to Moses, *'Therefore shall a man leave his father and his mother, and shall cleave unto his wife and they shall be one flesh.'* That is the Law." He paused again. He perceived Judah's reticence, so he decided he needed to lighten the moment. "My old rabbi used to say that a man wasn't a man until he was married and had added children to the congregation."

It was the first time the rabbi suggested anything concerning Judah's personal life. Judah was a little taken aback, and the effort to lighten the moment did anything but that.

"I don't know what to say, rabbi," Judah finally stumbled through an answer.

"I have been approached by three men in the congregation, all with marriageable daughters, who are interested in having me meet with you to discuss the possibility of marriage."

It took Judah some time to answer. He had thought about the possibility of marriage with some of the young girls he knew. But... He had considered how marriage would change his life. He was financially very well off. He lived in a palace with servants to clean and cook. He had access to everything he loved. He had spare time to sit in his roof garden and watch the beautiful sunset ending of each day. He had time to meditate and to pray. Time to enjoy his life. He had seen his friends who were married. They each had had children quickly. A wife and children made demands on their time. That changed their relationship with him and their other friends who were not married. They became different people. Judah liked the person he was and the one he was becoming.

"I am willing to meet with the men and their daughters to honor my friendship with you and because I respect you. But, I want you to know that I am not really interested in the idea of marriage right now."

"I will make the arrangements. The meeting will be here after service on Sabbath. You will make a good husband and father."

Judah returned home.

The sun had risen and set on many wonderful days in Alexandria. There were many successful days at the workshop. Many days working on projects for the synagogue and many days learning from the rabbi. Many days spent reading and studying at the library and many days spent just talking to his friend and mentor, Philo. Now the rabbi wants to help change that. Judah was distressed and conflicted.

Judah walked around Alexandria after his conversation with the rabbi. He needed some time to think. He walked down the Canopia Road past the square, past the Library and the Gymnasium, past the Emporium all the way to the wall that bordered the small port. He sat on the wall for a while, looking at the water and considering what the rabbi had said. The one person he trusted enough to ask for advice was Philo. He didn't know if Philo was married or not. Neither he nor Jesus ever asked, and he didn't remember ever seeing a woman in the four years they had class at his house. He would talk to Philo. That's what he would do.

Judah returned home.

It was nearing sunset and the end of Sabbath. He went to the rooftop garden. Flowers were blooming and a natural sugar scent filled the air. There was a soft breeze blowing. Judah lighted the ceremonial candles and sat where he could see the candles and the sunset. The ever-changing kaleidoscope of color reminded him of priceless art. The three stars appeared, signaling the end of Sabbath, and Judah blew out the three candles. And with that another new week began.

The furniture business occupied the first three days of the week. Judah sent one of the apprentices to Philo's house to see when he could talk with him. Friday afternoon was good with Philo.

Friday afternoon arrived and Judah made his way to Philo's house. Judah followed him to the roof garden where the two men sat on pillows under a colorful canopy to block the sun. Philo filled mugs with wine and started the conversation by asking how Judah was doing and if he had heard from Jesus. Judah reported on his activities and the success of the business. He said he and Jesus had talked briefly during

Passover in Jerusalem three years ago. Jesus was working with his father and brother. His younger brothers were growing and Jesus now had twin sisters, born shortly after the family had returned to Nazareth. With the pleasantries out of the way, Philo began the discussion.

"First of all, I want to tell you how proud I am of you, Judah. A teacher is judged by his students. You and Jesus have been my star students and I am proud to call both of you my students. Your apprentice said you had something you wanted to talk about."

"Philo, I have always been proud to say you were my teacher and I know the same is true of Jesus. It's been almost five years since Jesus and I were accepted into the congregation and were recognized as men. I don't think I ever told you about that trip. Jesus and I were both presented to the Court of the Israelites. We were asked to join the elder's class on the next day. We arrived early and took seats at the feet of the elder to listen. He had one of the men read from Exodus the story of the Israelites' departure from Egypt. He said that was an appropriate portion of the *Torah* for the group to discuss since we were celebrating Passover. Jesus and I sat and listened to the learned men present their ideas on the reading. I noticed that Jesus was fidgeting; I knew he was going to say something even though I wasn't certain it was appropriate. But, he did. He brought your belief of allegory in the *Torah*. Jesus was always good about asking a question that made a statement, so he asked how 600,000 men along with women and children and animals could cross the Red Sea in six hours. Then he asked what was more important, that the army of people and animals crossed the sea in six hours or the fact that our people were allowed to leave. That got the attention of the elder, and he wanted to know who had asked that question. Jesus answered and that gave me the opportunity to tell of your belief that the actual story could be an allegory to focus attention on the importance of the people leaving. That brought an end to the class. The elder wanted to discuss it with the rabbi before he answered. Jesus and I were asked to return to the class on the next day. We returned and were able to discuss David and Daniel, much as we did in your class. The learned men were amazed."

"Thank you for telling me your version of the elder's class story. I had heard about your performance from no fewer than a dozen of the men who were there. First, they wanted confirmation that you and Jesus were my students. Then they wanted confirmation of the story. You two caused quite a stir in Jerusalem. The rabbi told the elder that he was not to discuss the question of how the Israelites left Egypt. Then, your comments on the next day resulted in the rabbi stopping the discussion groups. I have to tell you that I can't help but smile every time I hear about those days in Jerusalem. And, I was proud to say you were my students and proud of what you two did. Now, what did you want to talk about?"

"Well, I'm conflicted by something the rabbi here in Alexandria wants me to do. You know I sit as an advisor on the rabbi's committee of the Law. I am oftentimes called on to comment on the actions of a congregation member and if they are in concert with the *Torah* and the other laws of Moses and the *Talmud*. The rabbi asked me when I was going to be married. He said that he had been approached by three of the men who had marriageable daughters who are interested in me. I'm happy as I am. I don't know what to do. Since I have never seen a woman here, my first question is are you married?"

"No, Judah, I am not."

"Since the law says *'and a man shall leave his father and mother and cleave to his wife and they shall be one flesh,'* the rabbi said that was God's command that a man should marry. He also said that many of the old rabbis said that a man wasn't a man or a part of the congregation unless he was married and contributing children to the Congregation. I am happy as I am now. I see many of my friends marry, have children and become a different person. As I said, I am happy as I am now. I don't want to change. What should I do?"

In true Socratic form, Philo gave Judah the perfect answer by asking the perfect question, "What do you think you should do, Judah?"

"Well, I said I would meet with the men and their daughters, so I am prepared to do that but, what should I do then?" Judah stood and started to pace.

"The only advice I have for you, Judah, is to look inside. Your heart and your soul will tell you what to do but, if you decide not to marry, you can tell the rabbi that Genesis was written over 1,400 years ago. At that time growing the number of people was important. Growing the congregation is important now and that is why it is important to the rabbi. Like the allegories, there is a point to what the laws say and a point to why they were written. What was written may have been true then and it may or may not be true now. But, the final test for each person, for you, Judah, is 'what is your heart and soul telling you?' So, make your meetings and then, do what you have always done. You told me that when you were doing your work as a student and had a problem, you would go on your rooftop, sit in your garden and meditate on God's answer. God will answer. He always has."

Judah stopped pacing. He took a moment after sitting on his pillow before he answered his teacher. "You have given me wise advice in the past and I believe this is wise advice today. God does provide the right answers and he gives me free will to decide what I will do."

Judah finished his wine, thanked Philo for taking time with him and started walking back to the shop. He was amazed at how simple the answer to his problem actually was. He had been considering all of the negative outcomes that were possible. The decision had built up to be insurmountable. But, the answer was simple. God would direct him just as he had always done before. The sun seemed more warming. He noticed that he was smiling as he returned to the workshop. Judah told the lead man in the shop to close at the regular time. He requested some bread, dried fruit, almond paste, honey and wine be delivered to him on the roof. Judah went to the roof. His favorite place was under the canopy that provided a shaded view of the sea and the lighthouse. It was where he sat anytime he needed to meditate. As he sat, he thanked God for providing this marvelous place. The food was delivered. He ate, prayed and meditated. Clarity seemed to come easily up on the roof.

Just before sunset, one of his servants brought a tray with all of the essentials for Judah to celebrate the beginning of Sabbath. Candles, candlesticks, wine in Kiddush Cup and the challah bread. The servant removed what was left of the fruit, bread and almond paste.

It was a glorious sunset for Judah. Colors reminded him of the meaning of Sabbath, the covenant between God and His chosen people. As the sun was setting, Judah lit the candles and placed them in the candleholders. He then sipped the wine, savoring the sweet taste. As he continued to sip the wine, he remembered the joy of his life and the celebrations of Sabbaths past. He took the challah and broke it into pieces. It was still warm. He held a piece. Looking at the bread, he prayed in Hebrew... "Baruch atah Adonai, Eloheinu Melech ha'lolam, hamotzi lechem min ha'aretz". (Blessed are you, Lord our God, King of the universe, who brings forth bread from the earth.) He then added, "Guide me in the decisions of coming weeks."

Joseph's Home and Family Were Growing

The decision to enlarge the house was a good one. Joseph, James and Jesus had to decide when to start the project and how long it would take. Mary helped them by announcing that she was pregnant again. So, the way it looked, they had about six months to complete the construction. They had most of the money they needed. They had a lot of the material. They had a workable plan for how to build it. They had the people who could do the work. What they didn't have was the available time to do the project. The meeting ended with an assignment for each person. Think about it. Pray about it. And be ready to discuss their ideas on the roof the next evening. They had to find a way to continue doing the work they had committed to and still have enough time to work on the expansion.

That night, Jesus asked his heavenly Father to help him. James and Joseph were praying the same prayer to their heavenly Father. The work went well the next day and, at its end, Mary brought mugs of wine to the trio as they were settling on the roof. Joseph led a short prayer and started the meeting by saying that he had an idea, but he wanted to hear from the others first. James looked at Jesus and said he should go first.

Jesus began his presentation by saying that he had prayed last night for divine guidance, and he had received an idea behind sleep. James and Joseph looked surprised but said nothing. Jesus then began. "We need to start an hour earlier and work an hour later. The first and the last hours would be dedicated to working on the expansion. We should be able to essentially complete the new addition before Mother presents us with a new addition. That is what I believe God is suggesting for us to do." Joseph and James were silent when Jesus finished. James looked at Joseph and then at Jesus. "That was my dream, too." Joseph was laughing. "That was my dream as well." So Jesus added, "Well, I guess God was communicating to the entire family at the same time."

They all agreed and work on the expansion began immediately.

Jesus decided he would accompany James to Sepphoris only one day each week. That way he could work on the addition one entire day each week. The cousins also agreed to work on it.

The expansion would more than double the space in the house. In addition to increasing the living space, the plan would increase the size of the food storage area. With Mary and Joseph's growing family, providing food was a primary concern. Also, the plan would increase the size of the cooking area. The new kitchen would include an oven. Bread was a staple for each meal. An oven would make baking much easier. Joseph had decided that any plan for the addition would include a bigger cooking area and an oven. The stable would be larger, as would the garden.

Work on the addition began early the next morning. It started with the outline of the walls and the rooms. This was actually drawn in the packed soil that surrounded the house. The exterior walls went up first. Then the cover of the stable. The openings were set to allow for positive airflow to help remove the smell the animals. The cover of the stable would actually be the floor of the new living area. The walls were a basic form of wood covered with a plaster mortar. When dried, the walls were virtually indestructible. It took four weeks to complete the new stable area, open up the kitchen area into the former stable area, and reconfigure the storage area and assure that it was sealed and vermin proof. The new kitchen was completed as well.

To celebrate the completion of the first level, Mary cooked a special meal for all of her men and the children. She prepared loaves of the children's favorite bread. Barley flour with fruit juice instead of water made the dough for the sweet bread. For the men, she used wheat flour and added fennel seeds and ground cumin. That was Jesus' favorite treat when dipped in the mixture of olive oil, vinegar and spices. It was Mary's specialty. She also made a lentil and vegetable stew. She called it Jacob's stew because it was mentioned in the story of Jacob and Esau in the *Torah*. Carrots and onions were added to the lentils and spices including garlic, cumin, hyssop, sumac and bay leaves. It had always been Joseph's favorite. Goat's milk cheese, dried fruit, dried olives and a relish made of dried figs, dates, pomegranates, ground fennel seeds blended in olive oil and sweet wine completed her special meal. It was a true celebration.

Work on the addition went smoothly. All of the men had prayed for God's strength and His guidance Everything was finished the day before Sabbath, 12 weeks later. It would be a day for the family to celebrate. Joseph, James, Jesus, the cousins, the children and Mary celebrated the beginning of Sabbath on the roof that evening. All of the prayers had special meaning for each of the family.

It was only three weeks until baby Simon would enter the world and join the family. Jesus was 18. He and James were running the business. Joseph had started building houses in Sepphoris. James and Jesus would take turns helping him while the others would be at the workshop. James the younger, as he was called since his older half-brother was also called James, was helping in the workshop. He was 14 and had completed synagogue school and had been accepted into the Nazareth Synagogue congregation. Jude was eight. So there were enough people to help Mary take care of the twins and the new baby and manage the house.

Joseph and Jesus collaborated on the design of the houses they were building. They incorporated many of the things they had seen in Alexandria, and the work they did was of high quality. So, they were always in demand.

Jesus had become a reader in the synagogue when he was 16 and had recently been asked to deliver sermons. Thanks to his education at the feet of Philo, he was able to add a more modern approach to the application of the Law than the old rabbi who had been at the synagogue for many years. They actually made a good team. The traditional approach from the rabbi and a contemporary approach by Jesus. He was careful to limit his comments about allegory in the *Torah* to a minimum.

His time in Nazareth was a happy time.

Baby Simon was still suckling. Mary was sitting with him on the roof when she heard Jesus come into the garden area from the workshop. She called to him. He came quickly to the roof thinking that something was wrong.

"What can I do for you, mother."

"I have been waiting for the right time to talk with you.

You are 18 years old, my son. Don't you think it is time for you to consider selecting a wife? Some of the women, the ones with marriageable daughters, have asked if you had been committed. It would be appropriate for you to be looking for the proper mate."

"I know all of the girls in the village. I believe that some would be good wives. But, I have never been moved to consider them. You know that I have a purpose; being here is not my choice. I will pray about what you ask. If it is in God's plan for me to take a wife, He will let me know who and when. But, because you have asked, I will pray about it. You should as well."

Baby Simon started crying. And from the smell, both Mary and Jesus knew there was a need to clean him. Mary told Jesus she would pray and they should consider the idea as soon as they had an answer.

Jesus and the entire family joined other families from Nazareth in making the trip to Jerusalem for Passover. A number of the young women asked to carry baby Simon. Their assistance was welcomed by Mary, but Jesus thought it was more to be obvious to him and to show that they were ready to have a family. Mary and Jesus were courteous, and baby Simon had nursemaids for the entire trip to and from Nazareth.

The Nazareth group selected the Jordan River Road and the Jericho Road to get to Jerusalem. It was a three and a half day trip. James the younger was 14 so he was interested in the girls who were hanging around baby Simon and Jesus. Jude was 8 and the twins were 4. For them the trip was an excellent opportunity to enjoy the company of the other children their ages. Joseph, James, and Jesus had responsibilities.

It was about two and a half days into the trip that the

caravan passed the place where Jesus prayed on their trip to Nazareth. He asked Joseph if he could visit his prayer spot and catch up to the group when he had finished his talk with God. He sat on the same rock he had sat on and this time dangled his feet in the gently flowing River Jordan. The water was slightly cooler than the surrounding air. The cooling effect was refreshing to Jesus. His prayer was one of praise, thanks and a few questions. Asking about a wife hadn't felt right until he was in this holy spot. So, Mary's question about a wife was among the questions he posed to his heavenly Father. He knew that God would answer him when the time was right.

Jesus' prayer time was about a half hour. He knew he wouldn't catch up with the group until they had selected a place to overnight. So, he took his time as he walked along the road. It was time to think about his life so far. He hoped Judah would be at the synagogue for Passover. He wanted to know how his friend was doing and what he was doing. He wanted news about Philo and others he had met in Alexandria. He was looking forward to being in God's house even though he knew he was in God's house as he was walking on the trail. He reached a clearing and saw the group. Jude came running to Jesus with a beautiful rock he had found. Jesus realized he left God's world and reentered man's world. He praised Jude for observing God's beautiful creation and suggested he keep the stone to remember his trip to Jerusalem.

The group arrived at Jerusalem. Each family had places to stay. Joseph and his family went to his uncle's house. He was expected, and there was a cousin's family staying there as well. Baby Simon was the center of attention, which was satisfying to him. There were children near the same age as the twins and Jude. They would be happy. Mary and baby Simon would be with the women, seeing to the needs of the kitchen. Joseph, James, Jesus, and James the younger gathered with the other men on the roof, waiting for the beginning of Sabbath. Family was what holiday celebrations were all about.

The Rabbi, the Fathers, the Girls, & Marriage

Judah enjoyed the beginning of the Sabbath on his rooftop garden. It was a glorious sunset. The wine was sweet and refreshing. The *challach* was filling. The raisins were sweet and the fruit relish and the goat cheese made a perfect meal to welcome *Shabbat*. He had refused to think about the meeting after *Sabbath* service with the would-be wife and her father.

This was his time and he felt like God was sitting next to him on the pillow on his rooftop garden. The soft breeze was playing music on the wind chime at the corner of the garden.

He dipped the bread in the fruit relish. It was sweet and, with a piece of cheese, made an excellent combination. Judah was in a world by himself, well actually, in a world with God. He enjoyed his world for half an hour without interruption. Slowly but surely he remembered what lay ahead of him following the *Sabbath* service. He realized that he wasn't prepared for the meeting with the girl who was interested in being his wife, and certainly not with her father. After a few minutes of concern, it became obvious that he needed some help—some divine help.

"God, I need Your help." He was praying aloud because he knew that God was sitting next to him on the pillow. "Tomorrow I will be meeting with a young woman who wants me to be her husband and with her father. I am not ready to make a decision. I'm not even sure I want to have a wife, much less a family. I need Your help—Your guidance." Silence replaced the sound of his voice. Only the quiet song being played by the wind chimes. "Well, God. I need Your help." That, too, was said aloud as if he expected God to verbally answer him. From somewhere in the back of his head, he heard a voice. A warm soothing voice that seemed like it was from someone sitting next to him. "Just listen. I will guide you. Just listen."

The silence was back. Even the wind chime was silent. Judah realized that was his answer and it would be the only answer he would get on this evening. Listen. Simple and direct.

Judah retired from the rooftop to his bedroom. He enjoyed one of the best night's sleep he had had in many days.

He was up early. A cup of hot tea and a piece of warm bread, and he was dressed and on his way to the synagogue. He did not know whom he would meet after the service but that didn't matter to him. He would be there. So would be the girl and her father. So would be the rabbi. And, so would be God.

Meeting #1

Following the service, one of the girls he had known his entire life showed up with her father and the rabbi. Judah and the girl chatted briefly. Judah asked her if she had wanted to be married to him. Her father interrupted and said Judah should direct his question to him. He was the one arranging the marriage. Judah, very quietly and respectfully answered the father. He said the possibility of marriage was between Judah and the girl, not the father. The father looked at the rabbi, as if to say something was wrong here. Judah again asked the girl if she wanted to marry him. This time the rabbi interrupted Judah.

"Judah, it is customary for the young woman's father to negotiate the potential marriage with the father of the potential husband. Since your father is in Jerusalem and you are older and well-educated, it was I that suggested that the father negotiate directly with you." With that, the rabbi was trying to smooth the feelings on both sides.

Judah sat quietly for a few minutes. Then he spoke to the father. "Sir, your daughter is a handsome and talented young woman. We have known each other as long as I can remember. Any man would be honored to be her husband. But, there is a lot of discussion that needs to take place between a man and his prospective wife. Otherwise, the woman becomes little more than a servant. I don't want a servant as a wife. I already have servants. I have spent a great deal of time praying about this since the rabbi mentioned that you were interested in me. And I appreciate that interest. But, I have decided that I want a wife who cares about me. And what I do. And what I think. I want her to come to me because she wants to, not because I have money or education or contacts or a big house and a lot of servants. Because she wants to be with me! I believe that is what God wants for me as well. So, sir, with great respect, that is why I asked the question of her." Judah looked at the young woman when he had finished. "Do you want to be married to me?" He saw what looked like a faint smile but nothing was said.

"Young man, I am not certain what to say to you. You should know that it is our custom to meet in this way. My daughter has nothing to say about these arrangements. It is my decision. You need to show some respect to me and to our traditions." The man's voice was getting louder. The rabbi interrupted him.

"There is no man in this congregation with more respect for our people than Judah. He came here today because he respected my invitation. You thought enough of him that you were willing to offer your daughter to him to marry him. I believe we should suspend this discussion and if you both agree, schedule a time to meet later after both of you have time to think and pray."

The father stood and turned to walk off. Judah and the daughter stood and embraced as friends. And she followed her father. Judah watched the two leave and when they were out of hearing, he turned to the rabbi. "Rabbi, you are my friend and in many ways, my mentor. If this is the way each of these encounters will go, we can cancel the rest. I would be interested in the girl as a wife but not him as a father-in-law."

"Judah, you are educated and you know the *halakha*, The Law, The *Torah*, the Prophets and the *Talmud* better than I. You know that he was following our tradition."

"But not my tradition, rabbi, and not what I was taught and not what I believe. For us to have a meaningful conversation about my marriage, he needs to recognize that my beliefs are as important as his. You need to tell him that, and I would hope you would discuss that with the other two men." Judah paused. "I have great respect for you, for the synagogue, for God and for our Law. But, in order to expect respect, one has to be willing to give respect."

"Judah, you are correct, but you must remember that you were taught by a very liberal teacher. Philo wasn't wrong but he is somewhat out of touch with the people of today. He is ahead of his time. I would ask you to be a little more tolerant of the traditions of our people." The rabbi paused and shifted the subject of his conversation with Judah. "Have you heard from your father? I hope to see him when we are in Jerusalem for Passover. I hope you will be going this year."

"The last I heard, my father was fine and well. I expect to see him at Passover as well and, yes, I am planning to go and will be traveling with the group from the synagogue. It has been too long a time since I was there and I want to see him and Jesus, too."

"Very good. I will let the other two men know what to expect. I believe the other meetings will go differently. *Shalom Shabbat*, my friend."

"*Shalom Shabbat*." Judas walked home. He was pleased that God had provided the words to state his case and express his feelings. Maybe he was a little too direct. He would watch that at the next two meetings. But he wasn't going to change his basic thoughts on marriage."

Meeting #2

In reality meeting #2 started on the evening of the ending of meeting #1. Judah again ended the *Sabbath* on his rooftop garden with a *kiddush* cup of sweet wine. As he was watching another glorious sunset, he prayed aloud. "God, today's meeting was troubling. I want to do Your will but I am not certain what Your will is. I know that The *Torah* says that You instituted marriage. You said You would make a suitable partner for man. It says that the two shall become one. I take that to mean that in a marriage the man and the woman are to be equals. In today's meeting, the young woman was the one treated with no respect. It was like she was an animal. Like when I buy a sheep or a goat. I believe we have distorted

Your meaning. When and if I marry, I want to marry my equal. Not a servant and not an animal. Please help me."

With that request, Judah decided he would sleep there on the roof. He pulled a couple of pillows together and snuggled into them. Sleep came quickly. His dream started with a flock of sheep. The number of sheep kept increasing. Before long there were sheep as far as the eye could see. He didn't see a shepherd anywhere. Suddenly, in the far distance he saw the outline of a person fully cloaked and with a shawl covering his head. The sheep would part as he moved to the front of the herd. Obviously he was the shepherd. When the shepherd was within a few feet of his view he took off the shawl and it was not a he at all, but his friend Ruth. She was radiant. Her dark curly hair actually shined as if there was light coming from within. She smiled at him but said nothing. And, there before his eyes she changed into a sheep with the same shawl draped around its neck. With that Judah awoke with a start. "Must have been the wine," he said.

He decided to move back to his bedroom. Now, in his bed, he quickly went back to sleep.

When he awoke again it was morning. He was refreshed and ready for a busy day at the shop. It was a busy day. He was even needed to finish building a lectern that Jesus had started but was unfinished because it hadn't been paid for. The rabbi had visited the shop that morning with the complete payment, wanting the lectern for the next Sabbath. It had been made of the finest olive wood, but he hadn't rubbed it with oil. He sent word to the Rabbi by an apprentice that the lectern would be ready for use in two days.

Sunset on that day found Judah back on his rooftop garden where he had decided he wanted to eat the main meal of the day. He had requested red lentil and vegetable stew, cheese, bread and dried olives and dried figs when he left that morning. He went to the roof to see the sunset and to discuss his dream with God.

The lanterns were lit. He had finished his meal and was enjoying the fruit and the wine. It wasn't long before he became sleepy. His pillow was against the wall so he leaned back and closed his eyes and started to pray. He had barely finished the "Thank you, God" when he was asleep. Another dream began. Two people were sitting on pillows on his rooftop. They were sitting close together watching a glorious sunset. He could hear the wind chimes. The point of view began to slowly move, to circle around the couple. The couple was Ruth and Judah. With that, he awoke with a start.

"Please, God. Reveal what You are trying to tell me."

He finished his wine and went to his bedroom and to bed.

The next night he was going to the market in his dream. Ruth was everywhere he looked. Not interacting with him but standing everywhere he looked. Again, her hair was glowing as if lighted from inside. He awoke, shook his head and prayed a short prayer, "God, give me peace."

Another day of work. But near the end of the day, he left the shop and walked to the market as in his dream. He looked for Ruth. He looked in the shops, on the street. He looked everywhere and didn't see her. He even walked by her house and she wasn't there either. He finished oiling the lectern and wiped it dry. It shined. Jesus has done a master's job with the construction. It was like the first one he had made. Holders for The *Torah* roll and a step that could be pulled out of the base that would allow the rabbi to stand taller when he was reading from The *Torah*. He had thought of everything. It would be ready for the rabbi when he came to pick it up on the next day.

Judah was hesitant about going to sleep. He was troubled by the dreams. He wanted to understand. He finally went to sleep. He was shocked when he awoke the next morning. No dreams.

He went to the rooftop for tea and warm bread and the fruit relish he loved and to watch the sunrise. The sun rose behind him. He realized that he had never watched a sunrise as long as he had lived in the palace. It was the reverse of the sunset but different. Many of the colors were the same but more muted. The sunsets were dramatic sharp colors. Defined. The morning colors were softer, calming. He made a mental note to come here at this time more often.

The day wasn't a memorable one. Closing time came. He had dealt with problems most of the day. The high point was when the rabbi came to pick up the lectern. "This piece of furniture is blessed."

It was the night before the beginning of *Sabbath*. He postponed sleep as long as he could. Sleep came to Judah, slumped on the pillow where he had eaten. His dream started with him leaving the palace, walking toward the center of Alexandria. Everyone he passed was one of the girls his age from the synagogue. They were everywhere. Each was beautiful in her own way. No one stood out. Ruth was there in his dream but not the focus of the dream, as in the other dreams. He got to the waterfront wall and turned around. They were all standing there looking at him. With that, the image went black and Judah woke. His neck was hurting from the way he had been sleeping. He was lying on his arm and it was tingling and his hand was numb. He went to his room and went to sleep.

It was Friday. The beginning of *Sabbath*. The workday felt like it was moving as fast as honey poured from a jar. Finally the end of the workday arrived. Judah went home to bathe before beginning the *Sabbath* celebration. When he thought about it, he decided it was more of a required activity than a cerebration. Just before sunset he settled into a pillow on the rooftop. The implements of the cerebration were delivered by a servant. Candles lit, wine drunk, prayers said. It was not like he was celebrating. With all of his duties completed, he poured another mug of wine. "God. No dreams please. Provide light tomorrow. I don't know who will be at the meeting with the Rabbi but I beg you to let it go smoothly." With that prayer he finished the wine and left the roof.

Sleep was dreamless. His head was clear when he awoke. He dressed and went to the synagogue for the service. His friend, the rabbi, began reading from the *Torah*.

"Therefore a man shall leave his father and mother and be joined to his wife, and they shall become one flesh.' It is important that they are to leave their fathers and mothers." The rabbi continued with his sermon, but Judah's mind was focused on the scripture. For the first time he recognized that the scripture said, *'They'*. Judah knew the definition of the word 'they' was to indicate two people who were basically equal. He was amazed that he had never thought about that before. So, The *Torah* was saying that marriage was between a man and woman who were equal. So it wasn't just his belief, it was biblical law. He wanted to go back in time to where the man he met with just a week earlier was sitting, to make certain that he had heard what the rabbi had said, what Moses had said, and what he had said. It only took a moment for him to remember the old Proverb, *"Do not answer a fool according*

to his folly, lest you also be like him." So the smile that was on Judah's face was a private moment, a private victory.

Judah found a comfortable place on the portico to wait for the rabbi and his potential family. Judah was dumbstruck when the rabbi showed up with Ruth and her father. Ruth's father was the leader of the legal advisory group for the synagogue. Judah was a part of it. Ruth's father was the first to speak. "Judah, you are a man I have great respect for. You know the Law, The Prophets and the *Talmud*. You are well educated even though Philo and I differ on certain points. Your father is a good friend and an honest businessman. And, you have been a good manager, from what I can tell. I know you know my daughter. When I started thinking about the possibility of marriage for my daughter, she and I had a discussion. Unlike many in our congregation, I wanted her to be in this process. I should tell you that she was enthusiastic about this meeting today. What are your thoughts."

Judah hesitated before he spoke. He decided he could be honest with Ruth's father. So he looked at him and said, "I greatly respect you, Sir. But, if I may, I would like to ask Ruth one question before we go on."

"Certainly, Judah. She and I have already discussed this."

Judah looked at Ruth. "Ruth, are you interested in being my wife?"

Ruth blushed and smiled and said, "Yes, Judah. I am."

"Alright, Sir, you may ask what you will."

"I already know you are committed to the synagogue. Please tell me about your business, or should I say your father's business."

Judah knew that was a fair question.

"My grandfather started the business. It was a small

woodworking shop in Jerusalem. He specialized in making oxen yokes. He actually made the best yokes in Jerusalem. His business grew and it was very profitable. My father started working with his father, and he started building furniture for the successful traders who were the successful business people in Jerusalem. They wanted high quality furniture for their homes. One person was hired before my father came into the business. My father's side of the business grew to the point where they had to add six craftsmen in Jerusalem. It wasn't long before my uncle took notice. He is my mother's older brother who sits on the Sanhedrin. He invested money with my father, and my father expanded the business. Now we have woodworking shops in Jerusalem, Cairo, Alexandria, Rome and Athens. We sell and take orders in at least thirty of the major markets in the Empire. Alexandria was the least profitable shop that we owned. I grew up and was educated by Philo here in Alexandria. My father asked me to move back here from Jerusalem and manage the shop. The family had a palace here so that was not a problem. Within the first year Alexandria was profitable and last year we were the most profitable of the six locations. All it took was good management and attention to quality. When I worked for my father here we had six craftsmen. Now we have 15 craftsmen, 20 apprentices, and we are the primary builder of quality furniture in Egypt. Thanks to the port, we ship to all of the major ports on the Mediterranean. We get orders here in Alexandria from Caesar even though we have a shop in Rome. My family has palaces in Jerusalem, Cairo, Alexandria and Athens and living arrangements at our shop in Rome.

"Our business has been very good because we build quality.

I have two younger brothers and they will be managing the business soon."

"Judah, you asked my daughter if she is interested in marriage to you. Are you interested in marriage to her?"

"Actually, Sir, until recently I had no interest in marriage at all. I was busy with the business and the synagogue. We have servants to clean and cook. I live in a beautiful home and have all of the money I need. Lately, I have been thinking about a wife. Ruth is one of the very few young women in Alexandria that I would be interested in. We have known each other for years. I respect her and she is very lovely. A woman I could be proud of."

Ruth blushed and smiled again.

"We are glad you are in Alexandria. You are an asset to the congregation and the city. I believe we have a lot to discuss concerning the marriage."

Judah smiled.

"Would you want the marriage here or in Jerusalem?" Judah asked the question almost in passing.

"Here, certainly. Why would we want the marriage in Jerusalem?"

"I expect that is where we will be living. As soon as I can find a replacement for me at the shop, I will be moving back to Jerusalem. I will be assisting my uncle in his duties at the Sanhedrin as soon as I arrive. However, I expect to be an advocating-lawyer because I know Mosaic Law and Roman Law. And I hope, not too long after moving to Jerusalem, to be appointed to the Sanhedrin." Judah had moved closer to Ruth.

"I don't know what to say, Judah. Ruth is my only daughter. I didn't know your plans included moving. Do you know that a trip to Jerusalem takes 40 days?"

"I do sir. I have made the trip a number of times."

"I will consider this, but I don't see any way I would agree to a marriage that would take my only daughter to another country over 40 days travel away from her mother and me."

Ruth started crying. Judah was considered the *catch* among marriageable young men in Alexandria. With that statement from her father, Ruth moved from number one on the list to not on the list at all.

"Well, Sir, I hope you and her mother will reconsider. But, I know I will be going to Jerusalem within two years."

The group stood. Ruth hugged Judah. She still had tears in her eyes. Her father and Judah parted with a smile.

Judah asked the rabbi what he thought of the meeting.

"It was a much better meeting but not much better ending. Well, we will see about next week.

"By the way, why did you choose that particular reading from The *Torah*, was it for my benefit?"

"No, Judah, although it was appropriate, don't you think? But I had scheduled it for today well over a month ago."

Judah went back to his palace.

An entire week passed with nothing special happening and no dreams.

It was late Friday afternoon. Judah was at his favorite place in the whole wide world, his rooftop garden. The requirements to begin Sabbath were delivered along with some warm bread, cheese, dried fruit and olives and his favorite fruit relish. Shortly after the food arrived, a servant came to the garden to announce that Philo was at the door and would like to celebrate the beginning of *Sabbath* with him.

Judah asked one of the servants to show him to the roof and bring more food, more wine and another kiddush cup.

As it got close to sunset, Judah asked Philo if he would like to handle *Sabbath* opening. Philo thanked him but said they were in Judah's house so it was appropriate for him to officiate.

Lanterns were lit as were the candles. Judah poured the wine. They enjoyed the sweet wine and the beginning of *Sabbath* in silence. Judah said the prayer and they drank more wine. It was officially the Lord's Day.

Judah turned to Philo and asked if something was wrong.

"Why do you ask, Judah."

"Well, this is the first time you have visited me at my house. I just assumed."

"No, not really wrong. I am just catching up. You came to my house asking about marriage. Then you have had meetings with at least two eligible young women and their fathers. You seemed like marriage was the most distant thing on your mind. Did that change?"

"I am glad you are here. I guess I do need your advice. At the first meeting I asked the girl if she was interested in marriage to me. That offended her father. I told him that I wanted a wife that was my equal. And, I told him I already had servants."

"You didn't say that, did you?"

"Yes I did. He told me that I needed to show some respect for the traditions of our people. Last *Sabbath*, I met with Ruth and her father. Philo, I think I would be interested in her. She is beautiful, she is educated and she seems to be smart. We almost finished with the interview and I mentioned I would be moving back to Jerusalem in a year or two. He said he would not permit her marriage to someone who would be leaving Alexandria. I sit with him on the *halakha* advisory. I feel like I can't challenge him now. This has been very disturbing." Judah cleared his throat, took a drink of his wine and leaned to Philo. I had a realization during last week's sermon. Did you know that Moses wrote in The *Torah*, that *'a man shall leave his father and mother and he shall cleave unto his wife and THEY shall be one flesh.'?* It actually said "they." The meaning, as I understand it, is that a husband and wife are to be equal. Why isn't it that way?"

"One of the great quandaries of Moses' Law, young one. There are others." Philo was smiling. A breakthrough for one of his students. A teacher is always judged by his students. Judah and Jesus were special students for Philo. "So, Judah, have you decided anything about your life?"

"Yes. I have. Among other things, I have decided I shall remain unmarried unless I can find my equal."

"A wise decision, my son. A wise decision."

Philo thanked Judah for his hospitality and headed back to his house.

Judah went to dreamless sleep and awoke in time for sunrise on the rooftop.

Meeting #3

After the sermon, Judah went to the portico and waited for the rabbi and the next round of the inquisition. Judah smiled when he described the meetings as inquisitions.

The rabbi showed up with the Ethnarch of Alexandria. He was the political leader of the members of God's Chosen People in Alexandria. He had his ugly, fat daughter in tow. The group sat where the two previous meetings took place. This time, Judah asked the rabbi where he wanted to start.

"I think we should let the Ethnarch begin."

"Judah, you are one of the most, if not *the* most desirable, marriageable young man in Alexandria. As the political leader of our people, I think it is almost essential that you be my son-in-law. My daughter is of marriageable age. I am well off and so are you, so there would be no need for a *mohar*, the traditional gift to seal the promise for marriage. I will tell you that I will be stepping down as Ethnarch in a few years, and I will assure you that you will be chosen to replace me."

Judah decided he would ask the same question. He looked at the young woman and asked, "Do you want to be married to me."

She whispered, "Yes."

"Why wouldn't she. You are a true find for a husband or a son-in-law."

Judah thanked them for the meeting. He said he would be making a decision following Passover, because he was staying with his father and mother with whom he wanted to discuss his marriage.

They left with hope.

Judah waited until they were out of sight before he spoke to the rabbi. "She is ugly," he paused, "and fat. She is ugly and fat. What were you thinking?"

"This one was purely political, Judah. When the Ethnarch heard you were meeting with the other young women, he insisted. You must remember, Judah, part of my job is political. You know that."

"Yes, I do. But, no more meetings, please. No more unless I request one. Agreed?"

"I agree Judah. *Shalom Shabbat*."

Judah walked home to find a note on his door from the Ethnarch, thanking him for the meeting.

Judah agreed to join the group from the Alexandria synagogue for the trip to Jerusalem for Passover. All three of the young women were in the group. Judah had a feeling that each was finding ways to be near him. After the 10h day, Judah started walking with the rabbi. He even started find a sleeping place near him. It worked for the most part. The group arrived in Jerusalem right on schedule. They split up each family heading to the place they would stay while in Jerusalem. Judah arrived at the family palace where he was quickly met by his mother with hugs, kisses, and tears. He may be a man in the eyes of the congregation, but to Leah, Judah was her little boy.

The rest of the day was filled with a never-ending selection of his favorites. It was as if Leah were trying to make up for the three years that Judah had been living in Alexandria. He finally had to say, "Mother, please. The servants in Alexandria have fed me well. And if you keep this up, I will need a strong donkey to ride back to Egypt because I will be too fat to walk."

She laughed.

Judah sent a message to Jesus' uncle's house with a note that he wanted to see Jesus if there was time. Jesus agreed and said he would visit the palace mid-morning the next day, which was Thursday.

The next morning Jesus was met by one of the servants at Simon's palace. But Judah ran to meet him as soon as he was inside the main gate.

They walked together to the rooftop garden. Judah had wine, warm bread, goat's milk, butter, cheese, and some fresh fruit. There was a big bowl of figs because Judah knew that Jesus liked figs. The two had been sitting under a canopy enjoying the wine, the food, the conversation, and the cooling breeze. Judah told Jesus about the young women who wanted to get married, and the dreams and the meetings, about Philo and his visit and what he had told Judah, about the success of the workshop and what he had decided he wanted to do. Jesus told Judah about his talk with Mary about marriage, about the new family members, the growth of the business in Nazareth and Sepphoris, about the expansion of the house and the idea of building houses, and about reading and teaching in the synagogue.

For those few hours, the two were teenage boys, even though they were responsible men when they weren't together. They talked on about their plans and their dreams. Judah realized they soon would need to get ready to celebrate the beginning of Sabbath. So, he asked Jesus if he wanted to stay for their opening celebration. Jesus declined saying he needed to return to his uncle's so he could be with his family. They agreed to meet again on Sunday since both synagogue groups weren't going to leave for home until Monday.

Simon had arrived home during Judah's talk with Jesus. He had been visiting the shop in Rome. He had stopped at Ascalon and bought a donkey to speed his return home. He wanted to be there to celebrate Sabbath with Judah. He was sitting in the main garden between the gate and the house. Like everything in his palace, his garden was a perfectly calming place to sit. Calm is what he needed after the trip to and from Rome and the problems he found there.

Judah and Jesus came down from the roof garden. Jesus had enjoyed catching up with Judah—boyhood friends telling stories. As they walked toward the gate, Judah embraced his father. He said goodbye to Jesus and walked with his father, arms around each other, to the back garden by the fountain. It was a couple of hours before the start of *Sabbath,* and Judah wanted to talk to his father. There was a quick update on the business in Alexandria—very profitable. Judah told his father of his plan—pick a manager to keep Alexandria profitable, and he would make annual visits to check on everything. He also had looked into the possibility of commuting to Alexandria. Half the time and very little increase in cost. He talked with Simon about wanting to assist Leah's brother, to be a lawyer-advocate and, hopefully, soon to be appointed to the Sanhedrin.

Simon was smiling because he had already discussed Judah coming to Jerusalem with Leah, and Judah working with her uncle. Then Judah started telling his father about the meetings with the young women. About the arrogance of the first father. About the beauty of Ruth and her father's unwillingness to approve for her to move to Jerusalem. About the Ethnarch and the offer to make him Ethnarch if he married his daughter.

"But, father she was ugly. Ugly and fat. I would be embarrassed to introduce her as my wife."

His story was interrupted by one of the servants. The *Sabbath* ceremony was about to start.

Sabbath ceremonies for Jesus and Judah were about as different as their births and circumcisions. Jesus celebrated at his great uncle's with about 60 of his close relatives. Judah celebrated at his family's palace with his father and his mother. After the closing prayer, Simon asked Judah to tell his mother about her new daughter.

Leah said, "What new daughter?"

Judah told his story again. It was amusing for Simon

listening to it again. He was waiting to see what Leah would say when Judah said the girl was ugly and fat. She laughed, then caught herself and told Judah that it wasn't polite to say that about a young woman.

"But it's true mother. Ugly *and* fat."

She was happy to hear that her son would be coming closer to her. "Your suite is ready for you, but I think we can build you your own home at the back of the garden. Couldn't we, Simon?" She directed the second part to Simon.

"I'm sure we can, my dear. I'm sure we can."

Judah started to say that wasn't necessary but decided to wait. He was quite accustomed to living by himself. Having his own home, even next to his parents, would be preferable to having a room in his family's house, no matter how big and glorious it may be.

They all went inside and to their bedrooms. Judah was too excited to go right to sleep. He had brought a few books from Alexandria, and there was a Septuagint in his room. He picked it up, flipped pages, and stopped on the prophet Jeremiah.

"Blessed is the man that trusteth in the LORD, *and whose hope the* LORD *is. For he shall be as a tree planted by the waters, and that spreadeth out her roots by the river, and shall not see when heat cometh, but her leaf shall be green; and shall not be careful in the year of drought, neither shall cease from yielding fruit. The heart is deceitful above all things, and desperately wicked: who can know it? As the partridge sitteth on eggs, and hatcheth them not; so he that getteth riches, and not by right, shall leave them in the midst of his days, and at his end shall be a fool."*

Judah read the passage twice. The second time, he concentrated on the last verse. His father had essentially said that to him many times. The way Simon said it was, "charge a man a fair price, do quality work, and have the work ready when you say it will be ready. Do these things and you will always be wealthy and on the right side of God." That is how Judah had gotten the Alexandria shop profitable and growing.

Sabbath was different. Jesus sat with the men in his family and Judah sat with his father and the leaders of the Jerusalem synagogue. Jesus was asked to read from the *Torah*. He stood behind the open scroll but quoted the passage from memory. Judah marveled at the change in Jesus and his presentation of Moses' words. He spoke as if he owned the words. The reading was the highlight of the service. Following the service Judah went to Jesus and waited until he could have a private word with him. Judah praised Jesus and the presentation.

"My friend, you read the *Torah* like you wrote the words."

Jesus answered him. "God has been speaking to me about His plan for me and for us. We have a lot to talk about, but this is not the right time. You must see about your life and I must see about mine. But, when the time is right, we will talk. I am glad you are moving back to Jerusalem. I know your mother and father are happy."

"They are already talking about building me a house behind the palace. And mother said she would talk to her brother about my work. I will be a lawyer-advocate here in Jerusalem. Maybe I can help you and what you are doing."

"I'm sure you will, my friend, Judah. I'm sure you will."

Judah's father had walked up and was waiting to interrupt. He and Jesus exchanged greetings and he said he had some people he wanted Judah to meet. People who could be valuable contacts for him when he moved to Jerusalem.

So the two parted. They would not see each other any more on that visit to Jerusalem. Jesus returned to Nazareth with his family and friends from the synagogue there. Judah was occupied by his father, introducing him to influential friends and by his family discussing his impending move from Alexandria to Jerusalem. Judah told his rabbi that he would be taking a boat back to Alexandria. It would be faster and he wouldn't have to continue to dodge the would-be wives and their fathers.

Back to Nazareth

Jesus, his family, and the rest of his friends from the Nazareth synagogue started their trip back to Nazareth. Jesus had already decided he would stop again at his holy place to pray.

The group made good time on their first day. They had reached the Jordan River and the rabbi decided they would overnight there. Jesus knew that he was a little over an hour from his holy place. He decided to stay with the group that evening, but he would leave around an hour before the group, giving him some time to pray before the rest of the group caught up with him.

At first light he was up and ready to go. He told Mary and Joseph where he would be and that he would join them when the group arrived at his prayer place. It was a little less than an hour when he arrived. He thanked God for a successful trip to Jerusalem, an opportunity to be with his family, being able to read at the synagogue, and the time he spent with Judah and everything in his life. He took off his sandals and tied up his robe. The water was cold but refreshing as it flowed across his feet. It was a wonderful feeling. He relaxed for a moment, allowing all of his cares and problems to flow with the river water into the Dead Sea—such an appropriate name.

He climbed on the rock and began talking to his heavenly

Father. He had a lot to talk about and a lot of questions to ask. Just as he was saying *amen*, he heard the sounds of the group approaching. He couldn't believe he had been sitting there over an hour. As he left the rock, he noticed a shiny stone in the water. He picked it up and blessed it.

"God I ask blessings on this stone. I know that this is a holy place. I will continue using this place as a place to pray. I ask that my ministry begin here."

And with that blessing and request, he tossed the stone into the middle of the river.

The group didn't even stop. Jesus joined his family and headed to Nazareth. They were singing as they walked. They had just begun a song when Jesus joined them,

By the rivers of Babylon, there we sat down,
Yea, we wept, when we remembered Zion.
We hanged our harps upon the willows in the midst thereof.
For there they that carried us away captive required of us a song; and they that wasted us required of us mirth, saying, Sing us one of the songs of Zion.
How shall we sing the LORD's *song in a strange land?*
If I forget thee, O Jerusalem, let my right hand forget her cunning.
If I do not remember thee, let my tongue cleave to the roof of my mouth; if I prefer not Jerusalem above my chief joy.
Remember, O LORD, *the children of Edom in the day of Jerusalem; who said, Rase it, rase it, even to the foundation thereof.*
O daughter of Babylon, who art to be destroyed; happy shall he be, that rewardeth thee as thou hast served us.

Jesus was smiling as he walked and sang. He knew the

meaning of the psalm. It was a hymn expressing the yearn-ings of the Jewish people during their Babylonian exile. In its whole form, the psalm reflects the yearning for Jerusalem as well as hatred for the Holy City's enemies. The hatred expressed sometimes in violent imagery. The Septuagint version of the psalm bore the inscription: "For David. By Jeremiah, in the Captivity."

The song and the timing made Jesus smile numerous times over the two and a half days it took the group to get to Nazareth.

††††

Life in Nazareth slipped back into its normal routine. Joseph and James began to spend full time building houses. Jesus, James the younger, the cousins, and the three craftsmen they had hired handled the woodworking business. Jesus would still bring furniture to Sepphoris. James would occa-sionally take a break from the houses and join Jesus at the great market.

The next two years passed quickly. Building houses was very profitable. The shop was making money as well. Joseph and his family made trips to Jerusalem for Passover. Everything was going well for Jesus and his family.

Back in Alexandria

Judah enjoyed his visit with his mother and father. He was able to discuss his future with his father and get his agreement on Judah's plan. Judah had already selected the man that he would recommend to be the manager, and his father agreed. He approached the idea of the house and was happily surprised that his father was totally in agreement. Leah had invited her brother to join them for an evening meal while Judah was there. Judah was able to discuss his idea with his uncle. He was in favor of having Judah assist him. He also confirmed that there was a need for a good Lawyer-Advocate in Jerusalem. He did say that the idea of moving into the Sanhedrin any time soon was probably premature. But he had many contacts that could use him as a lawyer.

Judah spent a day with his father at his shop in Jerusalem. They looked at the books. Judah looked closely at the operation. He knew that his father would rely on him to oversee the shop even though he would be a Lawyer-Advocate on his own. Judah made a couple of observations that would make the Jerusalem shop more profitable.

The cook made lamb stew, something she knew Judah liked. She liked Judah and was happy he was coming back to the palace. Judah didn't tell any of the servants, but they all knew. They had their own means of communications. Nothing, absolutely nothing, happened in that house that the entire servant staff didn't know about.

Judah had decided that he wanted to take a ship back to Alexandria, but he asked his father because the trip on the ship was expensive. But, he would be back in Alexandria in six days, not 40 days. He thought about telling Ruth's father about the six-day trip. But that would rekindle a situation he wasn't sure he wanted to deal with. Moving back to Jerusalem would be complicated if he had a wife. Devils are best left where they lay.

The next afternoon, Judah was packed and, with his mother and father in a buggy, headed to the port. He had a cabin to himself. There were no other passengers on the ship, just wheat. Wheat was grown all throughout Israel. Wheat from Israel brought a good price in Egypt.

Judah met the owner of the ship and gave him his fare, 127 denarii. His father was with him, and he knew the owner. Simon had made many trips with him, and he assured Simon that his son would be safe. Judah bid his mother and father farewell. He then moved to the front of the ship to watch as they left the harbor at Ascalon and moved into the great sea.

Author's Comment

Denarii

A denarii was a standard coin used for payment in the Roman Empire from the beginning of the 1st century BCE to around 34 CE. It was a silver coin containing 3.9 grams of pure silver. The trip to Alexandria from Ascalon cost 127 denarii or about $2,550.00 in today's money, adjusted for inflation. To put the value of a denarii into perspective, the payment for a common laborer was one denarii a day, a legion soldier was paid 225 denarii a year, a Centurion was paid 3,750 denarii a year and a Commander was paid 15,000 denarii a year.

DETAILS

The trip gave Judah time to think and plan. It also gave him time to read. The trip went relatively fast. He arrived at the port and hired a buggy to take him to his palace. His return wasn't expected so soon, so nothing was ready for him. He didn't care. He had not slept very well on the trip. He didn't get accustomed to the rocking of the ship, so he was ready for a good night's sleep in his bed.

He wanted to start fresh and begin to move forward. He was ready to be in Jerusalem.

The first thing, he talked to the craftsman that he wanted to take over the shop. The talk went well.

That afternoon, he went to talk to the director of the *mensarii*, the bank. The new manager of the shop would deposit profit into an account for Judah and his father. Simon already used that *mensarii*, so arrangements were quickly handled. Judah would visit the *mensarii* each quarter when he was in Alexandria to check on the business.

He was home. He had already completed two important business things. And, it would be another month before the group from the synagogue would be back. Even though the boat trip was expensive, he wondered why he hadn't thought about that sooner. *Having money does have its benefits.* As he thought, he smiled.

Judah wanted to have *Sabbath* one more time with the people of the synagogue before he left for Jerusalem. For the next three weeks, he was tying up loose ends, finishing woodworking projects he had started, assuring that the transition between him and the new manager would be smooth and just relaxing. Judah sent word to Philo that he would be leaving soon for Jerusalem and asked for some time. They settled on a time, and the pair enjoyed a few mugs on Judah's rooftop garden. Judah told Philo he would miss spending time talking. Philo said Judah was prepared for his new work and that he, too, would miss not being able to talk. Judah emphasized his invitation for Philo to come to Jerusalem, "You will always have a place in my home." Philo said the same, knowing that Judah would probably stay in the family's palace the next time he was in Alexandria.

He packed his books, clothes and personal items and was ready to go to Jerusalem.

It took the synagogue group three weeks to get back to Alexandria. They arrived on Wednesday. The next day, Judah visited with the rabbi. Both were saddened by the decision, but the rabbi said it would be a good move for Judah. It would represent the closing of a big chapter in his life.

The next evening, Judah celebrated the beginning of *Sabbath* in his rooftop garden. It would be the last time to see the beautiful sunset from this place for a while. As the time approached, he lit the candles, drank the wine, said the *kiddush* prayer, ate the bread, and then began talking to God.

"Thank you God. I have so much to be thankful for..."

His prayer lasted close to an hour. That night was a nightlong blissful sleep. He had completed everything he needed to do in preparing to leave. That *Sabbath* morning, the rabbi asked him to read from the *Torah*. The rabbi followed the reading with the announcement that Judah was moving to Jerusalem.

"God speed, Judah," was all that was said. Then he offered the teaching. At the close of the service, he invited all present to join him on the portico for a mug of wine to send Judah off. He enjoyed the wine, and he enjoyed talking to everyone, with the possible exception of the first girl's father and the Ethnarch. But, that was like putting a period at the end of a sentence.

By the end of the week, Judah was on a ship headed for Ascalon and then to Jerusalem. He arranged for four camels as soon as he arrived, found a place to secure his luggage, and ate a good evening meal at the inn where he would stay the night. It took three camels to transport Judah and his luggage to Jerusalem. They started early and were able to cover the entire 57 miles in one day. He knew that he couldn't have done that on donkeys, even though they were cheaper. He paid the camel owner/driver five denarii per camel and was happy to arrive at his family palace that same evening.

Sunrise brought the dawning of a new life for Judah.

Nazareth, Sepphoris, and Joseph

Days were busy in Nazareth. Jesus was called on by the synagogue to read and to teach. He was asked to do more work at the synagogue as work at the shop was increasing. Joseph was spending most of his time in Sepphoris building houses. He did excellent work, and the demand was increasing. James continued spending one day each week at the great market where he was booking furniture orders every week. He also was the contact point for Joseph's building company. Except for *Sabbath*, every day was busy.

Joseph took time to go to Jerusalem for Passover. He had so much to be thankful for, and he knew God was the source of his blessings.

Passover the next year found Jesus, Mary, Joseph and the rest of the family on their way to Jerusalem. Every time Jesus passed his special place along the River Jordan, he had to stop and pray. This time the entire family stopped. The synagogue group continued to their selected overnight place. Jesus was approaching 20. Young James was 16, Jude was 10 (soon to be 11 and old enough to think he was already a man), the twins were just six, and baby Simon had turned two. Simon was old enough to walk some of the way.

Jesus told everyone that this was a holy place, that he always stopped here to pray and talk to God.

Jude asked, "Does God talk to you?"

Jesus always had patience with the children. "Yes, Jude. He does, but not out loud like we are talking. I ask Him questions either out loud or in my mind, and He answers me in my mind."

"How does He do that?" Jude's questions captured the attention of the twins and they wanted to know as well.

"To begin with, God and I talk all of the time. And it works this way. Over six years ago, I got a feeling inside that I should stop here and let the caravan go on. I don't know how to describe the feeling, but I knew I should stop and pray. Have you ever felt like you needed to do something, Jude?"

"I guess I have. Is it sort of like I feel when I am hungry?"

"Sort of. You just know you have to do something. That was the feeling I had six years ago about this place. I knew I was to sit on that rock and talk to God. Well, I did and He told me that this was a holy place. So I always stop and talk to Him."

By that time the twins had lost interest in the discussion between Jesus and Jude, but Mary and Joseph were listening. It was Mary who joined the conversation.

"You know that you are on special terms with God when He talks to you or sends an angel to tell you something. That is how I knew that I would have your brother. An Archangel named Gabriel came to me at the well in Nazareth and told me I would soon be a mother—that I would give birth to a son and call his name Jesus."

"Really, Mother, an angel came to you, and you could see him?"

"Yes, Jude, he did. And the same angel appeared to your father and let him know as well."

"That is amazing. Real angels?"

"Yes, Jude. Amazing and very special. If your heart is right and you abide by the law, he may come to you as well. Okay, Jude. Now go watch about your sisters. They are playing in the water and I don't want anything to happen to them."

"I will, Mother."

After Jude was out of hearing distance, Joseph talked to Jesus. "Son, you have such a way with children. You make them feel important. You treat them as you would an adult and they know it."

"Thank you, father. They deserve respect, and the only way they can learn to be respectful is for them to be treated with respect. Now, I need some time with my other Father."

Jesus' conversation with God was short. The children enjoyed playing in the water. Mary, Joseph, James, and James the younger were sitting in the cool grass. They were all ready to go about the same time.

Joseph and family caught up with the group as they were beginning to settle in for the night. As a smaller group, they moved faster. They were now a day and a half from Nazareth. Joseph had spent the day thinking about the work that needed to be done in Sepphoris. Each one in the group had been lost in thought most of the day. Even the twins were quiet and not picking at each other. Jesus was contemplating his ministry, something he and God had been discussing at the holy place.

Jesus asked, "When?"

God answered, "Soon. I'll tell you."

The next year went smoothly, quietly, and quickly. As they were packing for the trip to Jerusalem, James said to Jesus, "I thought we were unpacking all this stuff just last week."

Jesus looked at James. "Thankfully, we had a good year. Good times seem to move by quickly. It's the bad times that hang around and take their time leaving."

Passover was an excellent opportunity for all of the family to get together. There were at least 60 people staying at the uncle's house. Jesus was again asked to read at the Passover service at the synagogue. He sat with the men of his family. Judah again sat with his father and the leaders of the synagogue. Jesus was able to visit Judah at his new house. It had recently been completed. You could approach the house through the main gate at the palace, but Simon had provided a private entrance for Judah at the back of the palace near his house. Jesus had only a small amount of time with Judah, but they arranged a longer meeting at Passover the next year.

With another Passover completed, the Nazareth group left for home. When they reached the holy place, Joseph had the entire family stop. Joseph knew it would be a good place for a short rest, and they could easily catch up with the group later. Jesus walked to the large rock. He was quickly aware that James the younger and Jude were following him to the prayer spot. He smiled as he climbed on the rock. Jude was the first to speak. "James and I think we should join you in prayer. Is that alright with you?"

Jesus said they would be welcome.

After about a half hour, Jude began to get restless. He and James walked back to where the rest of the family was waiting. Within a few minutes, Jesus said *AMEN* aloud and climbed down from the rock. Jude asked Jesus what he talked to God about.

"About you, little one."

"What did you ask?"

"I asked if you were going to be a good man?"

"What did He say?"

"He said that was up to you, but that you had a good start."

That was enough to keep Jude quiet for a little while. Joseph and family soon joined the Nazareth synagogue group. Another day and a half and they walked into their hometown.

Life went back to normal. Joseph and James returned to building houses in Sepphoris. Jesus and James the younger went to work in the shop. Jude and the twins were going to school at the synagogue, and baby Simon was with Mary.

A month passed. One day Mary met Joseph as he was returning from the house he was building. They met in the center of the courtyard. They whispered for a few minutes and then called the entire family to the courtyard. Joseph announced, "Mary has something she wants to tell you all."

Mary cleared her throat, "I want you to know that we will be having a new baby soon." Everyone was thrilled, some more thrilled than others. A new baby meant the jobs around the house would change. More work for some, different work for others. Joseph, however, was very happy.

Three months passed.

JOSEPH DIES

Jesus and James came into the courtyard leading a donkey. Joseph was lying on the donkey. He had passed out from the pain. Mary ran from the cooking area of the lower level of the house to find her husband holding on to the last strains of his life. Jesus carefully lifted Joseph from the donkey as James told Mary of Joseph's fall from the roof of the house they were building. Joseph was alive but just barely. It had been almost an hour donkey ride.

Jesus asked Mary to get some water and some clean woolen cloths. They cleaned Joseph, and Jesus asked Mary if she would let him see what he could do for Joseph. Mary gathered the children to her and James They all started praying for Joseph.

Jesus started talking to Joseph. "I heard what you told me in the stable in Bethlehem. You said you couldn't be happier even if you were my real father. That made me happy and calmed me down. I was looking for comfort, and that is exactly what you gave me. That is what I want to do for you now. I have asked my heavenly Father if I can save your life. He told me that He wasn't ready for me to use my power. He said He had a special task for you in Heaven. He said you had done your job here, and it was time for you to come home. He wants you to know that Mary and the children will be fine, and He has asked me to make sure of that. I assure you that I will do just that. I have been proud of you all of my life, and I want you to know that I am proud to be called your son. Now, my father, it is time for you to go home."

And with that, Jesus bent down and kissed Joseph's forehead. He called all of the other family members to come pay last respects. Each of the children from the youngest to the oldest came and kissed his forehead. Mary was the last. Still crying, she kissed him and whispered, "I love you," as he silently passed into the heavenly realm.

Mary called for Jesus. She looked at him through the tears. "You could have saved his life, couldn't you?"

The way Mary phrased the question, Jesus had to tell her that he thought he could, but God said no.

"I asked God if I could save Joseph's life. God said no. He said He wasn't ready for me to use my powers. He said that He had something He wanted Joseph to do in heaven. He said the children and I should look after you, and that we will all be fine. I asked God if I could. I wanted to, but God said no."

Jesus repeated himself for emphasis.

"I will take care of you and the children. Mother, my mission here on earth isn't ready to start yet. We will have all the time we need. I told him that I was proud to be called Joseph's son."

With that said, Mary started crying again, uncontrollably.

The women of the synagogue were notified and they came to help Mary and to prepare the body for burial. He was washed in accordance with the Law. Mary brought the Frankincense and Myrrh that the Eastern Kings had brought to the family when Jesus was born. She told the women to use just half of the portions to anoint his body for burial.

James had alerted the rabbi of Joseph's death and he joined the rabbi in telling all of the relatives that they should come to the family courtyard to pay last respects. That meant everyone in Nazareth. Everyone came. The women brought food. The men gathered, all offering to carry the body to the gravesite. Joseph would be buried in the family grave. The women had prepared the body by tying his hands and feet with strips of cloth and covering his face with a *sudarium*, a special burial cloth. Then he was tightly wrapped with a woolen shroud.

The men of the synagogue all volunteered to carry the hastily constructed stretcher to the grave. It was considered a sign of affection to be selected to carry the body to the tomb. In fact, Joseph's friends took turns carrying the body. The body would be placed in a crypt carved in the grave wall at a diagonal. Burial would take place within eight hours of death. It was customary to roll a stone to cover the entrance to the burial chamber. The stone would be painted with whitewash as a warning that the area was a gravesite. After the body was placed in the grave and the stone rolled to cover the entrance, it was also customary for all of the visitors to join a ritual drinking of wine and eating *the bread of mourning*. Everyone gathered at the courtyard. Mary was expected to be in mourning for her husband for 30 days following the burial.

† † †

A year later, Jesus, James, James the younger, and Jude opened the grave, retrieved the bones and placed them in an ossuary and marked it as *Joseph*. His ossuary was placed in the grave with his father and other family members of a number of past generations.

With the passing of the patriarch, Jesus and James shared

management for the family and all of the family business. James the younger joined his older brother in building houses in Sepphoris. Jesus was mostly managing the woodshop. They now had eight craftsmen, and Jude was their apprentice. He was recognized as a man and joined the men at the Nazareth synagogue. The twins were seven and able to start helping Mary. They took turns playing with and watching Simon who was three. Mary gave birth to another boy. The entire family agreed that he should be called Joseph in honor of his father.

The new baby made Mary start thinking about the need for Jesus to get married. The next time she was at the synagogue following *tumat yoledet*—impurity after childbirth—Mary started looking at the young women of marriageable age. She was certain that Jesus would be interested in getting married and starting his own family. Her job was complicated by family ties. She and Joseph were both from Nazareth, so almost everyone from Nazareth was related. After careful consideration, she found two young women who were likely prospects. She was reasonably certain that, if she approached Jesus directly with the idea of marriage, he would say no. So she invited her first choice, Ariel, to come to their house to visit her and the new baby on the next Sabbath afternoon. She knew Jesus would be there, probably playing with the baby.

As if it were planned, Ariel showed up, and Jesus was holding the baby. Mary made certain that Jesus knew the girl and then left to see what Simon was doing. Jesus knew that Simon was with the twins and needed no attention from his mother. The thinly veiled effort by his mother was more than obvious. He was courteous to Ariel, and when Mary returned, Jesus excused himself.

After everyone had gone to bed, Jesus sat on the roof with

his mother. There was a large full moon that illuminated the rooftop and the two sitting there.

"Mother, it was nice to see Ariel today."

"She is a lovely young girl, isn't she?"

"Yes she is. Did you know she was coming to visit?"

"Yes, I did. She would be an excellent wife for you, Jesus."

"I seem to remember your matchmaking a few years ago. I also remember that I said that I couldn't have marriage plans until I know my heavenly Father's plans for my ministry. And, even then, I may not be able to have a wife. Ariel is a lovely young woman and I am certain she would be a good wife. But—not now, please, mother."

"Alright, son. But, I am your mother, and I want the best for you. And you are so good with children. You should have some of your own."

"Mother!"

"Alright. No more matchmaking."

"Now, I need some prayer time."

Jesus was in prayer on the roof for hours.

When Mary saw him the next morning, he was smiling, and there was a calm look on his face. She knew that he and God had reached some decisions. She didn't expect that he would tell her, but she was happy for him. The entire family had been under a lot of strain since Joseph's death. A little happiness was a good thing.

Nazareth—The Next Six Years

L ife in Nazareth for the next six years was without major issues. Jesus was still not married. He was doing more teaching, reading, and ministering at the synagogue. He was studying the manuscripts that he was given by Philo. He was developing parables as illustrations of points he knew he would need when he began his ministry.

James the younger married Ariel, and they had two children. James had moved into a house in Sepphoris. So, Mary insisted that James and Ariel move into James' home. Jude had married. He was 19. They moved into the family house. One of the twins, Miriam, now 13, married and moved in with her husband's family. The other twin, Salome, was still at the house. Simon was nine and was an apprentice in the woodworking shop, anxiously awaiting his acceptance into the congregation and his manhood. Baby Joseph was seven.

It was the beginning of Sabbath. Jesus was sitting, just thinking, on the rooftop a little before sunset. So much had happened, and yet so much was still the same. He was still waiting for God's direction. Every night he prayed for direction. God answered, "Be patient."

It was two weeks before Passover. He had let everyone know that they were going to Jerusalem two days before the synagogue group. He wanted to talk with Judah. They had started getting ready for the trip. The family began to assemble for the beginning of *Sabbath*. Mary brought a tray with the candles and holders, the *kiddush* cups, a fresh loaf of *challah,* and a skin of wine. Mary lit the candles. They drank the wine. Jesus said the *kiddush* prayer and added a prayer of thanks for his family.

They would leave for Jerusalem first thing Sunday morning. That night, Jesus stayed on the roof. There was a full moon so he didn't need a lantern. He had been agitated all day. He had been short with Joseph because he was playing instead of doing his part of the packing. That was so unlike Jesus. He stopped and picked Joseph up and apologized to him. They shared a big hug and continued packing. He had been trying to be patient, but as each day passed he became more aware that he was ready. But, ready for what? That would be God's call. That evening he prayed for patience and support and for God to show him what he was to be doing.

Sitting on a pillow on the roof, Jesus began to feel at peace. As he sat, enjoying his new-found peace, he fell into a deep sleep. The Archangel Gabriel appeared to him behind sleep.

"Jesus, Most Holy One, your heavenly Father knows of your feelings. He knows that you are ready. You are prepared, you are educated, and you are ready to assume your role in His plan. But, there are many other people who will play a part in your ministry, and they are not yet ready. Some are not yet ready to hear your message. Some are not yet ready to join with you and support you. And, your family is not yet ready for you to leave them.

"God wants you to know that He is working in all of their lives to make them ready for His plan. During this next year, you will give more authority to your family and the craftsmen at the woodworking shop. You need to spend more time in the synagogue, more time teaching, more time dealing with people and their problems, and more time praying. A year from now, you will need to go to Capernaum and stay for a number of months. You will meet many of the people who will assist you.

You will be meeting with Judah on your trip to Jerusalem. You need to prepare him. You will need to call for his commitment to devote his life to your ministry. Like you, his entire life was in preparation for your ministry. His education, his career as a Lawyer-Advocate and his knowledge of Mosaic Law and Roman Law, his contacts, and his financial resources will be essential. And his commitment to give his life for you is also essential to God's plan. You need to meet with him in private, and God will provide the words you need.

"So, now, Most Holy One, you can continue your sleep and awaken refreshed and ready for a day of worship and rest." Gabriel touched Jesus forehead and disappeared in a flash of light.

Jesus slept. Mary was the first person he saw as he opened his eyes. She was saying it was time to begin preparation to go to synagogue. The family finally gathered in the courtyard. It was a short walk to the synagogue. When they arrived the family scattered. Each had their friends they wanted to see and talk to. The rabbi asked Jesus to read from The *Torah* at the service. He said the reading was from Jeremiah. Jesus agreed, and all who were assembled moved into the meeting room.

Jesus and the rabbi removed The *Torah* from the safety of its container—one that Joseph had made as a gift to the synagogue. It was placed on the lectern that Jesus had made as a gift for the synagogue.

The rabbi announced that the reading would be from the prophet, Jeremiah. Jesus moved to the scroll and looked at the verse he was to read. There was a moment of silence while he caught his breath. And then he started reading, *"Before I formed thee in the belly I knew thee; and before thou camest forth out of the womb I sanctified thee, and I ordained thee a prophet unto the nations."*

Jesus knew the passage well. Jesus knew it was Jeremiah giving God all of the reasons why he couldn't be a prophet. God said he should listen to Him, not his own ideas. God's answer was, *"Then the* LORD *put forth his hand, and touched my mouth. And the* LORD *said unto me, Behold, I have put my words in thy mouth."*

The rabbi started his teaching by saying this was a verse from the prophet Jeremiah but it was a description for all believers. "We are all prophets, and we are to tell the story to all nations."

Jesus listened to what the rabbi was saying, but he knew that the verse he read to the congregation on that *Sabbath*, was specifically for him. It was his commission, and he knew it was a message. He was ready. He was prepared.

"I will tell you when I am ready." It was a voice from across the years, but it was God speaking just to him, just now.

The angel had said that God was waiting until the people He needed were ready. And, now God was telling Jesus that He would tell him when He was ready. Jesus answered God in his mind, "In Your good time, my Father, in Your good time, and in Your good way."

Sabbath at Jesus' house was a happy day. The *Torah* said to do no work and not to talk of work, so it was a play day and a prayer day. Mary, James' wife, Ariel, and Salome had cooked the family's favorite the night before. It was a large pot of vegetable stew and Jesus' favorite dried fruit relish for his bread. Play started as soon as they arrived home. Joseph and James' two sons started a game of chase in the courtyard. Jesus joined in. Simon, age nine, thought he was too old to play with the young children, but when Jesus joined in, he brought out an old ball, and the entire group adjourned to the street for a game of kickball. James joined in, and so did a dozen of the neighbor children. It was a happy time for everyone involved.

Ariel appeared. She made one good kick and called the family in for their late afternoon/evening meal. The boys had worked up an appetite and were happy to see the big pot of stew. Jesus enjoyed the exercise, but he was ready to eat as well.

Everyone knew that they would need to be up early in the morning. Even Simon and Joseph were ready for bed at sunset. That gave Jesus some time for prayer. He thanked God for all of the lessons of that day. Just about everywhere he looked, God had a lesson for him. After everyone had retired, he went up on the roof. It was a short prayer time.

"God, thank you for all You showed me today."

The Beginning of the End

With first light, Jesus and the family set out for Jerusalem. They overnighted at their usual places the first and second nights. Everyone was in a good mood so the travel went smoothly. Simon was the first one to ask Jesus if he was going to stop and pray.

"Jude told me about the holy place. I want to pray there."

Joseph joined in, "Me too, Jesus. I want to pray at the holy place."

They got to the bend in the river. Jesus stopped, climbed on his rock and said, "Okay, everyone who wants to pray needs to at least walk in the water." Mary took the hands of James and Ariel's two children and walked toward the water. Simon, Joseph, Salome, and Jude all walked along the edge of the water. As they stepped in the river, Joseph said he wanted to be completely holy, so he sat in the water and splashed himself. He was totally soaked. James tied the two donkeys to a tree and joined his wife and children in the water. Everyone was enjoying the holy water. Jesus was the only one praying, and his prayer was short.

"Thank you, Father for this wonderful family. I am Your servant and I await Your instructions. Amen."

It took Jesus half an hour to collect all of the family on the trail. Joseph was soaked. Mary took a clean, dry cloak from their packed clothes and gave it to him to change. Everyone had some wet clothes, but Joseph was the only one who needed an entire fresh change of clothing.

So after the prayer and cleansing in the holy water, everyone was ready to finish the trip to Jerusalem. When they reached their overnight place, they knew they were just half a day away. Joseph, Simon, and Salome led the troupe at a fast pace. Everyone was happy that the young ones were leading since they were usually the ones playing and slowing the progress. It was midday when they arrived at the uncle's house. They were the first ones there, so they could pick their sleeping places.

Jesus asked Jude to walk over to Judah's palace to see if he could meet with him while the family was in Jerusalem. Jesus was surprised when Jude returned with Judah. Judah and Jesus embraced. It had been six years since they had seen each other. Jesus told Judah that he needed to talk to him in a private place. Judah suggested his roof garden at midday the next day.

"I have missed you, Jesus. I was so sorry to hear about Joseph's death. I knew he would be buried before I could get there. I decided I would pray for him and the family and would pay my respects when you were here. I knew we would need to have time together. Lately, I have been having dreams of our time in Egypt. Just last week I dreamed about the time you saved my life—and my commitment to you."

"That is what I want to talk about as well. But not here. Not now. Come. Let's go to the roof. We will have a mug of wine, and you can share what you have been doing."

Jesus asked for two mugs of wine, and the two friends moved to the roof. He asked for Mary to join them. Mary arrived and Judah started crying. Mary was like a second mother, and Joseph was also like a father to him. He sobbed for a few minutes as Mary embraced him. He explained why he didn't come to Nazareth. Mary said there was nothing he could have done. They both shared a few tears and continued the embrace. Mary separated and said she needed to be in the cooking area, helping the other women. One last quick embrace and she left the roof.

Jesus smiled. "Judah, she has loved you like she loves me." They sat quietly for some time. "Judah, I need some time to talk privately to you. Can I come to your house tomorrow afternoon? We can talk there."

†††

It was Friday, a little after noon, when Jesus arrived at Judah's family compound. The gate manager welcomed him and said that Judah was waiting for him on the roof of his house. He asked if Jesus needed him to show him the way. Jesus thanked him and said he knew the way.

When Jesus arrived on the roof, Judah was waiting with two freshly poured mugs of wine. A cooling breeze was blowing. There were soft pillows under the colorful woven mats that shaded the people on the roof from the midday sun.

They sat, and Jesus began the conversation. "So, Judah. What have you been doing?"

"You know that I managed the furniture business after you and your family moved to Nazareth. I think I told you that the rabbi asked me to sit on his legal advisory group. Thanks to Philo's lessons on Mosaic Law and Roman Law, the rabbi relied on my opinions. Did I tell you that the rabbi was trying to marry me off?"

"Yes. You did. My mother had picked out the perfect young woman for me. I told her I wasn't interested. So, James married her. They have two children."

"I guess matchmaking comes with the job of being a mother. She did arrange a meeting with her brother for me. My uncle sits on the Sanhedrin. I am now his assistant in addition to being a Lawyer/Advocate. I was shocked to find that Gamaliel was seated on the Sanhedrin and recognized as a Doctor of the Law. He even asked about you.

"I have become active in a group called the Zealotes. Philo introduced me to them before I left Alexandria. I believe your ministry may benefit from some of their beliefs. Judas of Galilee began the movement, inciting the people of Judea to rebel against the Roman government and take back the Holy land by force. They are fierce advocates for our God. There is a small group, whose members are very militant, located in Galilee. They are called the *sicarii*, or "dagger men," and they actually carry large daggers under their cloaks and reportedly kill our people who don't believe as they do. I'm not a part of that group. I believe that Gamaliel is sympathetic to their beliefs, but I can't be certain of that. He mentioned a young student, Paul, who is from Tarsus and has strong Zealot beliefs."

Judah continued telling Jesus what he was doing. When he was finished, Jesus began introducing him to the rest of his life.

"First, Judah, I need to make certain that you remember your commitment and ask if you are still willing to do what I ask."

"I owe you my life, Jesus, and everything I have. You had my pledge then, you have it now."

"That is good to hear Judah, because God has told me that you are to play a very important role in my ministry. I need you to travel with me. Take care of my money and organize the people who will be working with me. God has revealed that I am to gather a few good men and travel throughout Galilee telling all who will listen about my heavenly Father. There is a lot more He said that He would reveal to me. You already know of some of the powers I have been given. You know of my ability to heal. I wanted to heal Joseph, but God said He had work for him in heaven. I believe I could have saved him. Watching him die was the most difficult thing I have had to do. I loved him. God said it was all a part of His plan. I am learning that everything in my life has been and is a part of God's plan. And your going with me is also a part of God's plan."

"Within a month of my return to Nazareth, I am to go to Capernaum. There are people I need to meet there. I will be back next year at Passover. I hope you can arrange your life by then; I need you to leave with me. We are to go to Nazareth for a short while and then to Capernaum. I need you to help me select the people who will assist me. Your Zealot friends may be of some help. I will need some men of various backgrounds. Some strong who can help with security. Others from..." Jesus paused. "Well, like I said, varied backgrounds. But, I want you to be the manager of the finances of our group and keep the money. I need someone I can trust, and God has shown me that you should be that man. You are good with money, you know Mosaic Law and Roman Law, and you are good with people. Will you do that for me? I need someone who is completely loyal, and I know you would be."

Judah agreed.

They continued to talk. Jesus told Judah about the message

of his ministry. They talked about the group of men that Jesus would be recruiting. Judah said that the Zealots call their workers disciples. Jesus said he liked that word.

"I have one final request of you, Judah. Your name means 'The Praised One,' and I want to focus on that. And your father was from Kerioth. I want to honor your family, and I want people to know that you are from Judea. For my purposes, I want you to be called Judas from Kerioth. Judas Iskerioth or Judas Iscariot."

"Judas Iscariot is easier. That suits me."

From that point on *Judah* was Judah to his family and contacts in Jerusalem, and *Judas* to Jesus and everyone connected with Jesus and his ministry.

They realized that they had talked all afternoon when one of Judas' servants arrived with everything necessary to celebrate the beginning of Sabbath. Judas asked Jesus to celebrate the start of Sabbath there at his house. Jesus decided that he would stay since he wouldn't be able to get back to the uncle's before the start of their Sabbath celebration.

Wine was poured in the ceremonial *kiddush* cups. Judas asked Jesus to recite the *kiddush* prayer. Jesus added a personal prayer for thanks, guidance, and safety.

Jesus left following the ceremony. He was smiling the entire way back to his uncle's house.

The family left for synagogue together. Joseph, Simon, Salome, and Ariel sat with Mary and the other family women and children. Jesus, James, and Jude sat with the uncle and the rest of the family men. The rabbi asked Jesus to read, but he declined. He said he wanted to enjoy the service with his family. Judah was sitting with Simon and Gamaliel and the leaders of the synagogue. Judah was asked to read.

"I will be reading from the prophet Jeremiah. '*I know the thoughts that I think toward you, thus sayeth the* LORD, *thoughts of peace and not evil to give you my expected end.*'"

It was a special service for Jesus. The rabbi's teaching was on God's plan. It was meaningful to Jesus and to Judah. The rabbi said God had a plan for each of us. A plan that pleased God, like a path that led to His divine outcome. We did have free will and we could elect not to follow it. But, the rabbi said that, in his opinion, any time we decide not to follow the plan, God would provide events in our life that would help us choose to get back on the path. Following the path would be easy; choosing a different path would be difficult. But, it was still our choice.

Jesus noticed that Judah was looking at him. Looking as if to say, "Okay, Jesus, I get the message."

When Jesus and the men met the women and children on the portico, Judah was already there with Simon and Gamaliel. Gamaliel was the first to speak.

"I've been hearing a lot about you, Jesus. Your rabbi speaks with high praise. He reports to me of your activities because he thinks you were one of my students."

"I didn't suggest that; only that we met. I'm sure he knows I was a student of Philo. But, I am honored that he thinks I studied under you." Jesus didn't want to insult Gamaliel. He could be a valuable contact in the future—and now, for that matter.

"It is I who should be honored. A teacher is valued by the success of his students. You would have made me proud." He looked at Judah and Simon. "You too, Judah."

The group chatted about the overcrowding of Jerusalem, the buildings Herod was building, and the improvements he had made to the synagogue. When it was time to leave, Gamaliel embraced Jesus and said "God be with you, my son. *Shalom Shabatt.*"

Jesus was able to respond, "And with you. *Shalom Shabatt.*"

On their way home, Jesus' uncle said he was impressed that Jesus knew the chief doctor of law on the Sanhedrin. Jesus said that they had met when Joseph, Mary, and he were in Alexandria. Jesus let the conversation about Gamaliel end then. And he changed the subject.

The visit ended, and Jesus and the family joined the Nazareth group heading home. Joseph had told all of his friends about the holy place. They all wanted to pray in the holy water. The rabbi talked to Jesus since many of the parents were asking about stopping to pray at Jesus' special prayer place. The rabbi asked Jesus about the entire group stopping. Jesus said the adult parents would have to manage their children, but he was going to pray, so he would be stopping. Anyone else who wanted to pray was welcome.

After prayer time was finished at least one child from every family needed to change clothes. Everyone survived the prayer stop. The children were happy to have been able to take a prayer stop and bathe in the holy water. It actually made the rest of the trip a lot easier because the children were in a much better mood.

All of the residents of Nazareth slowly got back to normal. Jesus had a meeting with James the younger. He was managing the woodworking business. There were still six craftsmen working at the shop. Jesus revealed his plan to leave for Capernaum and that it was time for him to start his ministry. He asked James if he thought he could handle the business without his help. James said the woodworking business was doing well, and it was very profitable. And he felt that he could handle it. Jesus said he was certain that James could handle the business. He said he wanted to talk to him about the house building business.

James was still building houses in Sepphoris, and he had three craftsmen working for him. Jesus went to Sepphoris for a conversation with James. He told him of his need to spend some time in Capernaum and that within a year he would be starting his ministry and would be traveling around Galilee. Jesus' timing was perfect. James had turned 45, and he was ready to stop working so hard.

Jesus said, "It's God's plan."

James had one of his craftsmen in mind to sell his business to. He asked if James the younger was still living in his house. Jesus said he was, but there was room to build another house, or the younger James could move into his room. James could decide what would be best for him. Jesus said he would help him do whatever he decided. Jesus asked him to consider what he wanted to do and come to Nazareth for Sabbath. On Sunday they could discuss plans.

When Jesus returned from Sepphoris, he asked his mother to join him on the roof. Sunset in Nazareth was earlier because of the mountains that surrounded the town. Mary, carrying a lantern, arrived shortly before sunset. They sat on the pillows. The sunset was another art show.

"I love you, Mother. We need to talk. God has started telling me what He wants me to do. I have continually questioned Him even though I know He has a plan for me and my life."

"I love you too, son. I Remember that the rabbi said God has a plan for you. What has He told you to do? Are you are questioning His plan?"

"He has told me to recruit my friend, Judah. That I have done. Now He wants me to leave you and go to Capernaum for much of this year. I know it is His will, but I don't think I am ready to leave you and the family."

"Jesus, you are my son, but you are His son, as well. You came to earth because God had a plan for you and His people living here. You have a role, and the only way you can fulfill that plan is to listen to Him and to do what He tells you to do. When does He want you to go to Capernaum?"

"Right away."

"Well, why are we talking? You should be packing."

"But, Mother. I want to be certain that you and the family will be able to live and keep money coming in from the woodworking shop. I have talked to James, and he will come home from Sepphoris. But, still."

"You know better than this, my son. God put you here. Now your only job is to do what He wants you to do. Why are you even asking me?"

"I guess I wanted you to say, *stay*."

"You will never hear that from me. Pack and make the trip to Capernaum. It's only one day's travel away. You need to do what God wants you to do."

"I know you are correct, Mother. As soon as James is here, I will leave. But, I will start preparing tomorrow." Jesus paused, "I love you, Mother."

"And I love you, Jesus, and God loves you, too."

They moved down a level and went to sleep.

Next Stop Capernaum

Jesus knew James would soon be arriving at the house and that he would be leaving soon. He began gathering his clothes for the trip. One of the things he needed to do was talk to the rabbi. He knew the synagogue would be closed on Sunday, so it would be a good day to handle arrangements. Jesus talked to young James. He needed to know what was going on.

Jesus and James sat on the roof. There was a good breeze blowing so the roof was quite comfortable.

"James. A lot has been happening lately, and I need to catch you up on recent events. In a week or so I will be leaving for Capernaum. I expect to be there for a while, possibly a year. Your older brother is selling his home-building business in Sepphoris, and he will be returning home.

"The first thing I want you to know is that you are in charge of the woodworking shop. James and I have talked. He understands what I have just said, and he agrees. His primary job is to look after Mother. If you need his advice or his help, he will be available, but he is not to interfere with your management of the business. I have made clear with James, and now I want to be sure I am making that clear with you. Before you ask, you, Ariel and the children are to stay in the house as long as you wish. James will move into my room. The business will pay the bills, and James will contribute if he needs to. Is all of that clear?"

"Yes, Jesus. It is clear. But, what happens if we differ?"

"James, you are both adults. Reach a compromise."

"That is easy to say, but you won't be here."

"You know more about the woodworking business than he does. He has been away for four or five years. He will defer to you."

"What about dealing with Mother. What if we disagree?"

"You are both to act like adults. Agree on a compromise."

"But, I'm not sure."

"Listen, James. You both will be living together. You will be eating together. You will be going to synagogue together, and you are both adults. You will find a way to handle your disagreements."

James asked Jesus what he would be doing in Capernaum. Jesus said he didn't know, but God would direct him. "He has told me to go and He will show me what I should be doing."

The week dragged along. The rabbi said Jesus would be missed. The rabbi said he knew the rabbi in Capernaum. Jesus said the rabbi would be the first person in Capernaum he would seek out to meet.

It was the middle of the next week when James arrived. Jesus had a meeting with the two Jameses. Both agreed to work through any problems they had.

As the family was entering synagogue, the rabbi asked Jesus to read from The *Torah*.

Jesus stood before the unrolled scripture. "I will be reading from the Psalms.

"*The* LORD *reigneth; let the people tremble; he sitteth between the cherubims; let the earth be moved. The* LORD *is great in Zion;*

and he is high above all the people. Let them praise thy great and terrible name; for it is Holy. The king's strength also loveth judgment; thou dost establish equity, thou executest judgment and righteousness in Jacob. Exalt the LORD *our God, and worship at his footstool; for he is holy. Moses and Aaron among the priests, and Samuel among them that call upon His name; they called upon the* LORD, *and He answered them. He spake unto them in the cloudy pillar: they kept His testimonies, and the ordinances He gave them."*

"And such is the Psalm of David."

Jesus rejoined the family. The rabbi finished the service. Just before closing the day of worship, he announced that Jesus would be leaving for Capernaum. He announced that God had selected Jesus for a ministry project. The rabbi prayed that Jesus would be successful.

Jesus visited with the people of Nazareth for at least two hours. Offers of prayers for Jesus and for support and help for the family were made by almost everyone who was there outside the synagogue. Jesus thanked everyone for their support.

Back at the family compound, Mary, Ariel, and Salome had prepared a special meal for the family to honor Jesus. Everyone enjoyed the lamb stew with vegetables, fruit relish, bread with honey and wine. It was a great time for the family all together. Thanks to the conversation, the meal lasted till the end of Sabbath. Everyone moved to the roof. They were just in time to see the three stars and officially end that Sabbath, possibly the most important Sabbath for Jesus and his entire family.

Jesus closed out the night with a prayer for protection from his heavenly Father.

His morning began early. He hugged and kissed everyone

and began his journey. It would be a full day. The sun was sinking when Jesus reached the first inn near Capernaum. Jesus slept later than normal. His first stop was the synagogue. Jesus said he was looking for work and presented his qualifications to the rabbi. His reputation had preceded him. The rabbi knew Jesus as a reader and knew he was one of Philo's students. The rabbi said he looked forward to having him at the synagogue.

Jesus told the rabbi he would need a place to stay and possibly a place to work. The rabbi said he had a room Jesus could use until he found a place to rent. He suggested that Jesus should meet with Zebedee. He said that Zebedee operated a fish drying business and occasionally built fishing boats for his fishermen to use.

Author's Comment

Capernaum

Capernaum was located on the northwest corner of the Sea of Galilee. It was founded in the 3rd century BCE. It grew from a small fishing village to a town that covered 13 acres with a population of over 1,500 and was occupied until the 11th century BCE. The town was largely a Jewish town, and a synagogue was built in 1st century BCE. The synagogue was a large and impressive structure. It was built of large, white limestone blocks quarried from the hills of Galilee on the west side of the town. The prayer hall measured 60 feet by 67 feet, the courtyard was 67 feet by 36 feet and the entire building was surrounded by a 13 foot wide porch. Fishing the Sea of Galilee predates the establishment of Capernaum. The Galilee boat had been used from over a hundred years. All of the boats were similar. Measuring 27 feet long by 7.5 feet wide with a sidewall of 4.5 feet. The boat would easily accommodate two fishermen and could expand to three with a helper to pull the nets.

CAPERNAUM

J esus put his clothes in the room provided by the rabbi and
spent the next four days exploring the village and the hills
that surround the Sea. He found two places where he could sit
and pray and enjoy the beauty that was Capernaum. Each day
he would watch Zebedee's fishermen leave in the morning and
return in the early afternoon. They would wash the fish with
seawater and load their catch in the cart that carried them to
Zebedee's house. There they were cleaned and tied by the tail
to tree branch racks to dry. It was a good business. The fish
were free, the sun was free, and most of the fishermen were
family members. There was good demand for the dried fish,
and Zebedee's dried fish were known for their good quality.

It was Friday morning. Sabbath would begin that evening. The rabbi asked Jesus if he would join him for the
beginning of *Shabbat*. They met at the front portico of the
synagogue. The rabbi had all of the essentials for the celebration. He poured the wine and asked Jesus if he would recite
the *Kiddush* prayer. The rabbi broke the *challah*, and the two
sat, eating the bread, drinking the wine, and talking. They
discussed Jesus' education and the teaching of Philo.

The rabbi asked about Alexandria and the Great Library.
The rabbi said he loved books and would love to be able to
read the actual writing of the masters.

Jesus said he had read Aristotle and Plato. He had held the handwritten manuscripts by Sophocles, Aristophanes and Euripides.

"I know it isn't right for a rabbi to envy, but I envy the opportunity you had to learn from Philo and read the manuscripts of the intellectual masters. God forgive me."

"I'm certain He will." There was a few minutes of silence. "I learned a lot from Philo." Again a pause. "But I have learned so much more from just watching people and how they treat each other. I learned about God's love by seeing how my mother looked when my brothers and sisters were born. I learned about beauty looking at God's sunsets. I've learned about friendship from my friends, and I've learned about hatred from some of those same friends. I've learned about wisdom from Moses' Law, and I've learned about stupidity from Roman Law. And, I am learning something new every day."

"So true, Jesus, so true."

Jesus and the rabbi sat in silence for some time. The oil lamp provided little light, but the two men were lost in thought and that didn't require light.

"Will you read tomorrow? That would help me, and it would be a suitable introduction for you." The rabbi was still looking off into the blackness where the sea was.

"If that is your wish." Jesus was looking at the same sea.

"I will be here tomorrow." Jesus was the first to speak. "Do you have the reading picked out for tomorrow?" Jesus assumed he did.

"No. I will leave that to your judgment."

"I have an idea," Jesus replied. "Do you want to know what it is?"

"No. I will find out tomorrow."

The two split. Both men slept quietly with no dreams.
They awoke. It was Sabbath morning.

The rabbi welcomed everyone. And introduced Jesus.

Jesus was standing in the back of the Court of the Israelites. He was holding a lighted oil lamp. He walked slowly
to the lectern. He set the lamp next to the lectern and stood
behind the opened *Torah*.

"The reading today is from The Psalms. *"Thy word is a lamp
unto my feet, and a light unto my path. I have sworn, and I will
perform, that I will keep thy righteous judgments. I have inclined
my heart to perform your statutes alway, even unto the end."*

"Such are the words of King David."

With that, Jesus quenched the flame and sat in Elijah's chair.

The rabbi's teaching was that light symbolizes God's
eternal presence. He quoted verse after verse from Exodus.
He focused on the reason for lighting candles, to mark the
transition from the profane life we live to the sacred life we
should be living. With the closing prayer, Jesus followed the
rabbi out of the Court of the Israelites and onto the portico.
Quickly, they were joined by the leaders of the synagogue.
And shortly thereafter, eligible young women started walking
near the group. Jesus of Nazareth was introduced to many
people that noon. But the rabbi made certain of an introduction to Zebedee. With him were his two sons, James
and John. His three daughters were nearby, waiting to be
introduced to the new reader.

The rabbi mentioned that Jesus was a master carpenter.
And that he was looking for work and a place to stay. The
eldest of the daughters spoke softly to her father, "Father,
the watchman's house at the fish drying yard is available."

"So it is. So it is. Jesus, can you come to the dock tomorrow.

We can talk after fishermen leave for the day." Jesus agreed and excused himself. In his room he changed into his short robe and walked up to his special place in the hills. The late afternoon sun had turned the sea into a liquid field of precious gems—diamonds, rubies, emeralds—sparkling points of light.

A full moon replaced the sun. That made it easy for Jesus to find his way back to the rabbi's house. Sleep replaced consciousness as quickly as the moonlight had replaced sunlight.

Shortly after sunrise, Jesus was standing on the dock where James and John were preparing their boat for a day of fishing. Zebedee was there as he said he would be, and introduced Jesus to Andrew and Simon Peter, sons of his former partner, who had died. The boats were launched. Together Jesus and Zebedee walked to Zebedee's house. They sat together. Zebedee talked about the fishing business. He talked about the difficulty of getting well-made boats. He talked about constantly repairing the boats. He talked about the fish drying business and the available house.

Jesus mentioned that his father and grandfather had been carpenters. Zebedee said he knew of Joseph of Nazareth. By the end of the conversation, Zebedee had made Jesus an offer, and Jesus had accepted.

They moved back into the house for a cup of wine. Zebedee's eldest daughter, Hannah, meaning with favor and grace, brought the cups and wine and started pouring it. Jesus said he would go back to the rabbi's and get his possessions and return to the house.

"No. No. No. You can't."

"No/ What do you mean, *No,* daughter? I have decided."

"No. Father. "It hasn't been cleaned in over a month."

"First of all, Hannah, you don't interrupt men when they are talking, and you don't talk back to me. But, you are correct. We do want the house to be presentable for Jesus. You and your sisters will clean it today."

"I am sorry I interrupted you, Father, but the condition of the house would reflect poorly on you and the family. I will see that it is perfect for your friend, Jesus."

"Will that be good with you, Jesus?" Zebedee asked. "The girls will have it ready tomorrow."

Jesus agreed. He finished the wine and asked to be excused. "I have a few things I need to do before I return.

Jesus went to the synagogue. He found the rabbi to let him know the results of the meeting with Zebedee. He thanked the rabbi for the arrangements and asked what he owed him for the use of the room.

"Jesus. You owe me nothing. You have already contributed to our congregation. And, I hope you will continue."

"You know I will."

"I will be moving to Zebedee's extra house tomorrow. I am heading up into the hills to pray and meditate. I have found a special place where I can overlook the sea. It is a place where I can talk to God."

"Tell Him I said thank you for all of our blessings."

"I will, rabbi. I will."

Jesus walked up into the hills to his special place. He prayed and he listened. He enjoyed having time with his heavenly Father. He remembered to say *thank you* for the rabbi. Jesus continued his meditation.

It was afternoon, and the fishing boats were returning. Jesus watched. He recognized the boats of Zebedee. The brothers in each boat worked well together. They unloaded the Musht they had caught. Musht was the fish of choice. They had few bones, and they tasted good when dried. The brothers selected the ones that were about three pounds. The older fish didn't taste good when dried. They were easy to select because they had changed color. They were discarded. Biny Carp and Sardines were the other fish that they could catch, but they weren't good for drying so they too were discarded. They washed the catch before they put the fish in the cart.

Jesus knew that all of these activities were designed to save time when they got to the drying yard. Jesus knew that he would see the catch cleaned, prepared, salted, and drying in the sun when he arrived tomorrow. Jesus again thanked God for providing for him. He wanted to be back in Capernaum before sunset.

Shortly after midday, Jesus, carrying his clothes, walked to Zebedee's house. The house that he would use was behind the main house. It was built for a watchman to keep wild animals from destroying the drying fish. It had a storage room where the dried fish could be kept until they were sold. Thankfully, the smell of drying fish was an odor that you could get used to.

Zebedee escorted Jesus to the house. As Hannah had said she would, the house was immaculate. She had even placed a vase of flowers in the room. The lavender she included helped disguise the dried fish smell.

Jesus was at the boats the next morning. He was watching everything the brothers were doing. He analyzed the boat's design. He wanted to see how a design change would make the boat more efficient. He watched what the brothers were doing. They lost a lot of fish when they were pulling the nets over the high sides of the boats. There was no way to fill the boat with one day of fishing, so the sides could be at least a foot shorter in the center on each side. That would make getting the fish into the boat a lot easier.

That evening Jesus asked Zebedee if they could talk. Jesus had made a carving of what his idea for a fishing boat would look like. Jesus explained how the new design would work. Zebedee asked if he could take one of the older boats and make the change and refit the boat for fishing. Jesus said he thought he could.

For the next few weeks, Jesus worked on the old boat. The changes were easier to make than he thought. It took a month and Jesus was looking forward to having Andrew and Simon Peter try out the new boat design. Andrew said there was no way he was going to get in the deep water with the new boat that was certain to sink. James over heard what Andrew said. He was quick to better Andrew and Simon Peter. He volunteered for John and him to use the new boat.

The next day, the two brother teams gathered at the launch point. The new boat was lighter so James and John were fishing before Andrew and Simon Peter got their boat in the water. James and John filled their boat first because they lost fewer fish hoisting the nets into the boat. They were back at the launch point separating and washing the fish when Andrew and Simon Peter arrived.

Zebedee had brought two carts to make evaluating the new boat fair. At the end of the afternoon, James and John, Jesus, and Zebedee were sitting on the cart, waiting for Andrew and Simon Peter to finish the sorting and washing. James and John had caught a substantial amount more that Andrew and Simon Peter. Andrew was saying that James and John had found a better place to drag their nets. But Simon Peter said that the winner was obvious, and he wanted a new boat design.

Zebedee trusted Jesus from that point on.

Jesus noticed that the fish-drying yard was growing with each day's catch. Everyone was happy with the larger catch except Zebedee. Sales had not increased even though the supply was steadily growing. Zebedee asked Jesus what he thought. Jesus called a meeting of all of the brothers. Jesus presented the problem.

"You four are now catching more fish than you used to. All you need to do is look at the drying yard or look in the storage area. We need to *sell* more. I believe we are selling all we can here in Capernaum. We need to expand. My suggestion is that we find a new place to sell fish and someone willing to make the trip twice a week. Someone who is a good businessman and who is good with people. You know the people here in Capernaum much better than I. Do you have any suggestions?

They all started talking at once. Suggesting names, countering each other. That went on for some time when Andrew suggested Matthew.

Quickly there was consensus. All of the brothers agreed, Matthew would be the best choice. Matthew Levi was a little older that Jesus. He was from a family of tax collectors. He was a customs collector in Capernaum. He had gone to synagogue school in Jerusalem.

Andrew was selected to meet with Matthew and offer him the opportunity. Matthew wanted to meet with Zebedee and Jesus before agreeing to accept the position. Matthew knew Zebedee's fish well, but he wanted to know what he would get paid and what would be expected of him.

They talked, and he agreed to start with one day a week, mostly because he was impressed by Jesus and wanted to be able to learn more from one of Philo's students. So, he made a part of his payment a four-hour class with Jesus every other Sabbath afternoon. Jesus recommended that Matthew set up his business in Tiberias. Herod Antipas had made Tiberias the capital of the Tetrarachy of Galilee. It was also known for the 17 hot springs. And it was only a three-hour walk from Capernaum. It didn't take long for Herod Antipas to demand that his palace serve him Zebedee's fish.

So, within a few weeks of arriving in Capernaum, Jesus was already a part of the synagogue, had a place to live and a key part in one of the largest businesses. He knew that many of the contacts he had made would be essential to his ministry.

Selling fish in Tiberias was so successful that Matthew added a second day and was selling out every time he was there.

The rest of the year passed swiftly. Jesus was active in the synagogue. The rabbi had started hinting that there were marriageable young women who had asked about Jesus. He told the rabbi that he may be leaving Capernaum and so marriage wasn't in his plan.

All of Jesus' recommendations for Zebedee were working, and Matthew was very successful at selling fish in Tiberias. As Passover approached, Jesus was asking God for directions. He knew he was supposed to start his ministry soon.

It was a Sabbath afternoon after his meeting with Matthew. He had walked up into the hills to his special place where he prayed. He had been meditating for some time after his prayers. A strong wind blew through the hills. God spoke to him in the wind. Jesus was to return to Nazareth in time for the group to travel to Jerusalem for Passover. Judas was to return to Nazareth with Jesus and his family. Then Jesus was to separate himself from the family and spend 40 days in the wilderness where God would reveal the purpose of the ministry. With that, the wind stopped abruptly.

Jesus thanked God. He returned to his house. Zebedee was in his courtyard. Jesus asked for a few moments to talk to him. He told Zebedee that he would be returning to Nazareth soon. He said he needed to visit his family. Zebedee asked what he needed to do for Jesus to stay. Jesus thanked him but said he had put the programs in place and they would be successful.

"My house is always open to you, Jesus. Always."

The next morning he talked to the rabbi. That afternoon, Jesus met the brothers as they returned from the day's fishing. They were unhappy that Jesus was leaving. Jesus said he would be back, but he didn't know when. The meeting with Matthew went well. He was happy with his new business, but he, too, was unhappy with the loss of his teacher.

The next day, Jesus was packed and ready to head to Nazareth at sunup.

WHAT WAS HAPPENING IN JERUSALEM

Judah had discussed what he knew of Jesus' plan with his father. Jesus' father had worked for Simon, and so had Jesus, as a young man. Judah discussed his pledge but not the specifics of the reason. Simon had said he felt like he owed Joseph for everything he had done to grow hiss business. Simon wasn't happy with his son's decision but he agreed to support him.

Judah had a year to get ready to join Jesus. The time went a lot faster than he expected. He knew that Jesus and his family would arrive in Jerusalem a few days before Passover. That was two weeks away. Judah had cleared most of his legal business and had collected most of the money owed him. He expected that whatever Jesus had planned for him would require money. He had reduced what he was taking as much as he thought possible, but he would still need a donkey.

Jesus, his family, and the Nazareth congregation arrived as expected. They would again be staying with the uncle. Jesus had a lot of family details to take of since he would soon be leaving home. He sent word to Judah that they could talk after Sabbath had ended. Jesus was sitting with his family as usual. Judah was sitting with his father, the uncle who was in the Sanhedrin, and many of the important people in the synagogue. The rabbi asked Judah to read.

Judah stepped to the lectern and stood behind the opened *Torah*. "I will be reading from the prophet Jeremiah. '*I know the thoughts that I think toward you, thus saith the* LORD, *thoughts of peace and not evil to give you my expected end.*'"

The rabbi replaced Judah. "Today, I have happy and sad news for the congregation. Our friend Judah will be leaving us. God has called him to be a missionary. I know that he will return occasionally. It is always good for us to be ready to do God's plan. Our commitment is that we will do God's plan even when it isn't our plan. Just as God told Jeremiah that He knew what Jeremiah was to do, God has told Judah what He wants him to do. You know that part of Jeremiah, you know that Jeremiah tried everything to get out of doing God's will. But in the end, God won and Jeremiah lost. That was a classic battle of wills. And in a battle of wills, God will always win. So, it is good that Judah's answer to God's question reflects the same willingness as the Prophet Isaiah, "*I heard the voice of the* LORD, *saying, Whom shall I send, and who will go for us? Then said I, Here am I, send me.*" The rabbi went on with his teaching, but two people in the congregation were smiling—Judah and Jesus.

Judah was mobbed on the portico after the service. Good wishes and questions. His answer, "I will tell you all the next time I see you."

Jesus whispered, "Tomorrow my friend. Tomorrow."

Sabbath ended with every member of the congregation closing with prayer.

Jesus arrived at Judah's compound the next morning. He was welcomed and shown to the roof of Judah's house. Judah was there waiting for Jesus. He asked Jesus if he would like some wine. Jesus declined. Judah excused the servant.

"Tell me what you have been doing, Jesus, and what we will be doing." Judah was anxious to get started.

"Calm, my friend. In good time." Jesus encapsulated the last year in his life and told Judah about the people he met in Capernaum—Andrew, Simon Peter, James, John, and Matthew. "I think some or all of these men could be very helpful in my, our mission."

They talked for hours. Finally Jesus got to the information Judah wanted to know. "We will leave tomorrow morning heading for Nazareth. I still don't know everything, but God told me that on the road to Nazareth we would meet John the Baptist. Have you heard of him?" Judah nodded his head. "He is to baptize me. And you, if you like. Then I am to fast for 40 days in the wilderness, just like Elijah and Moses, and God will tell me more. But I know about the baptism and the fasting in the wilderness outside Jericho. You, my friend, are to go to Nazareth with my family. You will stay there while I am fasting, and I will tell you of our commission when I return home."

"That is my agreement, Jesus."

"We will be leaving tomorrow as soon as everyone is ready. I will see you there.

"Yes. I have some of my stuff on a donkey. Is that alright?"

"Yes. There are a couple of other donkeys on the trip. Some with two legs."

Judah and Jesus laughed.

"Starting tomorrow, you will be Judas Iscariot. It will be like a new life."

Jesus returned to the home of his uncle. Everyone was mostly packed for the trip to Nazareth. Jesus prayed with and for everyone and for a safe and uneventful trip home.

He took James and Mary aside and told them that he would be baptized on the trip and following that, he would spend the next 40 days in the wilderness outside of Jericho, and God would tell him what he is to do.

Mary was worried. She had many questions.

"How will you get food and what about water? What is this baptism? Why are you going to be alone? James can stay with you."

"God will provide, Mother. And I can take care of myself. Judas will be going with you. I want him to stay at the house. He can help you until I get back. It is necessary for my ministry, Mother."

"I don't understand."

"You will, Mother. Soon, you will. For now just know that it is God's will, and that Judas will be with you until I return."

The next morning the Nazareth synagogue group, along with Judas and his donkey, started on their trip. They over-nighted just south of Jericho. The next day, they headed north again.

Baptism & Temptation

The group encountered a large group of people at a bend in the river. No one was moving.

"What's the hold up?" One of the group asked.

"What's going on?"

"Why aren't we moving?"

Jesus and the rabbi worked their way to the front of the group that was blocking the way. Everyone was gathered around Jesus' holy place. There in the middle of the Jordan River was a wild man—ragged clothes and long, unkempt hair.

The rabbi told Jesus, "He was grabbing people and trying to drown them."

Jesus told the rabbi that it was the Essene practice of baptism. To that Jewish group it represented a commitment to God. Putting off the old ways of idolatry and accepting the new way of God. "They call it being reborn. I think this is something I need to do."

At that point, Jesus walked toward the man in the water. Jesus knew it was John. The crowd seemed to part for Jesus. John saw Jesus when he stepped into the water. He was transfixed, staring at Jesus. John smiled. He realized he was actually going to meet the man, Jesus.

"I am come to be baptized."

John replied, "I have need to be baptized of thee, and comest thou to me?"

"First things first, John."

So, John dipped Jesus in the waters of the Jordan River at the place that Jesus had had many conversations with his heavenly Father. His holy place.

"I baptize you in the Holy Name of our Lord, God."

He dipped Jesus in the river. There was silence at the place; everyone had stopped talking. The animals were silent. The children had stopped playing. Everyone was looking. As Jesus emerged from the water, he was glowing. And he was smiling. At that moment, a dove landed on his right shoulder.

Everyone assembled there at the holy place knew the symbolism of the dove. In Genesis account of the great flood, Noah released a dove, and it returned with a freshly picked olive leaf. It was a sign of life after the flood. The *Talmud* compared the Spirit of God, hovering over earth, to a dove hovering over her young. The dove also symbolized the people of Israel in the Song of Solomon, "*O my dove, thou art in the clefts of the rock, in the secret places of the stairs, let me see thy countenance, let me hear thy voice; for sweet is thy voice, and thy countenance is comely.*" And that image was repeated throughout The *Torah*. A dove was also the required sacrifice at the temple.

As the dove flew away, a voice was heard saying, "This is My beloved Son in whom I am well pleased."

Jesus exited the river on the other side and walked off toward Jericho.

The entire group was quiet. When Jesus was out of sight, John turned to the crowd and said, "The baptismal has ended for today, and those who were not baptized should return tomorrow." John was visibly shaken. So were many of the people who were watching. Mary didn't realize that Jesus would be leaving for his 40 days of fasting. Judas told her that he would be all right, but his assurance was of little consolation.

Mary and Judas returned to the group. She told the family that Jesus was going to fast in the wilderness, that he expected God would tell him what his ministry would be. Joseph and Simon started asking questions. Mary stopped them. "I have told you all I know. This isn't the first time Jesus has gone to meditate, and it probably won't be the last. Now, let's catch up to the group and go home. You all can ask Jesus your questions when he returns home."

The family had two days on the road. James asked Mary if that was really all she knew. She looked at him and said, "Do you think I would lie to the entire family?" He apologized and said he just didn't know what to think. Mary added, "That's just Jesus."

Jesus had walked for over four hours into the Judean wilderness as if he were in a trance. He had a skin for water, but it was empty. He was deep in the desert south of Jericho. He had left the lush forest-lined Jordan River, crossed the scrub-covered plain, walked over the low hills, crossed a dry riverbed, and was now in the desert. He stopped to take a sip of water and found the water skin empty. So he prayed.

"God, My heavenly Father, I am here to learn Your will. That is My spiritual need. Water is My physical need. I trust in You completely."

After He prayed, He found a rock not far away. He sat and meditated on the beauty of the desert. The colors He saw were beautiful but muted. The lines created by the sand and rocks were flowing and curves. Only the distant mountains were harsh and angular. Again He prayed.

"Thank you, God for allowing Me to see the beauty of the desert."

The beauty provided by God refreshed Him. He continued on His journey. Two more hours of walking and He saw a spot of green on the horizon. As He got closer, He realized that it was an oasis. A lush green spot in the middle of the desert with a fresh water spring.

"Thank You, God, for this refreshing spot and the water. This is more evidence of Your power and Your creation of this marvelous earth."

The sun was setting, so Jesus sat in the green spot next to a rock and watched the sunset. It reminded Him of Alexandria and the many sunsets He saw reflected in the great sea. Sleep came. His dreams were like a kaleidoscope of images, some of the past that He remembered. Then there were some of places, activities, and people He didn't know, but that would be in His future.

Morning came, and Jesus began day two of his 40 days in the wilderness. Most were like the first day. Jesus walked, meditated, and prayed. When He was hungry, He would find a date palm growing where He was walking. He could gather enough for a few days nourishment. Occasionally He would find a small pomegranate shrub. Water in His water skin would last for many days. At nights, He would see angels visiting Him. They would heal the damage that the rocks and hot sand had done to His feet. They would heal the burns from the hot sun. They would provide blissful sleep when He needed it. He would say later that He existed through His heavenly Father, who was His sustenance.

Nearing the end of the 40 days, Jesus had made His way to a tall mountain that He had seen in the distance. He reached Mount Quarantania. He wanted to be closer to God. He climbed to the top. There He sat and meditated for an entire day. It was there that God revealed events that would be in Jesus' life for the next three years. He also revealed that His death would be a necessary part of His ministry and that, through His death, His story would be told for centuries and in places all over the world. God closed the revelation by telling Jesus that He was not to fear because all that would happen was for a purpose.

He again said what He had said at the baptism, "You are My Son and I am well pleased with You and what You are doing."

With that, God left and angels gathered and provided a protective covering under which Jesus could sleep. It was restorative sleep.

Jesus awoke on the morning of the 40th day. He stood and was face to face with Satan.

"So, You are this Jesus I have been hearing about?"

"Yes. I'm Jesus."

"I'm Satan, and God has sent me to you to help You with Your ministry. How long have You been out here in the desert?"

"40 days."

"You must be hungry. Right?"

"Well, somewhat."

Satan bent down and picked up three stones that were on the mountaintop.

"I have the answer for You. Turn these stones into bread. You have the power and the bread will provide You sustenance."

Jesus thought. It would be unusual for His heavenly Father

to send any entity other than angels to Him. So He decided to counter but play along.

"Sir, the last book of The *Torah*, Deuteronomy, says, '*Man doth not live by bread only, but by every word that proceedeth out of the mouth of the* LORD *doth man live.*'"

"Well, that may have been true, but in this day and time, eating real food is important."

With that Satan disappeared. Jesus started praying for continued guidance.

It wasn't long before Satan appeared again.

"Jesus, my friend. You are a holy man. You have angels who watch over You. They assure You that You will have no harm. You will be going on Your ministry soon. We are some 1,200 feet from the desert floor. Jump from this peak. Your angels will catch You and not allow any harm to come to You. I know that from Your beloved book of Psalms that God '*shall give his angels charge over thee, to keep thee in all thy ways. They shall bear thee up in their hands, lest thou dash thy foot against a stone.*' And if Your angels aren't sufficient I will call Azazel, my angel who can, most certainly protect You against harm. So when You are saved, I will go with You and provide eye witness proof that You are holy."

"Sir, you have tempted Me with food. Now you offer a very tempting way for Me to prove that I am important, a God in myself. I need for you to consider what Moses wrote in Deuteronomy. Moses says, '*Thou shalt not tempt the* LORD, *Thou shalt fear the* LORD *thy God, and serve him, and shalt swear by his name. Ye shall not go after other gods.*'"

"Jesus, you need to start caring more about Yourself. I'll be back"

With that, Satan disappeared.

"God, I love You, and by honoring You I honor Myself." Jesus was speaking out loud.

There was a strong wind that picked Jesus up and carried Him 20 miles to the highest point on the Temple. From there He could see much of the known world. Jesus could see visions of all of the kingdoms in the world. This time Satan was sitting on His shoulder.

"Okay, Jesus. You have turned down both of my offers. Now You see all of the great kingdoms of the world and all of the wealth of the world. All of this I will give to You if You will just kneel before me and worship me."

"Satan, you anger Me. Again Moses tells us, *'Ye shall not tempt the* LORD *your God, For the* LORD *thy God is a jealous God and lest the anger of the* LORD *thy God be kindled against thee, and destroy thee from off the face of the earth.'* Get thee away from me."

With the refusal of the third temptation, Satan grabbed his cape with both hands and swirled, sending Jesus back to Mount Quarantania as he disappeared.

As soon as Jesus appeared atop the mount, angels brought a feast—food and drink. Ravens flew around Jesus as they did with Elijah. God spoke to Jesus.

"My Son, You honored Me. You never lost Your faith. You are My Son."

Jesus left the place of temptation and headed to Nazareth.

CHOOSING THE DISCIPLES

Jesus' trip to Nazareth was a happy one. As He walked along the Jordan River, it greeted Him as if it were a bunch of young children, the babbling of the flowing river as it tumbled seemed to be saying, "Don't forget the children." He found an injured bird. He healed its damaged wing. It was chirping as it flew off as if it were saying, "Don't forget the importance of healing." He passed a lion that roared his warning, as if to say "There are beasts with two legs that will challenge You. Remember, You are the Son of God."

He arrived at the edge of the mountain pass to Nazareth. He stopped for a moment, sat on a rock, and prayed, "Father, I have learned so much in the past few days. I appreciate the beauty of this earth that You made so many years ago. I have experienced the beauty of the desert, the wilderness, the mountains, the trees and the lush vegetation, the water from heaven, springs and rivers, and the animals large and small. The temptations of Satan showed Me that Your creations can be beautiful and ugly, but with Your help and guidance nothing can keep Me from Your plan. I know I am beginning the last phase of My life on this earth. Know that I love You, Father, and with Your guidance and help I will complete My mission."

He continued to His home in Nazareth.

Everyone was happy to see Him. He had a lot to tell the family and a lot to tell Judas.

Everyone gathered in the courtyard. He told them about how God had provided for Him in the desert. Everybody had questions, and they all tried to ask them at the same time. Jesus asked them all to wait until He was finished, and He would answer everyone's questions. That process took a little over two hours. Even the young ones had questions. *What did He eat? Were there any wild animals? What was Satan like?* When He had finally answered everyone's questions, He asked Judas to meet Him on the roof for a private conversation.

Jesus had told everyone He needed some time with Judas, so when they arrived on the roof it was just the two of them.

"Judas, we will be leaving for Capernaum soon. God has shown Me that we will need a group of dedicated men to travel with us. He said twelve. There are people I know there that I think will go with us. We will need people with different skills. You will be directing the specifics of our travel and the money, but you will need someone to help you. We will need some strong men to help protect us and help direct people. So many things. I worked with five men in Capernaum who I believe will join us. You will meet them very soon. Four of them are fishermen, so they are strong, and the fifth one is a tax collector who will be good to help you gather and take care of the money. God has already told Me that He will guide and direct us in our travels. We will come here first. The people here in Nazareth know Me, so it will be a good place to start. Are you ready?"

"Yes. When do we leave for Capernaum?"

"The day after Sabbath."

††††

Sabbath came. Jesus asked the rabbi to let Judas read.

"I will be reading from the Second book of Samuel. *'When your days are over and you rest with your ancestors, I will raise up your offspring to succeed you, your own flesh and blood, and I will establish his kingdom. He is the one who will build a house for my Name, and I will establish the throne of his kingdom forever.'"*

Jesus had selected the reading. It was a fitting start to His ministry.

Jesus spoke to the rabbi after the service. He said that God had spoken to Him, and that He would begin His ministry in a few weeks and that He would like to present His first preaching at the synagogue in Nazareth. The rabbi agreed and asked Jesus when did he want to preach?

"Two to three weeks. I have some preliminary work to do. But, I appreciate your willingness."

At sunup, Jesus and Judas left Nazareth with what they could carry for the expected two-week trip. They arrived at the rabbi's house in Capernaum just before dark. He was happy to see Jesus. The room was vacant, so Jesus and Judas moved in.

They were up early. Jesus took Judas to meet Zebedee. His business had continued to grow after Jesus had left. In addition to Andrew, Simon, James, and John, he had four other teams fishing for him. Three other men had joined Matthew in selling Zebedee Dried Fish. In addition to Capernaum and Tiberius, they were now selling fish in Magdala and Bethsaida. One of the men from the synagogue was interested in setting up a marketplace in Cana where he had family.

Zebedee addressed at Judas. "I owe all of this growth to your friend, Jesus. He certainly turned my business around."

"It was the hard work of you and the brothers that made the difference," Jesus added. "What I am planning will have a major impact on your business, My friend, I want to discuss it with you."

"Let's go up on the roof. There was a cool breeze blowing this morning and we can sit under the shade." Zebedee led the way. It was cooler up on the roof, just like Jesus remembered.

"My story started before I was born. My mother was visited by an angel who told her she would give birth to the Son of God. My earthly father was also visited by an angel telling him the same thing. My mother was pregnant even though she had never been intimate with any man. I was born. The family moved to Alexandria, Egypt, because King Herod wanted Me dead. I met Judas there. I knew I had special powers and even healed Judas from an injury that would have certainly killed him."

"That is true. I would have died that day in Egypt."

"My father told Me that I was the Son of God and destined to be minister to our people. God spoke to Me recently and told Me that My ministry was to start, and I would need 12 men whom I could trust to join Me in My ministry around Galilee. I asked for guidance in selecting the right men. And, that's why I am here."

"I appreciate the compliment, Jesus, but I am too old to be traveling around Galilee," Zebedee chuckled. "So, how can I help?"

"As much as I would love to spend time with you, My friend, I would like to personally, ask Andrew, Simon, James, John, and Matthew. I know that would affect your business, so I wanted to talk with you about the possibility, before I talk to them."

"Jesus, I owe the success of my business to You and Your suggestions. I now have four teams fishing and a list of other teams that want to work for me. Matthew is very successful, but I have a list of other people who want to sell fish. And, I started a boat building business after You left, and I have orders for a dozen boats. Your design has made fishing much easier. So, I guess I'm saying that I owe You. If the boys want to go with You, You and they have my blessing."

"I thank you, and I am proud to call you My friend." So, Jesus arranged to meet with the group on Zebedee's roof after they finished fishing.

After He and Judas left Zebedee's, He walked to Matthew's house. He was able to meet with Matthew, tell him about the idea and get his agreement. Jesus suggested that Matthew meet with the brothers at Zebedee's that evening.

The brothers had a good day of fishing so they were in a good mood. Jesus introduced them to Judas; student of Philo, lawyer, and advocate in Jerusalem, and now manager and keeper of the money for Jesus' group. He then started telling them about His birth and that He was starting His ministry. He told them that He had developed a great appreciation for each of them, and He wanted them to join Him because He had need of their skills. He told them about His powers and that the powers were from His heavenly Father. He told them that He had a mission and He was certain that each of them was essential to the success of His plan.

Finally He said. "You may not believe this, but I am the long-awaited Messiah. I need each of you. What do you say?"

Silence followed. Andrew was the first to speak. "Jesus, I don't know why, but I believe what You say." Simon told the group that there was no reason for them to believe what He had said. The others quickly agreed.

"Before we decide, what would be required of us?"

Jesus told them that they would be part a group that would travel with Him as He preached to people all over Galilee and possibly more of the country. Peter asked how long they would be needed. Jesus said that God, His Heavenly Father, had said a few years. Peter was quick to say that they had jobs with Zebedee, and some of them had wives and children. Jesus said He knew that, and that was why He had already talked to Zebedee and that he had given his blessing.

"I know this is a big decision. I want you to think about our conversation, and let's get back together tomorrow night. Right here, if that is permissible with you, Zebedee?"

Everyone agreed.

Jesus and Judas went back to the rabbi's house and their room. Judas slept, and Jesus prayed.

When they rose, the rabbi invited them for breakfast. He had pomegranate juice, *kikkar* and honey, and some fresh figs. It was a good way to start the day. Jesus told Judas that He wanted to talk to Matthew before the evening meeting. When they had finished, they walked to Matthew's house. Jesus asked to speak with him. Matthew lived in a nice house on the side of one of the large Galilean hills, not far from where Jesus prayed and meditated. Sitting in Matthew's roof garden, they had a view of the Sea of Galilee. They could see dozens of fishing boats.

"Matthew, you are important to My ministry plan. You are a good businessman. You were successful as a tax collector. Unlike most tax collectors, you are successful because of your ability to get along with people. You were successful in selling fish for Zebedee. Now, I need you and I need your skills. Have you thought about the idea of traveling with Me and with the group I will be putting together?"

"This is a big decision, Jesus. I would be leaving my family and friends and my job. I believe in You, but—"

"You will be working with the promised Messiah, Jesus Christ. I am a man with great insight, and a God with great power. I have seen that first hand, and if you travel with us, you will see it too." Judas had interrupted, and his comment was very timely.

"What do you mean, *God and great power?*" Matthew leaned forward as he asked the question.

Judas answered before Jesus could say anything. "As the promised Messiah. The One we have been looking for. He will deliver the people of Israel. He is Messiah ben David, the anointed One, and He is from the lineage of King David."

Before Judas could pick up his thought, Jesus spoke, "Matthew, I know you are Levi, and I know that you are a descendant of the family that provided priests for our people since the escape from Egypt. I know you. You and My friend Judas will handle our resources and see that our needs are met. My friend Judas is a well-respected lawyer. He knows Moses' Law and Roman Law. He was the trusted assistant of a member of the Sanhedrin. I know that you can write in Hebrew and Greek. I need someone to produce a record for the people who will follow us. I will only be here a short time. I need someone to record the miracles. I need someone to record the parables. I need you both, and I want you to join us. Follow Me."

Matthew was silent for a few moments. No one was

talking. Then a big smile crossed Matthew's face. "I think You're right, Jesus. I think this is for me. When do we start?"

Jesus told him that tonight's meeting would be important, and that he should be sure to be there.

Author's Comment

Levi Matthew

Levi was the third son of Alphaeus. He was 31 years old, married with four children, and lived in Capernaum with his parents. He was a customs—tax—collector, as were members of his family.

Tax collectors, next to the Samaritans, were the most hated of the Israelites. He was a man with moderate wealth. He was a good businessman and very likable, even for a tax collector. He was wholeheartedly devoted to Jesus and the ministry, a fact that Jesus recognized. He and Judas were the most educated, and they were designated to control the money for the group.

Matthew could write Hebrew and Greek, so he was commissioned by Jesus to chronicle His ministry. He faithfully recorded the words of Jesus. He was the first to hear "Follow Me" from Jesus. His gospel is the closest we can get to the actual words of Jesus.

Matthew died as a martyr in Ethiopia.

Fishing on the Wrong Side of the Boat

Jesus and Judas walked back to the rabbi's house. They skipped midday meal, as was Jesus' fashion. He preferred a good breakfast and a good evening meal.

As they walked, Jesus told Judas more about His plan. He was expecting a positive response from the brothers. As a group, they would go back to Nazareth. The rabbi had already said when He was ready, Jesus could begin His ministry at His home synagogue.

"Between now and then, I will be praying for God to show Me what He wants Me to do next."

Jesus told Judas that He wanted to go to His special place in the hills to pray and meditate. But, He wanted both of them to be at the seaside when the brothers came in from fishing.

Judas walked around Capernaum. It seemed to be a nice place to live.

The brothers' boats arrived. Simon and Andrew were arguing. It was a poor catch. Only a dozen usable fish were caught. Each of the brothers was blaming the other. Jesus and Judas were standing there when they exited the boats and pulled them up on the ground. They stopped arguing to say hello to Jesus and Judas. Then they went back to arguing. Jesus let the argument go on for a few minutes until there was a lull. Then He asked if they had considered the offer to join Him and Judas.

Simon, always the most forward and talkative of the two brothers, said, "How do You expect us to leave our family? We can't even catch enough fish to justify our day's work. And, because Andrew is the oldest, he insists that he knows where the fish are. We spent all day working and look what we have to show for it. Ten little fish!"

Jesus interrupted, "Simon, you shouldn't be so quick to blame your brother. You two were fishing on the wrong side of the boat."

"What?" Simon was almost yelling at Jesus. "Wrong side of the boat? You've got to be crazy."

"Well, if you will put your boat back into the water, I'll show you. You can catch fish right here in 10 feet of water."

Simon was still in a mood to argue. He threw the net back in the boat. "We'll, show you. It would take a miracle to catch fish in this shallow water."

Jesus answered him, "We'll see. Push the boat out about 20 feet. Leave the rope here with Me in case you need some help. And drop your net on the other side of the boat."

"Alright. Just to prove You wrong."

The brothers launched the boat, and as Jesus had instructed, they dropped their net on the opposite side from where they had been fishing. As soon as the net was submerged, there was a bubbling around the it.

"Now. Pull the net up."

Again, Simon said, "What? We haven't let any time go by to catch the fish. The nets will be empty." Andrew told

Simon to calm down, that they were going to do just what Jesus said to do.

They began pulling the net in. It was heavy. So heavy that the two of them were unable to get the catch in the boat. They asked for help.

Judas pulled the boat into shore with the rope, and they all dragged the net full of fish, even overflowing with fish. There were more fish in that one cast than a typical full day of fishing.

Simon was apologetic. "I am sorry, Jesus. This is a miracle. A true miracle. This has proven to me that You are who You say You are."

Jesus looked at the four fishermen, smiled, and said, "Andrew, Simon, James, and John, if you come with Me, I will make you more than fishermen, I will make you fishers of men."

The brothers said they liked the sound of that. Then they got busy, cleaning and preparing the fish.

✝✝✝

The group met at Zebedee's house that evening.

Jesus spoke first. "I am the One that was prophesied by Isaiah. *"The Spirit of the* Lord *God is upon me; because the* Lord *hath anointed me to preach good tidings unto the meek; he hath sent me to bind up the brokenhearted, to proclaim liberty to the captives, and the opening of the prison to them that are bound; To proclaim the acceptable year of the* Lord, *and the day of vengeance of our God; to comfort all that mourn."*

By the time the evening was over, everyone had agreed. Hannah had brought the wine and sat near enough to hear. She announced that she would like to join the group. That started the men grumbling, but it caught Jesus' attention. Having some women traveling with them could be very helpful. Cooking, washing clothes, and a woman's view of the work could be very beneficial. Jesus asked Hannah to come into the circle.

"Hannah. You again come from the edge of the group and show great wisdom. Traveling with a group of men will not be easy, but you can contribute greatly. If you are certain you want to go with us and your father agrees, you will be welcome."

Zebedee spoke up and said Hannah had always given sage wisdom and if she wanted to go, she would be in the company of her brothers; he was certain she would be safe.

Jesus brought her chair into the group. She moved it back somewhat and continued to listen.

James Zebedee Boanerges

James was the oldest son of Zebedee.

Zebedee, along with Jonah, the father of Andrew and Simon, had a very successful fishing business in Capernaum.

James was married and had four children. They lived near their parents, Zebedee and Salome. James was a fisherman with his brother, John. They were among the first of the disciples to see Jesus perform a miracle—the net full of fish. James had a fiery temper, which he called "righteous indignation." Jesus called James and his brother *sons of thunder*—Boanerges. He was the best orator of the disciples and was usually able to see both sides of a situation. He was a thinker and a planner. James was the first of the disciples to die as a martyr, killed by the sword of Herod Agrippa.

John Zebedee Boanerges

John was younger brother to James. He was known as the disciple that Jesus loved. He was the more ambitious of the brothers. He was thoroughly dependable, prompt, courageous, faithful, and devoted. John was a man of action. He was designated by Jesus as His personal agent in dealing

241

with all issues related to Jesus' family. He continued to hold this position with Mary after Jesus' death. John was the only one of the disciples to die at an old age of natural causes. He was in Ephesus.

Andrew bar Jonas

Andrew, along with his brother Simon, was a fisherman. His father, until he died, was a partner with Zebedee in the fish drying business. He was unmarried. He was never an effective preacher, but he was an excellent personal missionary. He was a good organizer and an excellent judge of people. Jesus considered Andrew as the chairman of the disciples. He would provide a prompt decision and, if he felt the issue was beyond his authority, he would immediately take it to Jesus. Andrew had been a follower of John the Baptist. Andrew was crucified on an X-shaped cross because he felt unworthy to die on an upright one like Jesus did. He was crucified on November 30, 60 AD, in the city of Patras in Greece.

Simon bar Jonas

Simon—*Cephas* in Greek, meaning Rock—was a fisherman with his brother, Andrew. Simon was married and had three children. Andrew and his mother lived with him. Simon was an eloquent speaker. He was dramatic and a natural leader but, even though he was a quick thinker, he was not a thorough thinker. He had a complex contradictory personality. He was fiercely loyal and yet denied he knew Jesus at the crucifixion. With a smile, Jesus called Simon Peter the Aramaic for Rock. Peter's wife, Petronilla, joined him in his service to Jesus. She was one of the women who traveled with the disciples.

Disciples

Simon was excited as he left the meeting. He had seen the miracle of the fish and, as a result, he was committed to being a part of Jesus' band. He fully believed Jesus was the Messiah. He went home. His wife was there to meet him as were their daughter and two other children. He told them of his meeting with Jesus and His miracle with the fishes.

"The net was so filled with fish that it started tearing as we pulled it on shore. I believe He is the Messiah that we have looked for for so long. And, He wants me to go with Him, Andrew, James and John, and Hannah."

Petronilla questioned him. Soon, she too, was excited. "Simon, I am your wife. I am committed to being with you. So, you tell this Jesus that we are a couple, and where you go, I go. That way I can take care of you."

In two days, the apostolic band left for Nazareth. Andrew, Simon, James, John, Matthew, Hannah, Petronilla, Judas, and Jesus. They talked with Jesus as they traveled. They talked about His powers. Jesus talked about the group and the makeup that God had shown Him that He needed. He said He knew that each member of the group had been destined to be working with Him and the ministry. He said that Andrew would be the main point person. He said Matthew and Judas would be the money people, and that Matthew was included because he was a tax collector. He knew how to handle money and business and because, as a tax collector, he was among the most hated people in Galilee. Just having Matthew would show no partiality. He said that the fishermen would show everyone that He was open to everyone. And He said He had seen how the brothers worked well together. He was proud to say each of them was with Him. He said there would be others.

"God had said there will be twelve."

Andrew asked, "What will we call ourselves, Jesus?"

There was a lot of discussion. Finally, it was Hannah who suggested they be called disciples. After a few minutes of silence, everyone agreed. *Disciples* is what they would be called.

The conversation continued for most of the two-day trip back to Nazareth. When they got to Jesus' home in Nazareth, the entire group was ready for sleep. Places were arranged for everyone, mostly on the roof garden.

The next day, Jesus talked to the rabbi about the Sabbath message. Jesus asked him to spread the word that the Messiah would be at the synagogue on Sabbath. Nothing more. Not that Jesus would be there, only the Messiah.

Sabbath arrived and there was a great atmosphere of anticipation. Virtually the entire town was there. When the rabbi introduced Jesus, there were rumblings in the synagogue.

"Is not this the carpenter's son? Is not his mother called Mary? And his brethren, James, and Joseph, and Simon, and Judas? And his sisters, are they not all with us? Whence then hath this man all these things?" And they were offended in him."

But Jesus said unto them, *"A prophet is not without honour, save in his own country, and in his own house."*

Jesus did many wonderful things that day, even after the

rumblings of disbelief. He healed the sick and infirmed. He cast out devils. That was what was required for the people in His hometown to set aside their disbelief. There were many that still didn't believe Him, even after the miracles.

Jesus returned to His home along with everyone in the group. He gathered the disciples on the roof. He said He had seen the need to concentrate the ministry in Galilee, not in Nazareth.

Three days later Mary suggested that Jesus accompany her to the marriage of her cousin in Cana, an hour and a half walking distance from Nazareth. Mary, Jesus and their family, along with the eight disciples, made their way to Cana.

The wedding was a happy occasion. Everyone was enjoying themselves. The cousin's father approached Mary and said they were out of wine. He told Mary that he had been responsible, and he had bought all that he could afford to buy. He asked Mary what he could do. His daughter, Mary's cousin, would be the joke of the town. She had invited everyone in town, and now they had used up all of the wine. He was frantic.

Mary said for him to give her a few moments. She called Jesus and said to Him, *"They have no wine. Jesus saith unto her, Woman, what have I to do with thee? mine hour is not yet come. His mother saith unto the servants, Whatsoever he saith unto you, do [it]. And there were set there six waterpots of stone, after the manner of the purifying of the Jews, containing two or three firkins apiece. Jesus saith unto them, Fill the waterpots with water. And they filled them up to the brim. And he saith unto them, Draw out now, and bear unto the governor of the feast. And they did. When the ruler of the feast had tasted the water that was made wine, and knew not whence it was: (but the servants which drew the water knew;) the governor of the feast called the bridegroom, And saith unto him, Every man at the beginning doth set forth good wine; and when men have well drunk, then that which is worse: [but] thou hast kept the good wine until now. This beginning of miracles did Jesus in Cana of Galilee, and manifested forth his glory; and his disciples believed on him."*

Many at the wedding heard the story of the water that became wine. The disciples marveled at what Jesus had done.

Jesus asked James if he would take the family home to Nazareth. He and Mary would stay the night in Cana. He told James that they may go to Capernaum, but He wasn't sure.

Jesus asked His great uncle if the family and His disciples could overnight at his house. Mary and the girls helped her aunt prepare the evening meal. Jesus and the disciples met on the roof. Jesus was concerned.

Alone, He prayed before they arrived on the roof. He wanted to get the entire group together. He wanted to have a schedule. He wanted to know what was happening. So He prayed. God answered. "I am in charge, just let Me be."

It was so simple. Why couldn't He have seen it.

The group met. Jesus said He wanted to complete the group. God had said there would be twelve. There were six.

"I have one person in mind." James spoke up first. "Philip, who lives in Bethsaida. As I recall, he isn't very imaginative but, we need a steward, and I believe he would be a good one."

Andrew interrupted James, "I know him. You are right; he isn't creative. But I believe he would follow through with anything he starts, and I think he would be a good steward."

"That's one idea," Jesus was standing by this time. "Does anyone else have any suggestions?"

Andrew continued, "There is one possibility right here in Cana. His name is Nathaniel. We met him at one of John the Baptist's meetings. I believe that he was at the wedding today. I think he is well educated. I remember he was a good storyteller, even humorous at times. We could meet him tomorrow."

"Good. We will. More suggestions?" Jesus asked.

"James, what about Thomas?" It was John who made the suggestion.

"I don't know, John. He always seemed to me to be a pessimist. He was skeptical of almost everything and very disagreeable. But, he was logical and well organized. He was a stonemason and lately a fisherman. He is strong. Maybe he would be a good addition to our group."

"And how about James and Jude?"

"That's a good idea, John. James and Jude are sons of Alpheus. Lately they have been fishing with us. They aren't very smart, but they will do anything we tell them to do. They could be ushers and organizers to help if the crowds get big."

John interrupted, "They will be two people we can trust to run errands. Do odd work. They would be great at that. They are humble men and generous to a fault."

"Where do they live?" Jesus asked.

"In Capernaum, not far from us."

"Well, we have almost filled out our twelve-man group."

"As long as you don't mind another Simon in the group, I know a man who I think would be a good contribution."

"What do you mean, Simon?" Jesus asked.

"Well, first of all, he is a Zealot." There was some grumbling about that.

"Go ahead, Simon."

"Okay, Jesus. Simon is very much a nationalist. We met him at one of John the Baptist's gatherings. He was a merchant, I believe. And, I think he would be very sympathetic with our cause."

"Where does he live, Simon?"

"He lives in Capernaum."

"We will see him when we are there. This settles it. We leave tomorrow for Capernaum. Hannah, can Mary stay with you?"

"Certainly. And I am certain that all of the men can stay in the watchman's house. There should be enough room."

"Good. To bed! Tomorrow will be a full day. We need to be at Capernaum tomorrow night."

†††

Andrew went early to talk to Nathaniel. He knew of Jesus and agreed to join. He and Andrew caught up with Jesus on the way to Capernaum.

It was Wednesday night when Jesus and the disciples reached Capernaum. Everyone was tired, so they all slept. Accommodations, as Hannah said, were adequate and everyone enjoyed a good night's rest.

The group got up with the sun. Mary, Hannah, and her sisters had prepared breakfast. Pomegranate juice, flat bread, fresh figs and dried fruit relish. Jesus divided the group and sent them out to talk with the people they had discussed to be disciples.

Everyone returned to Zebedee's house by early afternoon. Every man who had been suggested had agreed—except Thomas. Jesus asked John to take Him to talk with Thomas.

Thomas had a few reasons why he didn't think he would fit in, but Jesus assured him that he would. Then he had some additional questions. Finally, he had nothing more to say.

Jesus said, "Well, Thomas. Is there anything else we need to discuss?" Thomas looked at Jesus and said, "I don't think so." Jesus said, "Thomas, follow Me."

It was now Friday morning. In less than 12 hours, Jesus had completed His group of disciples: Andrew, Simon Peter, James Zebedee, John Zebedee, Levi Matthew, Philip, Nathaniel Bartholomew, Thomas Didymus, James the younger, Jude, Simon Zelotes, and His friend Judas.

Author's Comment

Philip

Philip, from Cana, was one of the common people in Jesus' band of disciples. He was recently married and had no children. Philip was a man who could accomplish *little things in a big way.* He was named the steward. He was methodical and thorough. His responsibility was the supplies and food. In that, he was intelligent and efficient. Philip's wife joined the women's corp. She was a fearless woman. She was stoned to death while continuing to recite the story of salvation by faith. Philip had a warm heart and a pessimistic head. He was crucified upside down in the city of Hierapolis, Greece.

Nathaniel Bartholomew

Nathaniel was a friend of Philip's. He wasn't married and lived in Cana. When Philip first told him about Jesus, he was the one who said, "Can anything good come out of Nazareth?" When he met Jesus, he quickly reversed his opinion. Nathaniel had a dry sense of humor and was the jester of the disciples. He was a good storyteller and entertained Jesus and the disciples with his stories, both humorous and serious. He was a son of Talimai, King of Geshur, and the only one of the disciples from royal blood. Nathaniel was martyred in Armenia where he was flayed alive and beheaded.

Thomas Didymus

Thomas lived in Tarichea, a town some eight miles south of Capernaum. He was a fisherman but had been a stonemason and was from Tiberias. Thomas was a twin, hence the name Didymus, Greek for *twin*. His twin sister died when she was nine years old, and that contributed to his temperament in later years. He had a superb analytical mind—logical and skeptical. He had little education and was considered disagreeable and quarrelsome. Even his wife was happy to see him leave with the disciples. Thomas was martyred in the Indian city of Myalpur near Madras in AD 72.

James bar Alpheus
Jude bar Alpheus-Thaddeus

James the Younger, because James Zebedee was older, and Jude were twin sons of Alpheus. They were from Galilee and were also fishermen. They were not educated or ambitious people. They were happy to be numbered along with the mighty men who made up the disciples. During philosophical or theological discussions, they were satisfied to sit and listen to the more learned. They were good-natured, simple-minded helpers. They were faithful, big-hearted, kind and generous. They were assigned the policing if there were multitudes and generally helped anywhere they were needed. James-Thaddeus was stoned to death in Jerusalem while preaching. Jude was martyred in Beirut, killed with an ax.

Simon Zelotes

Simon was the last of the disciples chosen. He was not married and lived in Capernaum with his family. He was a businessman, but he turned his entire attention to the patriotic organization of the Zealots. He was strongly committed to the idea of Jewish Nationalism and resented the control of Rome. He was an efficient organizer and was in charge of the recreation and play life of the disciples and the women's corp. He was martyred by being cut in half with a saw in Persia.

PASSOVER, PREACHING, AND HEALING
THE BEGINNING

That evening would be the beginning of Sabbath. Jesus, the disciples, and the women's corps celebrated Sabbath in Capernaum. After a restful day in the synagogue, the group made preparations for the trip to Jerusalem. Judas made arrangements for the entire group to stay at his family's palace.

Jesus Cleans the Temple

On the first day of Passover, Jesus and His entourage went to the temple. *"And found in the temple those that sold oxen and sheep and doves, and the changers of money sitting: And when He had made a scourge of small cords, He drove them all out of the temple, and the sheep, and the oxen; and poured out the changers' money, and overthrew the tables; And said unto them that sold doves, Take these things hence; make not my Father's house an house of merchandise."*

Then Jesus sent the disciples and the women out into the streets of Jerusalem to gather the sick and those inhabited by devils and bring them to Him. During the day He healed the sick and lame and cast out devils. And *"many believed in his name, when they saw the miracles which he did."*

Jesus Meets Nicodemus

At the end of the day, the group moved back to Judas' family palace. Simon, Judas' father, had prepared a feast for Jesus and the others. It had been a long day so most of them retired after eating.

Jesus went up to the roof garden to pray and thank God for the opportunities of the day. Once it was dark, Judas interrupted Jesus saying, "I am sorry to interrupt, but a friend from the Sanhedrin, a Pharisee, is here and would like to talk with You. Will you speak with Nicodemus?"

"Yes. Would you show him up?"

Jesus welcomed Nicodemus, "How may I help you?"

"Rabbi, I know that Thou art a teacher come from God: for no man can do these miracles that Thou doest, except God be with Him. How can I go to the Heaven you talked about?"

"Except a man be born again, he cannot see the kingdom of God."

"How can a man be born when he is old? Can he enter the second time into his mother's womb, and be born?"

"Except a man be born of water and of the Spirit, he cannot enter into the kingdom of God. That which is born of the flesh is flesh; and that which is born of the Spirit is spirit. So, ye must be born again. The wind bloweth where it listeth, and thou hearest the sound thereof, but canst not tell whence it cometh, and whither it goeth: so is every one that is born of the Spirit."

Nicodemus answered, *"How can these things be?"*

"You are a master of Israel, and you know not these things? We speak of that we know, and testify of that we have seen; and ye receive not our witness. I have told you earthly things, and ye believe not, how shall ye believe, if I tell you of heavenly things? He that came down from heaven is the Son of God which is in

heaven. Whosoever believeth in him should not perish, but have eternal life. For God so loved the world, that he gave his only begotten Son, that whosoever believeth in him should not perish, but have everlasting life. God sent not his Son into the world to condemn the world; but that the world through him might be saved. He that believeth not is condemned already, because he hath not believed in the name of the only begotten Son of God. You must believe. Do you?"

Nicodemus left without answering Jesus' question.

The Disciples are Baptized

On their way back to Cana, they passed Jesus' holy place on the Jordan River. Jesus said to the disciples and the women's corps, "It is My wish that each of you be baptized. This is the holy place where I was baptized. Let us stop here."

They stopped to rest before being baptized. Everyone, including Jesus, was surprised to see John the Baptist coming out of the trees on the other side of the river. He crossed the river, and he and Jesus embraced. Jesus introduced him to the disciples and the women. John said he already knew Andrew, Simon Peter, and Simon Zelotes. A number of John's followers joined him across the river. Jesus had already started baptizing the disciples and the women. Some of John's followers came to him complaining that Jesus, who only recently had been baptized by John, was in the river baptizing other people.

"A man can receive nothing except it be given him from heaven. I said, I am not the Christ, but that I am sent before him. He that hath the bride is the bridegroom: but the friend of the bridegroom, which standeth and heareth him, rejoiceth greatly because

of the bridegroom's voice: this my joy therefore is fulfilled. He must increase, I must decrease." John continued loud enough for all to hear. "He that cometh from above is above all: he that is of the earth is earthly, and speaketh of the earth: he that cometh from heaven is above all. For he whom God hath sent speaketh the words of God. The Father loveth the Son, and hath given all things into his hand. He that believeth on the Son hath everlasting life: and he that believeth not the Son shall not see life; but the wrath of God abideth on him."

John told Jesus that he was going back to Jerusalem. Jesus told John that He was on his way to Cana. John bid everyone farewell, and he and his group departed for Jerusalem.

The Woman at the Well

Jesus knew He had to go through Samaria. He estimated they could get to Shiloh before having to settle in for the night. So, He finished baptizing, said His prayer and the group headed out. They reached Shiloh near sundown and found a place to overnight. At sunrise they left Shiloh. Within hours, they were at a city of Samaria, which is called Sychar, near to the parcel of ground that Jacob gave to his son, Joseph. It was the location of Jacob's well.

Jesus was weary from His journey. He sat on the side of the well. About the sixth hour. *"There cometh a woman of Samaria to draw water. Jesus saith unto her, Give me to drink. For his disciples were gone away unto the city to buy meat. The Samarian woman saith unto him, How is it that thou, being a Jew, askest drink of me? I am a woman of Samaria. Jews have no dealings with the Samaritans. Jesus answered and said unto her, If thou knewest the gift of God, and who it is that asked, Give me to drink thou wouldest have asked of him, and he would have given thee living water."*

The woman saith unto Him, *"Sir, Thou hast nothing to draw with, and the well is deep: from whence then hast Thou that living water? Art Thou greater than our father Jacob, which gave us the well, and drank thereof himself, and his children, and his cattle?"*

Jesus answered and said unto her, *"Whosoever drinketh of this water shall thirst again. But whosoever drinketh of the water that I shall give him shall never thirst. The water that I shall give him shall be in him a well of water springing up into everlasting life."*

The woman said unto Him, *"Sir, give me this water, that I thirst not, neither come hither to draw water."*

Jesus said unto her, *"Go, call thy husband, and come hither."*

The woman answered and said, *"I have no husband."*

Jesus said unto her, *"Thou hast well said, I have no husband. For thou hast had five husbands; and he whom thou now hast is not thy husband."*

The woman said unto Him, *"Sir, I perceive that Thou art a prophet."*

The woman went into the town telling everyone she met that there was a holy man at the well who told her everything she had done. She returned to the well to tell Jesus that she would contribute her considerable wealth to His cause and that she would travel with the women's corps.

After two days, Jesus left with the group, now including Mary Magdalene, and returned to Cana in Galilee.

Healing the Nobleman's Son

When He returned to Galilee, the Galilaeans received Him.

Many of them had seen the things that He did at Jerusalem at the feast. Jesus came again into Cana of Galilee, where He made the water wine. And there was a certain nobleman, whose son was sick at Capernaum. When he heard that Jesus had come to Galilee, he went unto Him, and begged Him to come and heal his son, for he was at the point of death. *"The nobleman saith unto him, Sir, come down ere my child die. Jesus saith unto him, Go thy way; thy son liveth. And the man believed the word that Jesus had spoken unto him, and he went his way. And, as he was starting on his way, his servants met him, and told him, saying, Thy son liveth."*

Jesus and the disciples traveled around Galilee preaching, healing, and teaching. He wanted to be in Jerusalem for the Festival of Weeks, also called *Shavuot,* so the group left Galilee on the day following Sabbath. It would be a four-day trip. They were happy. This festival was to celebrate the receiving of The *Torah* and the Ten Commandments.

The Bethesda Pool

There is at Jerusalem, by the sheep market, a pool, which is called in the Hebrew tongue Bethesda. Bethesda Pool was actually an underground hot spring that would occasionally bubble up covering the immediate area with warmed water. A great multitude of the sick lay waiting for the pool to spread water over the area. It was considered to be healing water. There were blind, lame, withered and devil possessed waiting for the moving of the water.

It was said that *"An angel went down at a certain season into the pool, and troubled the water. Whosoever was first after the troubling of the water stepped in was made whole of whatsoever disease he had. A certain man was there, which had an infirmity thirty and eight years. When Jesus saw him lie, and knew that he had been now a long time, So he saith unto him, Wilt thou be made whole? The infirmed man answered him, 'Sir, I have no man, to put me into the pool when the water is troubled, but while I am coming, another steppeth down before me.' Jesus saith unto him, Rise, take up thy bed, and walk. And immediately the man was made whole, and took up his bed, and walked."*

The same day was the Sabbath. When the Jews saw the man walking away carrying his bed, they said it was not lawful for him to carry his bed on the Sabbath. He told them that a man had made him whole and said for me to take up his bed, and walk.

They asked him, *"What man is that which said unto thee, Take up thy bed, and walk?"*

But Jesus had already left. Later, Jesus found him in the temple, and said unto him, Behold, you are made whole—sin no more.

John the Baptist Martyred

Jesus was in Jerusalem when He heard that John the Baptist had been imprisoned at the Fortress of Machaerus. Built a hundred years before, the fortress sat atop a mountain overlooking the eastern shore of the Dead Sea. It was a two-day trip for Jesus and the disciples. Jesus wanted to provide support for His cousin and forerunner, so they set out for Machaerus. When they arrived, they learned that John was already dead. Tetrarch Herod Antipas had ordered him beheaded at the request of his second wife, Princess Herodias.

There was a band of John's supporters gathered outside

the fortress. Jesus and the disciples joined the group and prayed for Herod Antipas, Herodias, and all who took part in John's death. Jesus presented the story of His ministry and invited all those who agreed with Him to join the group, and some did.

Back to Capernaum

The 120-mile trip from Machaerus to Capernaum took five and a half days. The group had become so large that their progress was slowed. They traveled north on the eastern side of the Jordan River to the Sea of Galilee. They continued north around the Sea until they reached Capernaum.

It was the day before Sabbath when they arrived in Capernaum. On the Sabbath day Jesus entered the synagogue and taught. Those who heard Him were astonished at His doctrine. He taught them as one with power and authority.

There was a man who was possessed, and he cried out, *"What have we to do with thee, thou Jesus of Nazareth? I know you ... the Holy One of God."*

Jesus said, *"Devil spirit, come out of him now."*

There was a loud cry from the evil spirit as it came out of him. All who were at the synagogue were amazed. *What is this? A new doctrine? A new teacher with authority who can command evil spirits, and they obey him?* The people who were there spread the story throughout the region around Galilee.

Jesus left the synagogue with Simon and Andrew. They stopped at Simon's house because his mother-in-law had a fever. Jesus touched her hand and she was immediately healed. She washed Jesus' feet and Simon Peter's and Andrew's as well.

Preaching in Galilee and Healing the Leper

Jesus, the disciples and entourage left Capernaum. They spent the next months preaching and teaching in synagogues throughout Galilee. The number of people following Jesus was growing. At each stop, Jesus would heal all manner of sickness and disease, and He would cast out devils and evil spirits. The word of His miracles had reached throughout Galilee, Judea, into Syria, Samaria, Decapolis, and west of the Jordan. Sick people were coming to Him everywhere He went.

The disciples were having more and more trouble reserving time for Jesus to rest. But Jesus would allow the infirmed to come to him wherever they stopped. He had been preaching in the northern part of Galilee near Caesarea Philippi and was on His way back to Capernaum. He decided to rest under a tree. The disciples and some of the women had set up a perimeter. Jesus had asked everyone to sit, for they needed rest as well.

A leper had worked his way through the crowd since no one wanted to touch him. He had reached the disciples and asked to see the Master when Andrew had stopped him.

He cried out, *"Lord. Master. You can make me clean if You will."*

Jesus was moved with compassion for the man and called to Andrew to let him through. The leper ran to Jesus and dropped to his knees, face on the ground, before Him, weeping. Jesus touched him. There was a moan from the crowd because just touching a leper was a certain means to contract the disease. Scabs dropped from his lesions, and he was instantly and obviously healed.

Jesus whispered to the man, *"Go first to your priest. Show yourself and make the offering commanded by Moses."*

Jesus and the group continued back to Capernaum.

Back in Capernaum, Again

The group had grown to the point that only the disciples and a few of the women's corps were all that could stay at Zebedee's house. Many of the followers had brought their own bedroll so they could find a place to sleep where ever Jesus went. Other followers had relatives in Capernaum. Still others had asked the disciples to find them a place. Their needs were accommodated whenever possible.

Healing the Man Let Down from the Roof

Jesus would preach, teach, and heal everyday. There were Pharisees who were following Him wherever He went. They were seeking to find Him in violation of the Law. The rabbi invited Jesus to teach at his house where Jesus had stayed. Jesus agreed, and when He arrived a large crowd, including some Pharisees, was already there. The crowd separated to allow Jesus and two of the disciples to get to the front where there was a small porch. The crowd continued to press until there was no more room for anyone.

Two men had brought their younger brother, who was afflicted with palsy, to see Jesus and possibly be healed. They could not get the crowd to make a way for them to get to Jesus. So one said they should make their way to the roof of the house. They found a way onto the roof and made a bed by tying the corners of a mat with ropes that were on the roof. They got to the edge of the roof and decided there was only one way for him to see Jesus. So they let the makeshift bed down. The surprised crowd pressed back as the bed was let down, and the young man was at Jesus' feet.

One brother called down to Jesus, "My brother has been afflicted with palsy since birth. Soon he shall surely die."

"I see by the efforts of your family, that they love you very much, and I see that you and they have great faith in My ability to heal you. So, My son," Jesus took his hand, "I love you, and today you are healed. Arise, take up your bed, walk and all of your sins are forgiven."

The young man stood, embraced Jesus, rolled up the pallet and left, praising Jesus and crying. The crowd was cheering, and this time the crowd parted to allow the young man to leave.

One of the younger Pharisees whispered to the leader, "Did you hear that? He said 'your sins are forgiven.' That's blasphemy. It is God alone who can forgive sins." He didn't get an answer, but the group of Pharisees soon left.

Jesus continued to preach in Capernaum. More and more, He required a bigger space because the crowd had grown. He announced that He would talk to them all and for them to follow Him to a space where they all could hear and they should ask friends and family to join Him at the Horns of Hattin. He then asked them to let Him have some space to prepare. Soon it was only the disciples left. He asked Philip and Nathaniel to get James the younger and Jude and gather as many filled water containers as they could transport and come to the top of the Mount of Hattin where He and the rest of the disciples would be.

The Sermon on the Mount

Jesus called Matthew aside and asked if he had papyrus

sheets with him. He showed a stack of many pages in the sling he was carrying. Jesus said that He would be saying important things today and that Matthew's only responsibility was to record an accurate copy of His words. He asked His mother to tell the women that it would be important to see that anyone who was thirsty got water, and she should see to anyone who was injured.

Jesus sat under a tree to pray. He talked to God. He asked for the right words. He asked for clear hearing and understanding for the people who would be in the crowd. He asked for healing for all there and He asked for the ability for all there to hear every word. And, finally He asked for strength and for anointing so that He would speak the words that God wanted Him to speak.

After a few minutes of silent meditation, Jesus stood and walked to a rock on the top of the mount where He sat and began to talk.

"Blessed are the poor in spirit: for theirs is the kingdom of heaven.

Blessed are they that mourn: for they shall be comforted.

Blessed are the meek: for they shall inherit the earth.

Blessed are they which do hunger and thirst after righteousness: for they shall be filled.

Blessed are the merciful: for they shall obtain mercy.

Blessed are the pure in heart: for they shall see God.

Blessed are the peacemakers: for they shall be called the children of God.

Blessed are they which are persecuted for righteousness' sake: for theirs is the kingdom of heaven.

Blessed are ye, when men shall revile you, and persecute you, and shall say all manner of evil against you falsely, for my sake. Rejoice, and be exceeding glad: for great is your reward in heaven: for so persecuted they the prophets which were before you.

Ye are the salt of the earth: but if the salt have lost his savour, wherewith shall it be salted? it is thenceforth good for nothing, but to be cast out, and to be trodden under foot of men.

Ye are the light of the world. A city that is set on an hill cannot be hid.

Neither do men light a candle, and put it under a bushel, but on a candlestick; and it giveth light unto all that are in the house.

Let your light so shine before men, that they may see your good works, and glorify your Father which is in heaven.

Think not that I am come to destroy the law, or the prophets: I am not come to destroy, but to fulfill.

For verily I say unto you, Till heaven and earth pass, one jot or one tittle shall in no wise pass from the law, till all be fulfilled.

Whosoever therefore shall break one of these least command-ments, and shall teach men so, he shall be called the least in the kingdom of heaven: but whosoever shall do and teach them, the same shall be called great in the kingdom of heaven.

For I say unto you, That except your righteousness shall exceed the righteousness of the scribes and Pharisees, ye shall in no case enter into the kingdom of heaven.

Ye have heard that it was said by them of old time, Thou shalt not kill; and whosoever shall kill shall be in danger of the judgment:

But I say unto you, That whosoever is angry with his brother without a cause shall be in danger of the judgment: and whoso-ever shall say to his brother, Raca (liar without proof), shall be in danger of the council: but whosoever shall say, Thou fool, shall be in danger of hell fire.

Therefore if thou bring thy gift to the altar, and there remem-berest that thy brother hath ought against thee; Leave there thy gift before the altar, and go thy way; first be reconciled to thy brother, and then come and offer thy gift.

Agree with thine adversary quickly, whiles thou art in the way with him; lest at any time the adversary deliver thee to the judge, and the judge deliver thee to the officer, and thou be cast into prison. Verily I say unto thee, Thou shalt by no means come out thence, till thou hast paid the uttermost farthing (that you owe).

Ye have heard that it was said by them of old time, Thou shalt not commit adultery: But I say unto you, That whosoever looketh on a woman to lust after her hath committed adultery with her already in his heart.

And if thy right eye offend thee, pluck it out, and cast it from thee: for it is profitable for thee that one of thy members should perish, and not that thy whole body should be cast into hell. And if thy right hand offend thee, cut it off, and cast it from thee: for it is profitable for thee that one of thy members should perish, and not that thy whole body should be cast into hell.

It hath been said, Whosoever shall put away his wife, let him give her a writing of divorcement: But I say unto you, That whosoever shall put away his wife, saving for the cause of fornication, causeth her to commit adultery: and whosoever shall marry her that is divorced committeth adultery.

Again, ye have heard that it hath been said by them of old time, Thou shalt not swear but shalt perform unto the LORD thine oaths: for I say unto you, Swear not at all; neither by heaven; for it is God's throne: Nor by the earth; for it is his footstool: neither by Jerusalem; for it is the city of the great King. Neither shalt thou swear by thy head, because thou canst not make one hair white or black. But let your communication be, Yea, yea; Nay, nay: for whatsoever is more than these cometh of evil.

Ye have heard that it hath been said, An eye for an eye, and a tooth for a tooth: But I say unto you, That ye resist not evil: but whosoever shall smite thee on thy right cheek, turn to him the other also. And if any man will sue thee at the law, and take away thy coat, let him have thy cloak also. And whosoever shall compel thee to go a mile, go with him twain. Give to him that asketh thee, and from him that would borrow of thee turn not thou away.

Ye have heard that it hath been said, Thou shalt love thy neighbour, and hate thine enemy. But I say unto you, Love your enemies, bless them that curse you, do good to them that hate you, and pray for them which despitefully use you, and persecute you; That ye may be the children of your Father which is in heaven: for he maketh his sun to rise on the evil and on the good, and sendeth rain on the just and on the unjust. For if ye love them which love you, what reward have ye? do not even the publicans the same? And if ye salute your brethren only, what do ye more than others? do not even the publicans so? Be ye therefore perfect, even as your Father which is in heaven is perfect."

"Take heed that ye do not your alms before men, to be seen of them: otherwise ye have no reward of your Father which is in heaven. Therefore when thou doest thine alms, do not sound a trumpet before thee, as the hypocrites do in the synagogues and in the streets, that they may have glory of men. Verily I say unto you, They have their reward. But when thou doest alms, let not thy left hand know what thy right hand doeth: That thine alms may be in secret: and thy Father which seeth in secret himself shall reward thee openly.

And when thou prayest, thou shalt not be as the hypocrites are: for they love to pray standing in the synagogues and in the corners of the streets, that they may be seen of men. Verily I say unto you, They have their reward. But thou, when thou prayest, enter into thy closet, and when thou hast shut thy door, pray *to thy Father which is in secret; and thy Father which seeth in secret shall reward thee openly. But when ye pray, use not vain repetitions, as the heathen do: for they think that they shall be heard for their much speaking. Be not ye therefore like unto them: for your Father knoweth what things ye have need of, before ye ask him. After this manner therefore pray ye:*

Our Father which art in heaven, Hallowed be thy name.

Thy kingdom come. Thy will be done in earth, as it is in heaven.

Give us this day our daily bread.

And forgive us our debts, as we forgive our debtors.

And lead us not into temptation, but deliver us from evil:

For thine is the kingdom, and the power, and the glory, for ever. Amen.

For if ye forgive men their trespasses, your heavenly Father will also forgive you: But if ye forgive not men their trespasses, neither will your Father forgive your trespasses.

Moreover when ye fast, be not, as the hypocrites, of a sad countenance: for they disfigure their faces, that they may appear unto men to fast. Verily I say unto you, They have their reward. But thou, when thou fastest, anoint thine head, and wash thy face; That thou appear not unto men to fast, but unto thy Father which is in secret: and thy Father, which seeth in secret, shall reward thee openly.

Lay not up for yourselves treasures upon earth, where moth and rust doth corrupt, and where thieves break through and steal: But lay up for yourselves treasures in heaven, where neither moth nor rust doth corrupt, and where thieves do not break through nor steal: For where your treasure is, there will your heart be also.

The light of the body is the eye: if therefore thine eye be single, thy whole body shall be full of light. But if thine eye be evil, thy whole body shall be full of darkness. If therefore the light that is in thee be darkness, how great is that darkness!

No man can serve two masters: for either he will hate the one, and love the other; or else he will hold to the one, and despise the other. Ye cannot serve God and mammon.

Therefore I say unto you, Take no thought for your life, what ye shall eat, or what ye shall drink; nor yet for your body, what ye shall put on. Is not the life more than meat, and the body than raiment? Behold the fowls of the air: for they sow not, neither do they reap, nor gather into barns; yet your heavenly Father feedeth them. Are ye not much better than they?

Which of you by taking thought can add one cubit unto his stature?

And why take ye thought for raiment? Consider the lilies of the field, how they grow; they toil not, neither do they spin: And yet I say unto you, That even Solomon in all his glory was not arrayed like one of these. Wherefore, if God so clothe the grass of the field, which to day is, and to morrow is cast into the oven, shall he not much more clothe you, O ye of little faith? Therefore take no thought, saying, What shall we eat? or, What shall we drink? or, Wherewithal shall we be clothed? (For after all these things do the Gentiles seek:) for your heavenly Father knoweth that ye have need of all these things.

But seek ye first the kingdom of God, and his righteousness; and all these things shall be added unto you."

"Take therefore no thought for the morrow: for the morrow shall take thought for the things of itself. Sufficient unto the day is the evil thereof.

Judge not, that ye be not judged. For with what judgment ye judge, ye shall be judged: and with what measure ye mete, it shall be measured to you again.

And why beholdest thou the mote that is in thy brother's eye, but considerest not the beam that is in thine own eye? Or how wilt thou say to thy brother, Let me pull out the mote out of thine eye; and, behold, a beam is in thine own eye? Thou hypocrite, first cast out the beam out of thine own eye; and then shalt thou see clearly to cast out the mote out of thy brother's eye.

Give not that which is holy unto the dogs, neither cast ye your pearls before swine, lest they trample them under their feet, and turn again and rend you.

Ask, and it shall be given you; seek, and ye shall find; knock, and it shall be opened unto you: For every one that asketh, receiveth; and he that seeketh, findeth; and to him that knocketh it shall be opened.

Or what man is there of you, whom if his son ask bread, will he give him a stone? Or if he ask a fish, will he give him a serpent? If ye then, being evil, know how to give good gifts unto your children, how much more shall your Father which is in heaven give good things to them that ask him?

Therefore all things whatsoever ye would that men should do to you, do ye even so to them: for this is the law and the prophets.

Enter ye in at the strait gate: for wide [is] the gate, and broad is the way, that leadeth to destruction, and many there be which go in thereat: Because strait is the gate, and narrow is the way, which leadeth unto life, and few there be that find it.

Beware of false prophets, which come to you in sheep's clothing, but inwardly they are ravening wolves. Ye shall know them by their fruits. Do men gather grapes of thorns, or figs of thistles? Even so every good tree bringeth forth good fruit; but a corrupt tree bringeth forth evil fruit. A good tree cannot bring forth evil fruit, neither can a corrupt tree bring forth good fruit. Every tree that bringeth not forth good fruit is hewn down, and cast into the fire. Wherefore by their fruits ye shall know them.

Not every one that saith unto me, Lord, Lord, shall enter into the kingdom of heaven; but he that doeth the will of my Father which is in heaven. Many will say to me in that day, Lord, Lord, have we not prophesied in thy name? and in thy name have cast out devils? and in thy name done many wonderful works? And then will I profess unto them, I never knew you: depart from me, ye that work iniquity.

Therefore whosoever heareth these sayings of mine, and doeth them, I will liken him unto a wise man, which built his house upon a rock: And the rain descended, and the floods came, and the winds blew, and beat upon that house; and it fell not: for it was founded upon a rock. And every one that heareth these sayings of mine, and doeth them not, shall be likened unto a foolish man, which built his house upon the sand: And the rain descended, and the floods came, and the winds blew, and beat upon that house; and it fell: and great was the fall of it."

When Jesus had ended all of these sayings, the people were astonished. Even though His teachings were different from the scribes, He taught them things as one having authority. As one sent from God.

Parables

The throng followed Jesus and the disciples back into Capernaum. Jesus stopped at the Sea of Galilee where the fishing boats were kept. He asked if He could use one of the larger boats as a place to sit and speak to the multitude. The owner knew Jesus and welcomed Him. Jesus sat in the front of the boat and the owner rowed them a few feet off shore to give Him some space.

He again spoke to the crowd, this time in parables..

"A sower went forth to sow; and when he sowed, some seeds fell by the way side, and the fowls came and devoured them

*up. Some fell upon stony places, where they had not much earth
and forthwith they sprung up but because they had no deepness
of earth when the sun was up, they were scorched and because
they had no root, they withered away. Some fell among thorns;
and the thorns sprung up, and choked them. But other fell into
good ground, and brought forth fruit, some an hundredfold, some
sixtyfold, some thirtyfold. Who hath ears to hear, let him hear."*

*"The kingdom of heaven is likened unto a man which sowed
good seed in his field but while he slept, his enemy came and sowed
tares among the wheat, and went his way. When the blade was
sprung up, and brought forth fruit, then appeared the tares also.
So the servants of the householder came and said unto him, Sir,
didst not thou sow good seed in thy field? From whence then hath
it tares? He said unto them, an enemy hath done this. The servants
said unto him, Wilt thou then that we go and gather them up?
He said, Nay; lest while ye gather up the tares, ye root up also
the wheat with them. Let both grow together until the harvest
and in the time of harvest I will say to the reapers, Gather ye
together first the tares, and bind them in bundles to burn them:
but gather the wheat into my barn."*

*"The kingdom of heaven is like to a grain of mustard seed, which
a man took, and sowed in his field which indeed is the least of all
seeds but when it is grown, it is the greatest among herbs, and
becometh a tree, so that the birds of the air come and lodge in the
branches thereof."*

*"The kingdom of heaven is like unto leaven, which a woman took,
and hid in three measures of meal, till the whole was leavened."*

*"He that soweth the good seed is the Son of man; the field is the
world; the good seed are the children of the kingdom; but the tares
are the children of the wicked one; the enemy that sowed them is
the devil; the harvest is the end of the world; and the reapers are*

the angels. The tares are gathered and burned in the fire; so shall it be in the end of this world. The Son of man shall send forth his angels, and they shall gather out of his kingdom all things that offend, and them which do iniquity and shall cast them into a furnace of fire: there shall be wailing and gnashing of teeth. Then shall the righteous shine forth as the sun in the kingdom of their Father. Who hath ears to hear, let him hear."

"The kingdom of heaven is like unto a net, that was cast into the sea, and gathered of every kind of fish, which, when it was full, they drew to shore, and sat down, and gathered the good into vessels, but cast the bad away. So shall it be at the end of the world: the angels shall come forth and sever the wicked from among the just, and shall cast them into the furnace of fire: there shall be wailing and gnashing of teeth."

"Have ye understood all these things?"

Jesus asked the boat owner to return to shore. Before Jesus could exit the boat, He called to the disciples to get in the boat so they could go out on the Sea of Galilee where they would be safe. They made room for all of the disciples. Jesus called Matthew over to ask if he had written the events of the day and the words He had said. Matthew assured Him that, with the help of Judas, he had a complete and accurate writing. He also reported that they had been given generous contributions. Jesus was happy with the news. And with that good news, He settled in the stern of the boat and promptly went to sleep.

Jesus Calms the Storm

"And there arose a great storm of wind, and the waves beat into the ship, so that it was now full. And he was in the hinder

274

part of the ship, asleep on a pillow: and they awake him, and say unto him, Master, carest thou not that we perish? And Jesus saith unto them, Why are ye fearful? O ye of little faith? Then he arose, and Peace by Still, winds and the waves ceased and there was a great calm. The men marvelled, saying, What manner of man is this, that even the winds and the sea obey him!"

Encounter with a Demoniac

The owner of the boat put in at Gennesaret since it was time for the group to have some food.

And when he was come to the other side into the country to Gergesenes, there met a man possessed with two devils, coming out of the tombs, exceeding fierce and no man could bind him, no, not with chains because he had been often bound with fetters and chains, and the chains had been plucked asunder by him, and the fetters broken in pieces: neither could any man tame him and no man might pass by that way. But, when he saw Jesus afar off, the man ran to Jesus and worshipped him. Behold, the devils cried out, saying, What have we to do with thee, Jesus, thou Son of the most high God? Art thou come hither to torment us before the time? Jesus said unto the devil, Come out of the man, thou unclean spirit. And Jesus asked him, What is thy name? And he answered, saying, My name is Legion: for we are many. And there was a good way off from them an herd of many swine feeding. The devils besought him, saying, Send us into the swine, that we may enter into them. And he said unto them, Go, and when they were come out, they went into the herd of swine: and, behold, the whole herd of swine ran violently down a steep place into the sea, and perished in the waters. And they that kept the swine fled into the city, and told every one, every thing that had

*happened to the man that was possessed of the devils. They came
to Jesus, and saw him that was possessed with the devil sitting,
and clothed, and in his right mind: and they were afraid and
they began to pray him to depart out of their coast."*

So, Jesus and the disciples got back into the boat and the
owner directed it back to Capernaum. Jesus spoke to the
disciples with these parables.

*"And Jesus said unto them, No man putteth a piece of new cloth
unto an old garment, for that which is put in to fill it up taketh
from the garment, and the rent is made worse. Neither do men
put new wine into old bottles: else the bottles break, and the wine
runneth out, and the bottles perish: but they put new wine into
new bottles, and both are preserved."*

Jarius' Daughter and Other Miracles

When the boat carrying Jesus and the disciples pulled in
at Capernaum, a group of people was still waiting for Jesus
to return. The disciples were the first to exit the boat. They
pushed aside the people to allow Jesus space to leave the boat.
Jarius approached Andrew. Andrew knew Jarius was a ruler of
the synagogue in Tabgha some 20 minutes from Capernaum.
He asked to speak to Jesus about his 12-year-old daughter.

*"There came a certain ruler, worshipped him and, saying, My
daughter is even now dead: but come and lay thy hand upon
her, and she shall live. Jesus arose, and followed him, and so
did his disciples. A woman, which was diseased with an issue
of blood twelve years, came behind him, and touched the hem
of his garment. For she had said within herself, if I may but
touch his garment, I shall be whole. Jesus turned about, and
when he saw her, he said, Daughter, be of good comfort, thy*

faith hath made thee whole. And the woman was made whole from that hour."

"When Jesus came into the ruler's house, and saw the minstrels and the people making a noise. He said unto them, Give place for the maid is not dead, but sleepeth. And they laughed him and scorned him. But when the people were put forth, he went in, and took her by the hand, and the maid arose. And when Jesus departed thence, two blind men followed him, crying, and saying, Thou son of David, have mercy on us. When he was come into the house, the blind men came to him: and Jesus saith unto them, believe ye that I am able to do this? They said unto him, Yea, Lord. Then touched he their eyes, saying according to your faith be it unto you. Their eyes were opened; and Jesus straitly charged them, saying, See that no man know it. But they, when they were departed, spread abroad his fame in all that country."

"As they went out, behold, they brought to him a dumb man possessed with a devil. When the devil was cast out, the dumb man spake: and the multitudes marvelled, saying, It has never been seen in Israel." The Pharisees said, "He casteth out devils through the prince of the devils."

"And Jesus went about all the cities and villages, teaching in their synagogues, and preaching the gospel of the kingdom, and healing every sickness and every disease among the people."

Feeding the 5,000

Because of the size of the crowds that followed Jesus, He would use a boat to get to places near the Sea of Galilee. Jesus told Andrew that He was going north of Bethsaida to the desert to pray by Himself. The boat left leading north. The crowd saw the direction it was headed and started walking in that direction. The disciples followed along in case they were needed.

Jesus arrived in Bethsaida and started walking north toward the desert. The first of the crowd saw the direction Jesus was going and followed him. He sat in a quiet place and started to pray. He heard a clamor and looked back toward Bethsaida. He saw the multitude heading toward Him.

He was moved with compassion toward them, and he healed their sick and preached. And when it was evening, his disciples came to him, saying, "This is a desert place, and the time is now past to send the multitude away, that they may go into the villages, and buy themselves food." But Jesus said unto them, "They need not depart; give ye them to eat What have we here." And they say unto him, "There is a lad here, which hath five barley loaves, and two small fishes: but what are they among so many"? And Jesus said, "Bring them hither to me and make the men sit down". So the men sat down, in number about five thousand. He took the five loaves, and the two fishes, and looking up to heaven, he blessed, and brake, and gave the loaves to his disciples, and the disciples to the multitude. And they did all eat, and were filled: and they took up of the fragments that remained filled twelve baskets. And they that had eaten were about five thousand men, beside women and children."

Walking on Water

"And straightway Jesus constrained his disciples to get into a ship, and to go before him unto the other side, while he sent the multitudes away. And when he had sent the multitudes away, he went up into a mountain apart to pray: and when the evening was come, he was there alone. But the ship was now in the midst

of the sea, tossed with waves: for the wind was contrary. And in the fourth watch of the night Jesus went unto them, walking on the sea. And when the disciples saw him walking on the sea, they were troubled, saying, It is a spirit; and they cried out for fear. But straightway Jesus spake unto them, saying, Be of good cheer; it is I; be not afraid. And Peter answered him and said, Lord, if it be thou, bid me come unto thee on the water. He said, Come. And when Peter was come down out of the ship, he walked on the water, to go to Jesus. But when he saw the wind boisterous, he was afraid; and beginning to sink, he cried, saying, Lord, save me. And immediately Jesus stretched forth his hand, and caught him, and said unto him, O thou of little faith, wherefore didst thou doubt? And when they were come into the ship, the wind ceased."

A Hard Teaching

When they arrived at Capernaum, Jesus, the disciples, and the women who traveled with them went to Zebedee's house for some rest. Jesus called Matthew aside and asked if he had been faithfully recording the events of the past few days. Matthew said he had and he had a stack of papyrus pages to prove it. Jesus said he didn't need to see them. He just wanted to be certain.

It was Passover again. Realizing that many of the Jewish leadership sought to kill Him, Jesus began to avoid going into Jerusalem. Jesus asked the rabbi in Capernaum if He could celebrate Passover at the synagogue in there.

Jesus called the disciples to the synagogue when the women were preparing the Passover feast. He asked them to sit and listen.

"Then Jesus said unto them, Verily, verily, I say unto you, Moses

gave you not that bread from heaven; but my Father giveth you the true bread from heaven. For the bread of God is he which cometh down from heaven, and giveth life unto the world. Then said they unto him, Lord, evermore give us this bread. Jesus said unto them, "I am the bread of life: he that cometh to me shall never hunger; and he that believeth on me shall never thirst. All that the Father giveth me shall come to me; and him that cometh to me I will in no wise cast out. For I came down from heaven, not to do mine own will, but the will of him that sent me. And it is the Father's will which hath sent me, that of all which he hath given me I should lose nothing, but should raise it up again at the last day. This is the will of him that sent me, that every one which seeth the Son, and believeth on him, may have everlasting life: and I will raise him up at the last day. Jesus said unto them, Murmur not among yourselves. No man can come to me, except the Father which hath sent me to draw him: and I will raise him up at the last day. Verily, verily, I say unto you, He that believeth on me hath everlasting life. I am that bread of life. I am the living bread which came down from heaven: if any man eat of this bread, he shall live for ever: and the bread that I will give is my flesh, which I will give for the life of the world."

"Others have gone away from me. *Will ye also go away?*"

Then Simon Peter answered him, "Lord, to whom shall we go? Thou hast the words of eternal life. We believe and are sure that thou art that Christ, the Son of the living God."

Jesus was preparing the disciples for His death and their ministry. But they didn't understand. He had taught them through His preaching. He had shown them through His miracles. He had made the illustrations simple through His parables, but they still didn't understand. He knew He needed to continue preparing them.

Passover celebration was over, but the throng was still milling around Capernaum. It seemed that everyone was looking for the opportunity to see Jesus or hear Him or be healed by Him or just to touch Him. There was no peace for Jesus. He asked Mary to gather the women together and move to the south. He said that it was designed to attract the throng away from Capernaum. They did that the next morning. It worked. When Capernaum was clear, Jesus and the disciples started their trip to Phoenicia where He wasn't well known. There they could all get some rest. There would be time to regroup. Time to prepare for what He knew would be His last year. His plan was to go to Tyre on the Great Sea. They could make the trip in 10 hours.

Teaching, Preaching, and Healing
The Final Year

When they arrived in Tyre, Jesus met with Matthew and Judas. He told them that He knew that much of the finance from the ministry had come from their personal wealth. He said He knew He could rely on them, and that was why He had put that responsibility on them. He asked Matthew again if he was still recording the miracles and His sermons. Matthew assured Him that he had. Jesus thanked him and said that was very important—important to the ministry and the future. He dismissed Matthew saying He needed to talk to Judas.

He started by reminding Judas of his commitment. He told Judas that He would soon call on him and that, even though he wouldn't understand what he would be asked to do, his role was essential. Judas said that he didn't understand, but that he owed Jesus his life, and he would be faithful until his last breath.

Jesus said, "I will do many things that you won't understand. Everything will be for the purpose of the Kingdom."

When they rejoined the group, Jesus said He needed some time alone to pray and meditate. He said they were to find a place where they could relax; a place where they could watch the sunrise.

Andrew asked Judas what the Master had said to him. Judas said they were discussing money. The disciples knew that Jesus and Judas had been friends as children, but they were curious about the bond. There was a growing level of competition among the disciples for the attention of Jesus. Simon Zelotes asked Matthew to read Jesus' sermon to the 5,000 on Mount Hattin. That quickly refocused the group on the ministry, but the sparks of jealousy were there.

Jesus did not return until midday. A woman from Sidon had found the disciples and was asking to see Jesus. They told her that He wasn't there but she was insistent. When Jesus joined the group, Andrew asked Jesus to meet with her since she had been begging them for help since sunup.

The woman cried unto him, saying, "Have mercy on me, O Lord, thou son of David; my daughter is grievously vexed with a devil." He answered her not a word. And his disciples came and besought him, saying, "Send her away; for she crieth after us..." Then came she and worshipped him, saying, "Lord, help me." He answered and said, "It is not meet to take the children's bread, and cast it to dogs." And she said, "Truth, Lord: yet the dogs eat of the crumbs which fall from their masters' table. "Then Jesus answered and said unto her, "O woman, great is thy faith: be it unto thee even as thou wilt." And her daughter was made whole from that very hour.

The disciples asked Him to explain His words to the woman.

"But he answered and said, I am not sent but unto the lost sheep of the house of Israel."

Jesus and the disciples stayed a week. Jesus talked to them about many of the lessons He had already taught them. It was a time of review. Jesus knew that His time was nearing and He needed to reiterate the things He had taught them.

Next, they went to Caesarea Philippi. When they had stopped for rest and water and were refreshed. *"He asked his disciples, saying, Whom do men say that I the Son of man am? They said, Some say that thou art John the Baptist: some, Elias; and others, Jeremias, or one of the prophets. He saith unto them, But whom say ye that I am? And Simon Peter answered and said, Thou art the Christ, the Son of the living God. And Jesus answered and said unto him, Blessed art thou, Simon Barjona: for flesh and blood hath not revealed it unto thee, but my Father which is in heaven. And I say also unto thee, That thou art Peter, and upon this rock I will build my church; and the gates of hell shall not prevail against it. And I will give unto thee the keys of the kingdom of heaven: and whatsoever thou shalt bind on earth shall be bound in heaven: and whatsoever thou shalt loose on earth shall be loosed in heaven."*

"Then charged he his disciples that they should tell no man that he was Jesus the Christ. From that time forth began Jesus to shew unto his disciples, how that he must go unto Jerusalem, and suffer many things of the elders and chief priests and scribes, and be killed, and be raised again the third day."

"On next day Jesus taketh Peter, James, and John, and bringeth them up into an high mountain apart, And was transfigured before them: and his face did shine as the sun, and his raiment was white as the light. And, behold, there appeared unto them Moses and Elias talking with him. Then answered Peter, and said unto Jesus, Lord, it is good for us to be here. While he yet spake, behold, a bright cloud overshadowed them: and behold a voice out of the cloud, which said, This is my beloved Son, in whom I am well pleased; hear ye him. And when the disciples heard, they fell on their face, and were sore afraid. And Jesus came and touched them, and said, Arise, and be not afraid. When they had lifted up their

eyes, they saw no man, save Jesus only. And as they came down from the mountain, Jesus charged them, saying, Tell the vision to no man, until the Son of man be risen again from the dead."

Jesus and the disciples went straightway to Capernaum and to Zebedee's house where they met the women. Jesus called the entire group together. But, before He could talk to them, Andrew asked, *"Who is the greatest in the kingdom of heaven?" And Jesus called a little child unto him, and set him on His knee and in the midst of them, He said, "Verily I say unto you, Except ye be converted, and become as little children, ye shall not enter into the kingdom of heaven. Whosoever therefore shall humble himself as this little child, the same is greatest in the kingdom of heaven. And who so shall receive one such little child in my name receiveth me. But who so shall offend one of these little ones which believe in me, it were better for him that a millstone were hanged about his neck, and that he were drowned in the depth of the sea."*

"Again I say unto you, That if two of you shall agree on earth as touching any thing that they shall ask, it shall be done for them of my Father which is in heaven. For where two or three are gathered together in my name, there am I in the midst of them."

The next day, Peter came to Him and said, *"They that received taxes came to me, and said, Doth not your master pay tribute?"*

Jesus answered, *"Notwithstanding, lest we should offend them, go thou to the sea, and cast an hook, and take up the fish that first cometh up; and take it to them and when thou hast opened his mouth, thou shalt find a piece of money: that take, and give unto them for me and thee."*

In Capernaum, people were following Jesus and the disciples everywhere they went. *"And there came to Him a certain man, kneeling down to him, and saying, Lord, have mercy on my son: for he is lunatick, and sore vexed: for oft times he falleth into the fire, and oft into the water. I brought him to thy disciples, and they could not cure him. Then Jesus answered and said, O faithless and perverse generation, how long shall I be with you? how long shall I suffer you? bring him hither to me. And Jesus rebuked the devil; and he departed out of him: and the child was cured from that very hour. Then came the disciples to Jesus apart, and said, Why could not we cast him out? And Jesus said unto them, Because of your unbelief: for verily I say unto you, If ye have faith as a grain of mustard seed, ye shall say unto this mountain, Remove hence to yonder place; and it shall remove; and nothing shall be impossible unto you."*

Jesus and the followers went down to Judea. They stopped to preach at a synagogue at Jericho. A large crown gathered to hear Jesus. There were many Pharisees in the crowd. Jesus started with a discussion of eternal life.

An educated man standing near the back of the group spoke up and tempted him by saying, *"Master, what shall I do to inherit eternal life? Jesus said unto him, "What is written in the law? how readest thou?" The man answering said, "Thou shalt love the* LORD *thy God with all thy heart, and with all thy soul, and with all thy strength, and with all thy mind; and thy neighbour as thyself". And Jesus said unto him, "Thou hast answered right: this do, and thou shalt live." But he, willing to justify himself, said unto Jesus, "Who is my neighbour?" Jesus answering said, "A certain man went down from Jerusalem to Jericho, and fell among thieves, which stripped him of his raiment, and wounded him, and departed, leaving him half dead. By chance, there came down a certain priest that way and when he saw the injured man, he passed by on the other side. And likewise a Levite, when he was at the place, came and looked on him, and passed by on the other side. But a certain Samaritan, as he journeyed, came where the injured man was and when he saw him, he had compassion on him. He went to him, and bound up his wounds, pouring in oil and wine, and set him on his own beast, and brought him to an inn, and took care of him. On the morrow, when he departed, he took out two pence, and gave them to the host, and said unto him, 'Take care of him; and whatsoever thou spendest more, when I come again, I will repay thee.' Which now of these three, thinkest thou, was neighbour unto him that fell among the thieves?" The educated man said, "He that shewed mercy on him." Then said Jesus unto him, "Go, and do thou likewise."*

When Jesus was finished preaching, He and the disciples continued south from Jericho to Bethany. There was a brother there and two sisters that Jesus wanted to visit. *"A woman named Martha received him into her house. She had a younger sister called Mary, which also sat at Jesus' feet, and heard his word. But Martha was cumbered about much serving, and came to him, and said, "Lord, dost thou not care that my sister hath left me to serve alone? bid her therefore that she help me." And Jesus answered and said unto her, "Martha, Martha, thou art careful and troubled about many things but one thing is needful and Mary hath chosen that good part, which shall not be taken away from her."*

Jesus and the disciples left Bethany and traveled east to the edge of the Judean Desert. Jesus found a good place, an oasis with shade and good water. He stopped. He said that He needed to pray.

When He was finished praying, one of His disciples said, "Master, teach us to pray as John also taught his disciples."

"Jesus said unto them, When ye pray, say,

Our Father which art in heaven,
Hallowed be thy name.
Thy kingdom come.
Thy will be done, as in heaven, so in earth.
Give us day by day our daily bread.
and forgive us our sins,
for we also forgive every one that is indebted to us.
And lead us not into temptation,
but deliver us from evil. Amen."

When Jesus finished, He told the disciples that He wanted to go to the synagogue in Jerusalem to teach. Jerusalem was a short walk from where they were. In less than an hour, the group was standing on the portico. Jesus had started preaching about a heavenly kingdom when a young man was brought to Him who was possessed by a devil that had made him blind and dumb *"and he healed him, insomuch that the blind and dumb both spake and saw. And all the people were amazed, and said, Is not this the son of David? But when the Pharisees heard it, they said, "This fellow doth not cast out devils, but by Beelzebub the prince of the devils." and Jesus knew their thoughts, and said unto them, "Every kingdom divided against itself is brought to desolation; and every city or house divided against itself shall not stand and if Satan cast out Satan, he is divided against himself; how shall then his kingdom stand?"*

"In the mean time, when there were gathered together an innumerable multitude of people, insomuch that they trode one upon another, he began to say unto his disciples, "first of all, Beware ye of the leaven of the Pharisees, which is hypocrisy. For there is nothing covered, that shall not be revealed; neither hid, that shall not be known. Therefore whatsoever ye have spoken in darkness shall be heard in the light; and that which ye have spoken in the

ear in closets shall be proclaimed upon the housetops. And I say unto you my friends, Be not afraid of them that kill the body, and after that have no more that they can do. But I will forewarn you whom ye shall fear: Fear him, which after he hath killed hath power to cast into hell; yea, I say unto you, Fear him. Are not five sparrows sold for two farthings, and not one of them is forgotten before God? But even the very hairs of your head are all numbered. Fear not therefore: ye are of more value than many sparrows."

"He spake also another parable. A certain man had a fig tree planted in his vineyard; and he came and sought fruit thereon, and found none. Then said he unto the dresser of his vineyard, Behold, these three years I come seeking fruit on this fig tree, and find none: cut it down; why cumbereth it the ground? And he answering said unto him, Lord, let it alone this year also, till I shall dig about it, and dung it, and if it bear fruit, and if not, then after that thou shalt cut it down."

"Behold, there was a woman which had an infirmity eighteen years, and was bowed together, and could in no wise lift up herself. When Jesus saw her, he called her to him, and said unto her, Woman, thou art loosed from thine infirmity. And he laid his hands on her: and immediately she was made straight, and glorified God."

Jesus' words angered the Pharisees. They directed the group to pick up stones and be prepared to stone Jesus, but none would. Jesus finished what He was saying and left the temple.

Jesus went from Jerusalem to Paraea on the other side of the River Jordan. Many of the crowd followed Him. He approached a flat place and asked them all to sit.

He then said, "Ask what you will."

"Then said one unto him, "Lord, are there few that be saved?" And he said unto them, "Strive to enter in at the strait gate: for

many, I say unto you, will seek to enter in, and shall not be able. When once the master of the house is risen up, and hath shut to the door, and ye begin to stand without, and to knock at the door, saying, 'Lord, Lord, open unto us; and he shall answer and say unto you, I know you not whence ye are.' Then shall ye begin to say, We have eaten and drunk in thy presence, and thou hast taught in our streets.' But he shall say, 'I tell you, I know you not whence ye are; depart from me, all ye workers of iniquity.' There shall be weeping and gnashing of teeth, when ye shall see Abraham, and Isaac, and Jacob, and all the prophets, in the kingdom of God, and you yourselves thrust out. And they shall come from the east, and from the west, and from the north, and from the south, and shall sit down in the kingdom of God. And, behold, there are last which shall be first, and there are first which shall be last."

During Jesus' answer a Pharisee ran up to the crowd and yelled at Jesus. *"Get thee out, and depart hence: for Herod will kill thee." Jesus said unto him, "Go ye, and tell that fox, Behold, I cast out devils, and I do cures today and tomorrow, and the third day."*

Jesus continued healing and casting out devils. The crowd was amazed that Jesus would continue what He was doing even after being told that Herod was planning to kill Him.

Jesus knew that there were Pharisees, lawyers, and advisors to the Sanhedrin in His audience. So, in order to make His point He told this parable.

"There was a certain man before Him which had the dropsy. And Jesus answering spake unto the lawyers and Pharisees, saying, "Is it lawful to heal on the sabbath day?" And they held their peace. So, He took him, and healed him, and let him go. And answered them, saying, "Which of you shall have an ass or an ox fallen into a pit, and will not straightway pull him out on the sabbath day?" They could not answer Him again to these things."

Some of the Pharisees moved to the edge of the crowd and left where Jesus was speaking.

"If any man come to me, and hate not his father, and mother, and wife, and children, and brethren, and sisters, yea, and his own life also, he cannot be my disciple. And whosoever doth not bear his cross, and come after me, cannot be my disciple."

Jesus then took the opportunity to speak parables to the group.

"Which of you, intending to build a tower, sitteth not down first, and counteth the cost, whether he have sufficient to finish it? Lest, after he hath laid the foundation, and is not able to finish it, all that behold it begin to mock him, saying, 'This man began to build, and was not able to finish.'"

"I am judged by My followers. I chose them, and they are important to Me.

"Salt is good: but if the salt have lost his savour, wherewith shall it be seasoned? It is neither fit for the land, nor yet for the dung-hill; but men cast it out. He that hath ears to hear, let him hear."

"I do not wish to lose even one of my followers, for, as I said, they are important to me."

"What woman having ten pieces of silver, if she lose one piece, doth not light a candle, and sweep the house, and seek diligently till she find it? And when she hath found it, she calleth her friends and her neighbours together, saying, Rejoice with me; for I have found the piece which I had lost. Likewise, I say unto you, there is joy in the presence of the angels of God over one sinner that repenteth."

"Money is important but people are more so."

"A certain man had two sons. The younger of them said to his father, 'Father, give me the portion of goods that falleth to me. And he divided unto them his living.' And not many days after, the younger son gathered all together, and took his journey into a far

country, and there wasted his substance with riotous living. When he had spent all, there arose a mighty famine in that land; and he began to be in want. He went and joined himself to a citizen of that country; and he sent him into his fields to feed swine. And he would fain have filled his belly with the husks that the swine did eat: and no man gave unto him. When he came to himself, he said, 'How many hired servants of my father's have bread enough and to spare, and I perish with hunger! I will arise and go to my father, and will say unto him, Father, I have sinned against heaven, and before thee, and am no more worthy to be called thy son. Make me as one of thy hired servants.' He arose, and came to his father. But when he was yet a great way off, his father saw him, and had compassion, and ran, and fell on his neck, and kissed him. And the son said unto him, 'Father, I have sinned against heaven, and in thy sight, and am no more worthy to be called thy son.' But the father said to his servants, 'Bring forth the best robe, and put it on him; and put a ring on his hand, and shoes on his fee. And bring hither the fatted calf, and kill it; and let us eat, and be merry. For this my son was dead, and is alive again; he was lost, and is found.' And they began to be merry. Now his elder son was in the field: and as he came and drew nigh to the house, he heard musick and dancing. He called one of the servants, and asked what these things meant. He said unto him, 'Thy brother is come; and thy father hath killed the fatted calf, because he hath received him safe and sound.' And he was angry, and would not go in: therefore came his father out, and intreated him. And he answering said to his father, 'Lo, these many years do I serve thee, neither transgressed I at any time thy commandment: and yet thou never gavest me a kid, that I might make merry with my friends. But as soon as this thy son was come, which hath devoured thy living with harlots, thou hast killed for him the fatted calf.' His

*Father said unto him, 'Son, thou art ever with me, and all that
I have is thine. It was meet that we should make merry, and be
glad: for this thy brother was dead, and is alive again; and was
lost, and is found.'*

And the Pharisees also, who were covetous, heard all these
things and derided him. *"He said unto them, Ye are they which
justify yourselves before men; but God knoweth your hearts: for
that which is highly esteemed among men is abomination in the
sight of God."*

There was grumbling among the Pharisees who were still
there and among the leaders of the synagogues and the advisors to the Sanhedrin. Hearing the grumbling, Jesus told
another parable that He knew would make them think.

*"There was a certain rich man, which was clothed in purple
and fine linen, and fared sumptuously every day. And there was
a certain beggar named Lazarus, which was laid at his gate, full
of sores, desiring to be fed with the crumbs which fell from the rich
man's table. Moreover the dogs came and licked his sores. And it
came to pass, that the beggar died, and was carried by the angels
into Abraham's bosom. The rich man also died, and was buried,
and in hell he lift up his eyes, being in torments, and seeth Abraham afar off, and Lazarus in his bosom. And he cried and said,
'Father Abraham, have mercy on me, and send Lazarus, that he
may dip the tip of his finger in water, and cool my tongue; for I
am tormented in this flame.' But Abraham said, 'Son, remember
that thou in thy lifetime receivedst thy good things, and likewise
Lazarus evil things but now he is comforted, and thou art tormented. Beside all this, between us and you there is a great gulf
fixed, so that they which would pass from hence to you cannot;
neither can they pass to us, that would come from thence.' Then
he said, 'I pray thee therefore, father, that thou wouldest send*

him to my father's house, for I have five brethren, that he may testify unto them, lest they also come into this place of torment.' Abraham saith unto him, 'They have Moses and the prophets, let them hear them.' And he said, 'Nay, father Abraham: but if one went unto them from the dead, they will repent.' And Abraham said unto him, 'If they hear not Moses and the prophets, neither will they be persuaded, though one rose from the dead.'"

Jesus continued talking to the crowd, now mostly followers. He talked about the kingdom of heaven and about the new Law. When He dismissed the crowd, He gathered His disciples and said that He needed to return to Judea. They crossed the Jordan River and made their way to Qumran.

Simon Zelotes spoke up and said he knew many people there. "That is where John the Baptist called home."

Qumran was only a little over an hour from where they were in Peraea.

The group arrived at Qumran and they were greeted by Zealot members—some Simon knew; some, he didn't. Simon introduced Jesus. Most of the Zealots were happy to meet Him. Most knew that He and John were cousins, and they knew that John had baptized Jesus. Jesus spoke words of condolence regarding the martyring of John. He spoke of the promise of the kingdom of heaven.

The community invited Jesus and the disciples to join them in the evening meal.

MARTHA, MARY, AND LAZARUS
THE END APPROACHES

B efore Jesus and the disciples left on the next morning, they received word that Lazarus, the brother of Martha and Mary, was sick. *"Therefore his sisters sent unto him, saying, Lord, behold, he whom thou lovest is sick. When Jesus heard that, he said, This sickness is not unto death, but for the glory of God, that the Son of God might be glorified thereby. Now Jesus loved Martha, and her sister, and Lazarus. When he had heard therefore that he was sick, he abode two days still in the same place where he was. Then after that saith he to his disciples, Let us go into Judaea again to the town of Bethany. His disciples say unto him, Master, the Jews of late sought to stone thee; and goest thou thither again? Jesus answered, "Our friend Lazarus sleepeth; but I go, that I may awake him out of sleep". Then said Jesus unto them plainly, Lazarus is dead."*

"And I am glad for your sakes that I was not there, to the intent ye may believe; nevertheless let us go unto him. Then said Thomas, which is called Didymus, unto his fellow disciples, "Let us also go, that we may die with him." Then when Jesus came, he found that he had lain in the grave four days already. Now Bethany was nigh unto Jerusalem, about fifteen furlongs off. Many of the Jews came to Martha and Mary, to comfort them concerning their brother.

Then Martha, as soon as she heard that Jesus was coming, went and met him: but Mary sat still in the house. Then said Martha unto Jesus, "Lord, if thou hadst been here, my brother had not died. But I know, that even now, whatsoever thou wilt ask of God, God will give it thee." Jesus saith unto her, "Thy brother shall rise again." Martha saith unto him, "I know that he shall rise again in the resurrection at the last day." Jesus said unto her, "I am the resurrection, and the life: he that believeth in me, though he were dead, yet shall he live. And whosoever liveth and believeth in me shall never die. Believest thou this?" She saith unto him, "Yea, Lord: I believe that thou art the Christ, the Son of God, which should come into the world." And when she had so said, she went her way, and called Mary her sister secretly, saying, "The Master is come, and calleth for thee." As soon as Mary heard that, she arose quickly, and came unto him. Now Jesus was not yet come into the town, but was in that place where Martha met him."

The Jews then which were with her in the house, and comforted her, when they saw Mary, that she rose up hastily and went out, followed her, saying, "She goeth unto the grave to weep there." Then when Mary was come where Jesus was, and saw him, she fell down at his feet, saying unto him, "Lord, if thou hadst been here, my brother had not died." When Jesus therefore saw her weeping, and the Jews also weeping which came with her, he groaned in the spirit, and was troubled. And said, "Where have ye laid him?" They said unto him, "Lord, come and see." Jesus wept. Then said the Jews, "Behold how he loved him!" And some of them said, "Could not this man, which opened the eyes of the blind, have caused that even this man should not have died?" Jesus therefore again groaning in himself cometh to the grave. It was a cave, and a stone lay upon it. Jesus said, "Take ye away the stone." Martha, the sister of him that was dead, saith unto Him, "Lord, by this

*time he stinketh: for he hath been dead four days." Jesus saith
unto her, "Said I not unto thee, that, if thou wouldest believe,
thou shouldest see the glory of God?" Then they took away the
stone from the place where the dead was laid. And Jesus lifted
up his eyes, and said, "Father, I thank thee that thou hast heard
me. And I knew that thou hearest me always. But because of the
people which stand by I said it, that they may believe that thou
hast sent me."*

*"And when he thus had spoken, he cried with a loud voice,
"Lazarus, come forth." And he that was dead came forth, bound
hand and foot with grave clothes and his face was bound about
with a napkin. Jesus saith unto them, "Loose him, and let him go."
Then many of the Jews which came to Mary, and had seen the
things which Jesus did, believed on him. But some of them went
their ways to the Pharisees, and told them what things Jesus had
done. Then gathered the chief priests and the Pharisees a council,
and said, "What do we? for this man doeth many miracles. If we
let him thus alone, all men will believe on him and the Romans
shall come and take away both our place and nation." And one
of them, named Caiaphas, being the high priest that same year,
said unto them, "Ye know nothing at all, Nor consider that it is
expedient for us, that one man should die for the people, and that
the whole nation perish not." And this spake he not of himself
but being high priest that year, he prophesied that Jesus should
die for that nation. And not for that nation only, but that also
he should gather together in one the children of God that were
scattered abroad."*

*"Then from that day forth they took counsel together for to put
him to death. Jesus therefore walked no more openly among the
Jews; but went thence unto a country near to the wilderness, into
a city called Ephraim, and there continued with his disciples."*

Ephraim, a town on the border with Samaria, north and west of Jericho was a two-hour walk for Jesus and the disciples. They bypassed Jerusalem, heading to the Jordan River, then north past Jericho and west to Ephraim.

"And as he entered into Ephraim, there met him ten men that were lepers, which stood afar off And they lifted up their voices, and said, Jesus, Master, have mercy on us. And when he saw them, he said unto them, Go shew yourselves unto the priests. And it came to pass, that, as they went, they were cleansed. And one of them, when he saw that he was healed, turned back, and with a loud voice glorified God, And fell down on his face at his feet, giving him thanks: and he was a Samaritan."

Jesus took advantage of the disciples' time in Ephraim to teach the twelve.

"And He spake a parable unto them to this end, that men ought always to pray, and not to faint, saying, There was in a city a judge, which feared not God, neither regarded man And there was a widow in that city; and she came unto him, saying, Avenge me of mine adversary. And he would not for a while: but afterward he said within himself, Though I fear not God, nor regard man yet because this widow troubleth me, I will avenge her, lest by her continual coming she weary me. And the Lord said, Hear what the unjust judge saith, shall not God avenge his own elect, which cry day and night unto him, though he bear long with them? I tell you that he will avenge them speedily."

He then perceived that some of the disciples were thinking themselves more righteous than the people they were to minister to and even more righteous than their fellow disciples. So, Jesus told them this parable.

"Two men went up into the temple to pray; the one a Pharisee, and the other a publican. The Pharisee stood and prayed thus

298

with himself, God, I thank thee, that I am not as other men are, extortionist, unjust, adulterers, or even as this publican. I fast twice in the week, I give tithes of all that I possess. The publican, standing afar off, would not lift up so much as his eyes unto heaven, but smote upon his breast, saying, God be merciful to me a sinner. I tell you, this man went down to his house justified rather than the other: for every one that exalteth himself shall be abased; and he that humbleth himself shall be exalted."

Jesus always used little children as examples of how the disciples were to live. Little children have no unjust motives and they have no reason to lie.

Women from Ephraim came with their children. *"They brought unto him little children, that he should put his hands on them, and pray: and the disciples rebuked them. But Jesus said, "Suffer little children, and forbid them not, to come unto me: for of such is the kingdom of heaven." And he laid his hands on them, and they departed thence."*

Others from Ephraim came to see and hear Jesus. And some came to be healed.

And, behold, one came and said unto Him, "Good Master, what good thing shall I do, that I may have eternal life?" He said unto him, "Why callest thou me good? there is none good but one, that is, God. But if thou wilt enter into life, keep the commandments." He saith unto Jesus, "Which?" Jesus said, "Thou shalt do no murder, Thou shalt not commit adultery, Thou shalt not steal, Thou shalt not bear false witness, Honour thy father and thy mother: and, Thou shalt love thy neighbour as thyself." The young man saith unto Him, "All these things have I kept from my youth up. What lack I yet?" Jesus said unto him, "If thou wilt be perfect, go and sell that thou hast, and give to the poor, and thou shalt have treasure in heaven: and come and follow me." When the young man heard that saying, he went away sorrowful: for he had great possessions."

Jesus turned to His disciples and taught them saying, "*What profitith a man to gain the whole world and lose his own soul?*"

Jesus knew that the time was approaching for Him to celebrate Passover with the disciples and He knew that it would be the end of His ministry on earth. He wanted to prepare the disciples and He wanted to confirm what He needed Judas to do to fulfill the prophesies. So, He sent the people from Ephraim home to have some private time with the disciples.

He knew they would soon be going up to Jerusalem, so He took the twelve disciples and said unto them. "*Behold, we go up to Jerusalem; and the Son of man shall be betrayed unto the chief priests and unto the scribes, and they shall condemn him to death, and shall deliver him to the Gentiles to mock, and to scourge, and to crucify him: and the third day he shall rise again.*"

And they understood none of these things. and this saying was hidden from them, neither knew they the things which were spoken.

They overnighted at Ephraim for Jesus knew the time was near. Once all were settled, Jesus called Judas aside.

"Judas, My friend, the time is come for you to repay the debt you owe. When we arrive in Jerusalem, you are to go to the High Priest, Caiaphas, and tell him that you know that I have been guilty of blasphemy against Moses Law, and that I have committed sedition against Roman Law. You are to tell them that, according to temple custom, a payment of 30 pieces of silver is due to you for reporting this. Also suggest that you will, at the proper time, kiss Me on the cheek to reveal My identity to the authorities."

"Jesus, you are my best friend. Since childhood we have been such. I owe the debt to You, but we do not know what the Sanhedrin will do. Neither do we know what the Roman authority will do. You certainly know that sedition is punishable by death."

"Yes, I know, but you and I are part of a plan that is essential to My ministry. As I said earlier, *we go up to Jerusalem; and the Son of man shall be betrayed unto the chief priests and unto the scribes, and they shall condemn Him to death, and shall deliver Him to the Gentiles to mock, and to scourge, and to crucify Him.* Death is My destiny, My friend, and you are to be the one that provides the key to the fulfillment of the prophets and My ministry. Are you still willing?"

There was a moment of silence. Judas had to weigh the oath he had given Jesus with the knowledge that what he was being asked to do would result in the death of his friend.

"My oath is my bind. I will do as you ask, but it will be the hardest thing I have ever done."

"The others are to know nothing of this. You will be considered an evil one, a betrayer. But, this is necessary."

Judas walked around Ephraim that night trying to find a way out but none revealed itself.

The Die is Cast

The next morning, Jesus and the disciples began the short trip to Jerusalem. They walked through Jericho. *And Jesus entered and passed through Jericho. And, behold, there was a man named Zacchaeus, which was the chief among the publicans, and he was rich. And he sought to see Jesus who He was; and could not for the press, because he was little of stature. So, he ran before, and climbed up into a sycamore tree to see Him: for He was to pass that way. When Jesus came to the place, He looked up, and saw him, and said unto him, "Zacchaeus, make haste, and come down, for to day I must abide at thy house." And he made haste, and came down, and received Him joyfully. When they saw it, they all murmured, saying, That He was gone to be guest with a man that is a sinner. And Zacchaeus stood, and said unto the Lord "Behold, Lord, the half of my goods I give to the poor; and if I have taken any thing from any man by false accusation, I restore him fourfold." Jesus said unto him, "This day is salvation come to this house, forsomuch as he also is a son of Abraham. For the Son of man is come to seek and to save that which was lost."*

Jesus and the disciples and the entire group stayed the night with Zacchaeus. The next morning they made the four-hour walk to Bethany and the home of Martha, Mary, and Lazarus. Martha had planned a dinner for the group in honor of Jesus and the miracle he had performed in bringing Lazarus back to life.

There they made Him a supper; and Martha served: but Lazarus was one of them that sat at the table with Him. Then took Mary a pound of ointment of spikenard, very costly, and anointed the feet of Jesus, and wiped his feet with her hair: and the house was filled with the odour of the ointment. Then saith one of his disciples, Judas Iscariot, Simon's son, which should betray him, "Why was not this ointment sold for three hundred pence, and given to the poor?" Then said Jesus, "Let her alone: against the day of My burying hath she kept this. For the poor always ye have with you; but Me ye have not always." Much people of the Jews therefore knew that He was there: and they came not for Jesus' sake only, but that they might see Lazarus also, whom He had raised from the dead. Now, the chief priests consulted that they might put Lazarus also to death, Because that by reason of him many of the Jews went away, and believed on Jesus.

The group stayed the night with Martha, Mary, and Lazarus.

Less than an hour's walk from Bethany was Bethphage and the Mount of Olives. Jesus said he wanted to stop and pray and to prepare for His entrance into Jerusalem. Jesus called James the Younger and Jude, *"Saying unto them, Go into the village over against you, and straightway ye shall find an ass tied, and a colt with her. Loose them, and bring them unto me. And if any man say ought unto you, ye shall say, The Lord hath need of them; and straightway he will send them."*

Jesus instructed the group to find places to rest. Then He separated Himself from the group to pray.

"All this was done, that it might be fulfilled which was spoken by the prophet, saying, Tell ye the daughter of Sion, Behold, thy King cometh unto thee, meek, and sitting upon an ass, and a

colt the foal of an ass. And the disciples went, and did as Jesus commanded them. They brought the ass, and the colt, and put on them their clothes, and they set him thereon."

"And a very great multitude had gathered along the way and they spread their garments in the way; others cut down branches from the trees, and strawed them in the way and the multitudes that went before, and that followed, cried, saying, Hosanna to the son of David: Blessed is he that cometh in the name of the Lord; Hosanna in the highest."

"And when he was come into Jerusalem, all the city was moved, saying, Who is this? And the multitude said, This is Jesus the prophet of Nazareth of Galilee. And Jesus went into the temple of God, and cast out all them that sold and bought in the temple, and overthrew the tables of the moneychangers, and the seats of them that sold doves, And said unto them, "It is written, My house shall be called the house of prayer; but ye have made it a den of thieves."

He sat where the vendors were and directed the disciples to gather all who needed healing be brought to Him. *"And the blind and the lame came to him in the temple; and he healed them. And when the chief priests and scribes saw the wonderful things that He did, and the children crying in the temple, and saying, Hosanna to the son of David; they were sore displeased, And said unto him, "Hearest thou what these say?" And Jesus saith unto them, "Yea; have ye never read, Out of the mouth of babes and sucklings thou hast perfected praise?" And he left them, and went out of the city into Bethany; and he lodged there."*

On His way back to Bethany, He again stopped at the Mount of Olives. *"He hungered. And when he saw a fig tree in the way, he came to it, and found nothing thereon, but leaves only, and said unto it, Let no fruit grow on thee henceforward for ever. And presently the fig tree withered away. And when the disciples saw it, they marvelled, saying, the fig tree it withered away as we watched! Jesus answered and said unto them, "Verily I say unto you, If ye have faith, and doubt not, ye shall not only do this which is done to the fig tree, but also if ye shall say unto this mountain, Be thou removed, and be thou cast into the sea; it shall be done. All things, whatsoever ye shall ask in prayer, believing, ye shall receive."*

The next morning, Jesus and the disciples were again in the Temple, and Jesus was teaching. *"And when He was come into the temple, the chief priests and the elders of the people came unto Him as He was teaching, and said, By what authority doest thou these things? and who gave thee this authority? Jesus answered and said unto them, "I also will ask you one thing, which if ye tell me, I in like wise will tell you by what authority I do these things. The baptism of John, whence was it? from heaven, or of men?" And they reasoned with themselves, saying, If we shall say, From heaven; he will say unto us, Why did ye not then believe him? But if we shall say, Of men; we fear the people; for all hold John as a prophet. And they answered Jesus, and said, "We cannot tell." And he said unto them, "Neither tell I you by what authority I do these things."*

Jesus continued to teach the people gathered around Him. *"A certain man had two sons; and he came to the first, and said, Son, go work to day in my vineyard. He answered and said, I will not: but afterward he repented, and went. And he came to the second, and said likewise. And he answered and said, I go, sir: and went not. Whether of them twain did the will of his father? They say unto Him, The first. Jesus saith unto them, Verily I say unto you, That the publicans and the harlots go into the kingdom of God before you. For John came unto you in the way*

*of righteousness, and ye believed him not: but the publicans and
the harlots believed him: and ye, when ye had seen it, repented
not afterward, that ye might believe him."*

Jesus began again, teaching them with parables. *"The kingdom of heaven is like unto a certain king, which made a marriage
for his son, And sent forth his servants to call them that were
bidden to the wedding: and they would not come. Again, he sent
forth other servants, saying, Tell them which are bidden, Behold,
I have prepared my dinner: my oxen and my fatlings are killed,
and all things are ready: come unto the marriage. But they made
light of it, and went their ways, one to his farm, another to his
merchandise and the remnant took his servants, and entreated
them spitefully, and slew them. So, when the king heard thereof,
he was wroth: and he sent forth his armies, and destroyed those
murderers, and burned up their city. Then he saith to his servants, The wedding is ready, but they which were bidden were
not worthy. Go ye therefore into the highways, and as many as
ye shall find, bid to the marriage. So those servants went out
into the highways, and gathered together all as many as they
found, both bad and good: and the wedding was furnished with
guests. And when the king came in to see the guests, he saw there
a man which had not on a wedding garment And he saith unto
him, Friend, how camest thou in hither not having a wedding
garment? And he was speechless. Then said the king to the servants,
Bind him hand and foot, and take him away, and cast him into
outer darkness, there shall be weeping and gnashing of teeth. For
many are called, but few are chosen."*

Jesus continued to teach, but soon a group of Pharisees
approached Him with the intent of having Him stumble
on His own words. *"Then went the Pharisees, and took counsel
how they might entangle him in his talk. And they sent out unto*

him their disciples with the Herodians, saying, Master, we know that thou art true, and teachest the way of God in truth, neither carest thou for any man: for thou regardest not the person of men. Tell us therefore, What thinkest thou? Is it lawful to give tribute unto Caesar, or not? But Jesus perceived their wickedness, and said, "Why tempt ye me, ye hypocrites? Show me the tribute money." And they brought unto him a penny. Then He saith unto them, "Whose is this image and superscription?" They say unto him, "Caesar's." Then saith he unto them, "Render therefore unto Caesar the things which are Caesar's; and unto God the things that are God's." When they had heard these words, they marveled, and left him, and went their way."

"The same day came to him the Sadducees, which say that there is no resurrection, and asked him, Saying, "Master, Moses said, If a man die, having no children, his brother shall marry his wife, and raise up seed unto his brother. Now there were with us seven brethren and the first, when he had married a wife, deceased, and, having no issue, left his wife unto his brother. Likewise the second also, and the third, unto the seventh. And last of all the woman died also. Therefore in the resurrection whose wife shall she be of the seven? for they all had her." Jesus answered and said unto them, "Ye do err, not knowing the scriptures, nor the power of God. For in the resurrection they neither marry, nor are given in marriage, but are as the angels of God in heaven. But as touching the resurrection of the dead, have ye not read that which was spoken unto you by God, saying, I am the God of Abraham, and the God of Isaac, and the God of Jacob? God is not the God of the dead, but of the living." When the multitude heard this, they were astonished at his doctrine. But when the Pharisees had heard that he had put the Sadducees to silence, they were gathered together."

*"Then one of them, which was a lawyer, asked him a question, tempting him, and saying, "Master, which is the great command-ment in the law?" Jesus said unto him, "Thou shalt love the L*ORD *thy God with all thy heart, and with all thy soul, and with all thy mind. This is the first and great commandment. And the second is like unto it, Thou shalt love thy neighbour as thyself. On these two commandments hang all the law and the prophets."*

Condemning the Scribes and Pharisees

The learned people of the synagogue were in the group, and they were the ones questioning Jesus. Their concerns were selfish and self-centered. They were protecting their positions. So Jesus spoke directly to them.

"*Woe unto you, scribes and Pharisees, hypocrites! for ye shut up the kingdom of heaven against men. For ye neither go in yourselves, neither suffer ye them that are entering to go in. Woe unto you, scribes and Pharisees, hypocrites! for ye devour widows' houses, and for a pretense make long prayer,: therefore ye shall receive the greater damnation. Woe unto you, scribes and Pharisees, hypocrites! for ye compass sea and land to make one proselyte, and when he is made, ye make him twofold more the child of hell than yourselves. Woe unto you, ye blind guides, which say, Whosoever shall swear by the temple, it is nothing, but whosoever shall swear by the gold of the temple, he is a debtor! Ye fools and blind, for whether is greater, the gold, or the temple that sanctifieth the gold? And, Whosoever shall swear by the altar, it is nothing, but whosoever sweareth by the gift that is upon it, he is guilty. Ye fools and blind, for whether is greater, the gift, or the altar that sanctifieth the gift? Whoso therefore shall swear by the altar, sweareth by it, and by all things thereon. And whoso shall swear by the temple, sweareth by it, and by him that dwelleth therein. And he that shall swear by heaven, sweareth by the throne of God, and by him that sitteth thereon.*"

"*Woe unto you, scribes and Pharisees, hypocrites! for ye pay tithe of mint and anise and cumin, and have omitted the weightier matters of the law, judgment, mercy, and faith: these ought ye to have done, and not to leave the other undone. Ye blind guides, which strain at a gnat, and swallow a camel. Woe unto you, scribes and Pharisees, hypocrites! for ye make clean the outside of the cup and of the platter, but within they are full of extortion and excess. Thou blind Pharisee, cleanse first that which is within the cup and platter, that the outside of them may be clean also. Woe unto you, scribes and Pharisees, hypocrites! for ye are like unto whited sepulchers, which indeed appear beautiful outward, but are within full of dead men's bones, and of all uncleanness.*

"*Even so ye also outwardly appear righteous unto men, but within ye are full of hypocrisy and iniquity.*"

"*Woe unto you, scribes and Pharisees, hypocrites! because ye build the tombs of the prophets, and garnish the sepulchers of the righteous, And say, If we had been in the days of our fathers, we would not have been partakers with them in the blood of the prophets. Wherefore ye be witnesses unto yourselves, that ye are the children of them which killed the prophets.*"

"*Fill ye up then the measure of your fathers. Ye serpents, ye generation of vipers, how can ye escape the damnation of hell?*"

When Jesus finished, the learned men left. They were talking to each other, plotting against Jesus.

Those who had heard Jesus reported to the Sanhedrin. Jesus asked all but the disciples to go home. He sat with them to talk. "*And it came to pass, when Jesus had finished all these sayings, He said unto his disciples, "Ye know that after two days is the feast of the Passover, and the Son of man is betrayed to be crucified.*" But they didn't understand.

When they left Jesus, the scribes, Pharisees, and learned

men returned to the synagogue to meet with Caiaphas and the assembled members of the Sanhedrin to report on what they had heard. "*Assembled together the chief priests, and the scribes, and the elders of the people, unto the palace of the high priest, who was called Caiaphas, And consulted that they might take Jesus by subtlety, and kill him. But he said, "Not on the feast day, lest there be an uproar among the people."*

"*Then came the day of unleavened bread, when the Passover meal must be served. And He sent Peter and John, saying, "Go and prepare us the Passover, that we may eat." And they said unto him, "Where wilt thou that we prepare?" And he said unto them, "Behold, when ye are entered into the city, there shall a man meet you, bearing a pitcher of water. Follow him into the house where he entereth in. And ye shall say unto the goodman of the house, 'The Master saith unto thee, Where is the guest chamber, where I shall eat the Passover with my disciples?' And he shall show you a large upper room furnished and there make ready. And they went, and found as he had said unto them: and they made ready the Passover."*

Author Comment:

We are so accustomed to seeing the DaVinci painting of "The Last Supper" that we think that is the way Jesus' last supper actually took place. The *Seder* meal was most likely presented at a *triclinium*—U shape table. Jesus and the disciples would have eaten in a reclining position, lying on cushions on their left side, allowing them to eat with their right hand, which was considered their *clean* hand.

There was also an acceptable seating hierarchy dictating where people would sit. Jesus would have been very aware of this, so he was using the last meal with the disciples to continue His teaching. If you are looking at the table, the left side was where the host would sit—not in the center as most often depicted. Jesus would be seated in the second position, as was the custom. John would have been in the first position, which would allow him to "lean on the bosom of Christ to ask the identity of the betrayer." Judas would have been seated in the seat to Jesus' left—considered the seat of honor—which would allow them to eat from the same bowl.

Peter would have been seated across from John at the first position on the right side—the seat of the servant who would wash the feet of the guests. The disciples would have known about the seating plan. This would have made Jesus' decision to wash the disciples feet even more meaningful. Also, it would have pointed the disciples to His statement that he who would be first must be last. And, it explains Peter's comments about Jesus washing his feet John 13:6-8.

THE LAST SUPPER

"Now when the even was come, He sat down with the twelve. And as they did eat, he said, Verily I say unto you, that one of you shall betray me. And they were exceeding sorrowful, and began every one of them to say unto him, Lord, is it I? And he answered and said, He that dippeth his hand with me in the dish, the same shall betray me."

"The Son of man goeth as it is written of him: but woe unto that man by whom the Son of man is betrayed! it had been good for that man if he had not been born. Then Judas, which betrayed him, answered and said, Master, is it I? He said unto him, Do as thou has said. And as they were eating, Jesus took bread, and blessed it, and brake it, and gave it to the disciples, and said, Take, eat; this is my body. And he took the cup, and gave thanks, and gave it to them, saying, Drink ye all of it; For this is my blood of the new testament, which is shed for many for the remission of sins. But I say unto you, I will not drink henceforth of this fruit of the vine, until that day when I drink it new with you in my Father's kingdom."

He then said to Judas, "Go, do what I have asked you to do. And do it quickly."

"And the other disciples began to enquire among themselves, which of them it was that should do this thing. And there was also a strife among them, which of them should be accounted the *greatest. And he said unto them, "The kings of the Gentiles exercise lordship over them; and they that exercise authority upon them are called benefactors. But ye shall not be so: but he that is greatest among you, let him be as the younger; and he that is chief, as he that doth serve. For whoever is greater, he that sitteth at meat, or he that serveth? is not he that sitteth at meat? but I am among you as he that serveth."* And with that He called for a basin, filled with water. *"And began to wash the disciples' feet, and to wipe them with the towel wherewith he was girded. Then cometh he to Simon Peter: and "Peter saith unto him, Lord, dost thou wash my feet?" Jesus answered and said unto him, "What I do thou knowest not now; but thou shalt know hereafter." Peter saith unto him, "Thou shalt never wash my feet." Jesus answered him, "If I wash thee not, thou hast no part with me." Simon Peter saith unto him, "Lord, not my feet only, but also my hands and my head." Jesus saith to him, "He that is washed needeth not save to wash his feet, but is clean every whit: and ye are clean, but not all."*

"So after he had washed their feet, and had taken his garments, and was set down again, he said unto them, "Know ye what I have done to you? Ye call me Master and Lord: and ye say well; for so I am. If I then, your Lord and Master, have washed your feet; ye also ought to wash one another's feet. For I have given you an example, that ye should do as I have done to you. Verily, verily, I say unto you, The servant is not greater than his lord; neither he that is sent greater than he that sent him. If ye know these things, happy are ye if ye do them."

"Ye are they which have continued with me in my temptations. And I appoint unto you a kingdom, as my Father hath appointed unto me; That ye may eat and drink at my table in my kingdom, and sit on thrones judging the twelve tribes of Israel." And the

Lord said, "Simon, Simon, behold, Satan hath desired to have you, that he may sift you as wheat But I have prayed for thee, that thy faith fail not, and when thou art converted, strengthen thy brethren." And he said unto him, "Lord, I am ready to go with thee, both into prison, and to death." And he said, "I tell thee, Peter, the cock shall not crow this day, before that thou shalt thrice deny that thou knowest me." And he said unto them, "When I sent you without purse, and scrip, and shoes, lacked ye any thing?" And they said, "Nothing."

And when they had sung a hymn, they went out into the Mount of Olives.

"When he was at the place, he said unto them, Pray that ye enter not into temptation. He was withdrawn from them about a stone's cast, and kneeled down, and prayed, saying, "Father, if thou be willing, remove this cup from me, nevertheless not my will, but thine, be done. There appeared an angel unto him from heaven, strengthening him. And being in an agony he prayed more earnestly, and his sweat was as it were great drops of blood falling down to the ground. When he rose up from prayer, and was come to his disciples, he found them sleeping for sorrow, And said unto them, "Why sleep ye? rise and pray, lest ye enter into temptation."

"While he yet spake, behold a multitude, and he that was called Judas, one of the twelve, went before them, and drew near unto Jesus to kiss him."

"But Jesus said unto him, "Judas, Friend, wherefore art thou come?"

"Then came they, and laid hands on Jesus and took him. And, behold, then Simon Peter having a sword drew it, and smote the high priest's servant, and cut off his right ear. The servant's name was Malchus. Jesus answered and said, "Suffer ye thus far." And he touched his ear, and healed him. Then said Jesus unto Peter,

Put up thy sword into the sheath: the cup which my Father hath given me, shall I not drink it? But all this was done, that the scriptures of the prophets might be fulfilled. Then all the disciples forsook him, and fled."

"Then the band and the captain and officers of the Jews took Jesus, and bound him, and led him away to Annas first; for he was father in law to Caiaphas, which was the high priest that same year."

"Then took they him, and led him, and brought him into the high priest's house. And Peter followed afar off. When they had kindled a fire in the midst of the hall, and were set down together, Peter sat down among them. But a certain maid beheld him as he sat by the fire, and earnestly looked upon him, and said, "This man was also with him". And he denied him, saying, "Woman, I know him not". And after a little while another saw him, and said, "Thou art also of them." And Peter said, "Man, I am not." And about the space of one hour after another confidently affirmed, saying, "Of a truth this fellow also was with him: for he is a Galilaean." And Peter said, "Man, I know not what thou sayest." And immediately, while he yet spake, the cock crew. The Lord turned, and looked upon Peter. And Peter remembered the word of the Lord, how he had said unto him, Before the cock crow, thou shalt deny me thrice. Peter went out, and wept bitterly."

Annas was conflicted with Jesus and didn't know what to do. So he told the Captain of Guard to take Jesus to Caiaphas and the Sanhedrin.

"Now the chief priests, and elders, and all the council, sought false witness against Jesus, to put him to death, But found none. Yea, though many false witnesses came, yet found they none. At the last came two false witnesses, and said, "This fellow said, I am able to destroy the temple of God, and to build it in three

days." And the high priest arose, and said unto Jesus, "Answerest thou nothing? What is it which these witness against thee?" But Jesus held His peace, And the high priest answered and said unto Him, "I adjure thee by the living God, that thou tell us whether thou be the Christ, the Son of God." Jesus saith unto him, "Thou hast said: nevertheless I say unto you, Hereafter shall ye see the Son of man sitting on the right hand of power, and coming in the clouds of heaven."

"Then the high priest rent his clothes, saying to all gathered, "He hath spoken blasphemy; what further need have we of witnesses? Behold, now ye have heard His blasphemy."

Then Caiaphas said to the gathered members of the Sanhedrin. *"What think ye?" They answered and said, "He is guilty of death." Then did they spit in his face, and buffeted him; and others smote him with the palms of their hands."*

"Then led they Jesus from Caiaphas unto the hall of judgment: and it was early; and they themselves went not into the judgment hall, lest they should be defiled; but that they might eat the Passover. And when they had bound him, they led him away, and delivered him to Pontius Pilate the governor."

"Pilate then went out unto them, and said, "What accusation bring ye against this man?" They answered and said unto him, "If he were not a malefactor, we would not have delivered him up unto thee." Then said Pilate unto them, "Take ye him, and judge him according to your law." The Jews therefore said unto him, "It is not lawful for us to put any man to death." That the saying of Jesus might be fulfilled, which he spake, signifying what death he should die. Then Pilate entered into the judgment hall again, and called Jesus, and said unto him, "Art thou the King of the Jews?" Jesus answered him, "Sayest thou this thing of thyself, or did others tell it thee of me?" Pilate answered, "Am I a Jew?

Thine own nation and the chief priests have delivered thee unto me. What hast thou done?" Jesus answered, "My kingdom is not of this world. If my kingdom were of this world, then would my servants fight, that I should not be delivered to the Jews but now is my kingdom not from hence."

"Pilate therefore said unto him, "Art thou a king then?" Jesus answered, "Thou sayest that I am a king. To this end was I born, and for this cause came I into the world, that I should bear witness unto the truth. Every one that is of the truth heareth my voice." Pilate saith unto him, "What is truth?" And when he had said this, he went out again unto the Jews, and saith unto them, "I find in him no fault at all. But ye have a custom, that I should release unto you one at the Passover: will ye therefore that I release unto you the King of the Jews?"

"Then cried they all again, saying, "Not this man, but Barabbas." Now Barabbas was a robber.

Judas was at the back of the gathering wearing a scarf over his head. He was hoping that Pilate would simply scourge Jesus and let Him go. But, it looked like the outcome would be as Jesus said it would be.

Then Judas, when he saw that he was condemned, knew what he had to do, *"so he brought again the thirty pieces of silver back to the chief priests and elders, saying, I have sinned in that I have betrayed the innocent blood."*

He then said that he knew it was the Temple custom that if a person who had been paid by the temple for reporting someone who was violating Moses' Law, recanted his report and returned the money, both would be forgiven.

"And they said, What is that to us? see thou to that. And they refused the money. So, he cast down the pieces of silver in the temple."

"Then said Pilate to the chief priests and to the people, "I find

no fault in this man." And they were the more fierce, saying, "He stirreth up the people, teaching throughout all Jewry, beginning from Galilee to this place. Surly He is guilty of sedition and dangerous to Rome. When Pilate heard of Galilee, he asked whether the man were a Galilaean. As soon as he knew that he belonged unto Herod's jurisdiction, he sent him to Herod, who himself also was at Jerusalem at that time."

"And when Herod saw Jesus, he was exceeding glad, for he was desirous to see Him of a long season, because he had heard many things of Him, and he hoped to have seen some miracle done by Him. Then he questioned with Him in many words; but Jesus answered him nothing. And the chief priests and scribes stood and vehemently accused him. And Herod with his men of war set him at nought, and mocked him, and arrayed him in a gorgeous robe, and sent him again to Pilate."

"And Pilate, when he had called together the chief priests and the rulers and the people, Said unto them, "Ye have brought this man unto me, as one that perverteth the people: and, behold, I, having examined Him before you, have found no fault in this man touching those things whereof ye accuse him. No, nor yet Herod: for I sent you to him; and, lo, nothing worthy of death is done unto him. I will therefore chastise him, and release him." Pilate therefore, willing to release Jesus, spake again to them. But they cried, saying, Crucify him, crucify him. And he said unto them the third time, "Why, what evil hath he done? I have found no cause of death in him. I will therefore chastise him, and let him go."

"And they were instant with loud voices, requiring that he might be crucified. "Crucify him, crucify him." And the voices of them and of the chief priests prevailed. And Pilate gave sentence that it should be as they required."

"Then released he Barabbas unto them: and when he had scourged Jesus, he delivered him to be crucified."

Judas had returned to the crowd to hear the judgment of Pilate. He watched for a short time.

"Then the soldiers of the governor took Jesus into the common hall, and gathered unto him the whole band of soldiers. And they stripped him, and put on him a scarlet robe. And when they had platted a crown of thorns, they put it upon his head, and a reed in his right hand: and they bowed the knee before him, and mocked him, saying, :Hail, King of the Jews!" And they spit upon him, and took the reed, and smote him on the head. And after that they had mocked him, they took the robe off from him, and put his own raiment on him, and led him away to crucify him."

Judas could take no more. He left Pilate's castle and ran to the edge of the city where he found a tree. He had brought rope with him. He threw the loop over a sturdy branch. He secured the rope around his neck, stood on a nearby stump, prayed one last prayer for forgiveness and jumped. He dangled for a few minutes, screaming for help, but the rope stifled the sound. His body jerked one last time. And he hung there, dead.

"And as they came out, they found a man of Cyrene, Simon by name: him they compelled to bear his cross. And when they were come unto a place called Golgotha, that is to say, a place of a skull, They crucified him, and parted his garments, casting lot, that it might be fulfilled which was spoken by the prophet, They parted my garments among them, and upon my vesture did they cast lots."

"There were many sitting down they watched Him there. And one of them set up over his head his accusation written, This Is Jesus The King Of The Jews."

"There were two thieves crucified with him, one on the right hand, and another on the left. And they that passed by reviled

him, wagging their heads, and saying, "Thou that destroyest the temple, and buildest it in three days, save thyself. If thou be the Son of God, come down from the cross." Likewise also the chief priests mocking him, with the scribes and elders, said, "He saved others; himself he cannot save. If he be the King of Israel, let Him now come down from the cross, and we will believe Him. He trusted in God; let God deliver Him now, if he will have Him for he said, 'I am the Son of God.'

"The thieves also, which were crucified with him, cast the same in his teeth. Now from the sixth hour there was darkness over all the land unto the ninth hour. And about the ninth hour Jesus cried with a loud voice, saying,"

"Eli, Eli, lama sabachthani?" that is to say, "My God, my God, why hast thou forsaken me?"

"Some of them that stood there, when they heard that, said, "This man calleth for Elias. And straightway one of them ran, and took a spunge, and filled it with vinegar, and put it on a reed, and gave him to drink."

"The rest said, "Let be, let us see whether Elias will come to save him."

"Jesus, when he had cried again with a loud voice, "Father, into thy hands I commend my spirit" and having said thus yielded up the ghost."

"And, behold, the veil of the temple was rent in twain from the top to the bottom; and the earth did quake, and the rocks rent. And the graves were opened; and many bodies of the saints which slept arose, and came out of the graves after his resurrection, and went into the holy city, and appeared unto many."

"Now when the centurion, and they that were with him watching Jesus, saw the earthquake, and those things that were done, they feared greatly, saying, "Truly this was the Son of God."

322

"Many women were there beholding afar off, which followed Jesus from Galilee, ministering unto him. Among which was Mary Magdalene, and Mary the mother of Jesus, James and Joseph, and the mother of Zebedee's children."

"But when the soldiers came to Jesus, and saw that he was dead already, they brake not his legs but one of the soldiers with a spear pierced his side, and forthwith came there out blood and water. For these things were done, that the scripture should be fulfilled, A bone of him shall not be broken. And again another scripture saith, They shall look on him whom they pierced."

"When the even was come, there came a rich man of Arimathaea, named Joseph, who also himself was Jesus' disciple went to Pilate, and begged the body of Jesus. Then Pilate commanded the body to be delivered. And when Joseph had taken the body, he wrapped it in a clean linen cloth, and laid it in his own new tomb, which he had hewn out in the rock and he rolled a great stone to the door of the sepulcher, and departed."

It was only after Jesus was in the grave that Judas was discovered. His body was taken by his father who had it prepared for burial. His body was placed in a family grave. Judas was honored in death even though Jesus was not.

"Now the next day, that followed the day of the preparation, the chief priests and Pharisees came together unto Pilate, saying, "Sir, we remember that that the deceiver Jesus, said, while he was yet alive, After three days I will rise again. Command therefore that the sepulcher be made sure until the third day, lest his disciples come by night, and steal him away, and say unto the people, He is risen from the dead." Pilate said unto them, "Ye have a watch: go your way, make it as sure as ye can."

"So they went, and made the sepulcher sure, sealing the stone, and setting a watch."

"At the end of the Sabbath, as it began to dawn toward the first day of the week, came Mary Magdalene and Mary the mother of Jesus to see the sepulcher. And, behold, there was a great earthquake and the angel of the LORD *descended from heaven, and came and rolled back the stone from the door, and sat upon it. His countenance was like lightning, and his raiment white as snow and for fear of him the keepers did shake, and became as dead men. The angel answered and said unto the women, "Fear not ye: for I know that ye seek Jesus, which was crucified. He is not here: for he is risen.. Come, see the place where the Lord lay and go quickly, and tell his disciples that he is risen from the dead."*

AFTERWORD

I t is said that Gamaliel was impressed by Jesus when he met Him as a small child. As an adult, in his position as a leading authority of the Sanhedrin and a Doctor of the Law, he would have known about the comings and goings of Jesus and His ministry. It is also said that he was a believer, and that he was baptized by John. Regardless of the hearsay, Acts of the Apostles Chapter 5 verses 34-42, says that Gamaliel advised the Sanhedrin to treat the apostles with care. Gamaliel's comment was chiefly responsible for the light sentence imposed on them. Instead of having them stoned to death, the Sanhedrin just had them beaten and told them not to speak the name of Jesus. They left rejoicing and, of course, preaching the gospel of Jesus the Christ to everyone they met.

"Then stood there up one in the council, a Pharisee, named Gamaliel, a doctor of the law, having a reputation among all the people, and he commanded to put the apostles forth a little space; And said unto the members of the Sanhedrin, "Ye men of Israel, take heed to yourselves what ye intend to do as touching these men. For before these days rose up Theudas, boasting himself to be somebody; to whom a number of men, about four hundred, joined themselves. He was slain; and all, as many as obeyed him, were scattered, and brought to nought. After this man, rose up Judas of Galilee in the days of the taxing, and drew away much people

after him. He also perished; and all, even as many as obeyed him, were dispersed. And now I say unto you, Refrain from these men, and let them alone. For if this counsel or this work be of men, it will come to nought. But if it be of God, ye cannot overthrow it; lest haply ye be found even to fight against God." And to him they agreed: and when they had called the apostles, and beaten them, they commanded that they should not speak in the name of Jesus, and let them go. And they departed from the presence of the council, rejoicing that they were counted worthy to suffer shame for his name. And daily in the temple, and in every house, they ceased not to teach and preach Jesus Christ.

Acts Chapter 5 verses 34-42 (KJV)

Appendices

Travel Distances and time

Bethlehem to Alexandria–912 miles–42 days (7 hours a day)
Cana to Capernaum–21 miles–7 hours
Cana to Jerusalem–100 miles–4 1/2 days
Capernaum to Jerusalem–80 miles–3 1/2 days
Machaerus to Capernaum–120 miles–4 1/2 days (5 1/2 days with a large group)
Nazareth to Alexandria–940 miles–43 days
Nazareth to Bethlehem–120 miles–4 1/2 days
Nazareth to Cana–10 miles–1 1/2 hours
Nazareth to Capernaum–30 miles–7 hours
Nazareth to Jerusalem–120 miles–4 1/2 days (along the Jordan River with the group)
Nazareth to Jerusalem–90 miles–3 to 4 days (through Samaria)
Nazareth to Sepphoris–3.2 miles–1 hour

A Donkey travels a little over 4 miles per hour
A Camel travels between 5–9 miles per hour
A Horse walks at 4 miles per hour
A Person walks 3.1 miles per hour

GLOSSARY

Adar: Twelfth month in the Jewish calendar. Part of February and March.

Av: Fifth month in the Jewish calendar. Part of July and August.

Barley Groat Tea: relieves heartburn and stomach cramps

Bris: short for the circumcision

Brit Milah: Actual name for the circumcision ceremony

Cheshvan: Eight month in the Jewish calendar. Part of October and November.

Elul: Sixth month in the Jewish calendar. Part of August and September.

Fomentations: a cloth folded in preparation for making a compress or poultice

Groats: grains or kernels

Iyar: Second month of Jewish calendar. Part of April and May

Izmal: the ceremonial circumcision knife

Jewish Calendar: Lunar calendar based on the phases of the moon.

Kislev: Ninth month of the Jewish calendar. Part of November and December.

Minyan: official observers at the *Bris*

Mohel: a Jew trained in the practice of brit milah, the "covenant of circumcision."

Nidddah: time when a new mother is considered unclean

Nisan: first month in Jewish calendar. Part of March and April.

Roman Roads: A network of stone paved roads all over the Roman Empire making it easier to move the Roman Legions to all parts of the Empire.

Rosh Hashanah: The first day of that month according to the Hebrew calendar. On this day forgiveness of sins is also asked of God.

sandak: Godfather

Shabbat: Sabbath

Shalom Zakhar: A Shalom Zachar, is a gathering which takes place in Ashkenazi Jewish circles on the first Friday night after a baby boy is born.

Shevat: Eleventh month in the Jewish calendar. Part of January and February.

Sivan: Third month in Jewish calendar. Part of May and June.

Tammuz: Forth month of Jewish calendar. Part of June and July.

Tevet: Tenth month in the Jewish calendar. Part of December and January.

Tishri (Ethanim): Seventh month in the Jewish calendar. Part of September and October

Yom Kippur: Yom Kippur, also known as the Day of Atonement, is the holiest day of the year in Judaism.

Typical 1st century Nazareth house

Houses in Nazareth had a flat roof with exterior stairs at the side and an awning of woven goats' hair to protect against the sun. This was used by the women as a work-space, an extra room.

The inside of the house was minimalist by our standards. There were raised platforms with cushions and mats for sitting and sleeping. The walls were covered with plaster, rubbed flat with a stone and painted with geometric patterns. Niches were cut into the wall, and these provided storage for bedrolls and clothes.

The inside rooms of the house were small and dark, so the courtyard and roof were important work areas, with better light for tasks like spinning and weaving.

The roof was also a cool place to sleep in hot weather

Down in the courtyard was the cooking area, with an open fire, an oven and an array of cooking utensils. There was a mortar and pestle for grinding small amounts of grain and a covered area where people sat while they worked or talked. Large amounts of food—jars of oil and olives, etc., were kept in separate storage areas, secure against mice. That is also where the stalls for animals were. This space served as a daily workplace—the weather was dry for most of the year.

The courtyard often contained a mikveh for ceremonial

purification, and the family latrine as well, which was emptied every day into a communal manure pit.

BIBLIOGRAPHY

The King James Version of the Bible
    Exodus 1:15-16
    Leviticus 12:1
    Luke 1:26-80
    Matthew 1:18-25
The New International Version of the Bible
    Micah 5: 2-4
    Womeninthebible.net
    Wikipedia
    I Judas—a novel by Taylor Caldwell and Jess Stearn
    Britannica Online
    baslibrary.com
    esv.org
    hope-of-israel.org
    myjewishlearning.com
    chabad.org
    mechon-mamre.org
    heathline.com
    bible.ca
    conformingtojesus.com
    crosswalk.com
    biblicalarchaeology.org
    gotquestions.org

churchofjesuschrist.org
biblestudy.org
politico.com
biography.com
reformjudiasm.org
israelyoudidntknow.com
blessitt.com
juicyecumenism.com
biblestudy.org
jesus-story.net
jpost.com
israelyoudidntknow.org
medicalbag.com
bibleodyssey.org
haaretz.com
thebiblejourney.org
uccalpena.org
udayton.edu
ebible.org
Journal of Hebrew Scripture—Joshua Berman
The Works of Philo trans C.D. Yonge
iep.utm.edu
belie4fnet.con
nationalgeographic.com
loyolapress.com
commevtarymagazine.com
jewishencyclopedia.com
livescience.com

ABOUT THE AUTHOR

Ralph E. Jarrells entered the field of writing novels late in his life. He retired from corporate America eight years ago and began an award winning video production company that specialized in creating video programs for ministry and mission organizations. So far, his work has received 18 international creative awards.

He retired from a successful career in marketing, advertising and publishing that included senior executive positions with major corporations—Sr. VP Marketing with an international franchise company, VP Marketing with a NYSE company, VP Account Supervisor for the world's largest advertising company and Editorial director for a major trade magazine publishing company.

Connect with Ralph online at:
https://www.jesus-judas.com/

Made in the USA
Columbia, SC
03 October 2021